M

Grie

"A brutal yet compassionate portrait of a family at war, My Therapist Says This Grief Journal Is a Good Idea *faces our darkest impulses without losing its faith in humanity."*

—*Stephanie Feldman, author of* Saturnalia

"An unflinching look at family trauma...Katz refuses easy answers and captures a bewildering process of grief with compassion, dark humor, and a belief in the transformative power of writing."

—*Barbara Barrow, author of* An Unclean Place

"Charming, brutal, savage, and hysterical, Andrew Katz's My Therapist Says This Grief Journal Is a Good Idea *is a profound study of family, friendship, mental health, and the very nature of literature itself. It'll make you giggle, then kick you in the gut, spit in your face, and give you a wink and a smirk before finding new and clever ways to repeat that cycle—often on the same page. Katz does it again. Get reading!"*

—*Nick Gregorio, author of* Launch Me to the Stars, I'm Finished Here

Praise for
The Vampire Gideon's Suicide Hotline and Halfway House for Orphaned Girls

"A cross between Nathaniel West's Miss Lonelyhearts *and John Fowles's* The Collector*...Damned impressive!"*

—*Samuel R. Delany, author of* Dhalgren

*"While there are smiles aplenty, Katz also tackles the serious issues of alienation, depression, and mental health in his novel and does so in both a sympathetic and honest manner...*The Vampire Gideon's Suicide Hotline & Halfway House for Orphaned Girls *is a hugely satisfying book on many levels, and I can't wait to see what Katz writes next."*

—*Charles de Lint for* Fantasy & Science Fiction

My Therapist Says This Grief Journal Is a Good Idea

Also by Andrew Katz

The Vampire Gideon's Suicide Hotline and Halfway House for Orphaned Girls

My Therapist Says This Grief Journal Is a Good Idea

by Andrew Katz

LANTERNFISH PRESS
Philadelphia

MY THERAPIST SAYS THIS
GRIEF JOURNAL IS A GOOD IDEA

Lanternfish Press
P.O. Box 34569
Philadelphia, PA 19101
lanternfishpress.com

Cover Design: Kimberly Glyder

Printed in the United States of America.
28 27 26 25 24   1 2 3 4 5

Library of Congress Control Number: 2024935344
Print ISBN: 978-1-941360-8-59
Digital ISBN: 978-1-941360-8-66

Dedication

This book is for Richard Katz, Philip Katz, and Bridgette Maynfeld, aka Dick and the Gerder, for providing the love and support that only family can.

June 3, 2019

In my fifteenth summer, my father and I started building the house in which he would eventually kill himself.

That's where I'm starting.

So, in 2007, my father, mother, brother and I moved from Randolph, New Jersey, where my father worked as an electrician, to the rural mountains of Pennsylvania. When we got to the mountains, the property we found was nothing but a wooden fence, a mid-sized cabin, and a field of grass that went on forever. It smelled like pollen. But mostly what I remember from that day was the way my mother—she raised us to call her by her first name, Francine—dumped herself down in the middle of the cabin and cried. My dad—Kyle—and I stood there holding her bags. My nine-year-old brother, Nicholas, walked up from behind us, dragging Francine's purse by its long strap. He sat down next to her and joined in crying. I'm pretty sure he didn't know why.

There's some backstory here that's probably pretty important.

I am writing this grief journal at the repeated advice of my therapist. I'm writing it to myself, as my own reader. I hate readers. Mostly because I hate myself.

Dear reader, you are me. I am you.

Where do our issues begin? I don't want to do this stupid journal. When you've burned through seven other counselors and connected with zero of them, you try to hang on to the one you like. I'm going to do my best to listen to her. I call her Dr. Discipline Pills, because of all the pills we've tried, searching for the cocktail which will help me function and live a life worth living or whatever. She doesn't like the nickname. I shortened it to DDP to see if that worked for her. She didn't love that either, but she gets me. She made a joke about how she will not, under any circumstances, have her initials misconstrued as Dr. Double Penetration. So then I assured her people would think of the old WWF (back when it was WWF) wrestler, Diamond Dallas Page, about whom she knew nothing. His finishing move was the Diamond Cutter. So then I tried calling her DC, but neither of us felt that was quite right. Finally I made a joke that we should just use the nickname Diamond, because she's such a fucking gem. It also kind of works with the slant rhyme for Simon Says. Diamond Says. That's fun. I'll run with that at some point. Holy shit.

My father, Kyle Green, Sr., used to say, "Procrastination is the weakest nation."

He killed himself two months ago today. Maybe I wish he'd procrastinated a little longer.

Enough, K.J.

Let's get into it.

Diamond Says: Process.

These events took place what feels like forever ago. Memory is a thickening fog and the accuracy will be around eighty percent at best. Eighty percent is a lofty goal.

Hubris, thy name is Kyle Green, Jr., and your father killed himself, and if you don't let yourself start working through some of this shit, you may not end up far behind him.

Drama, thy name is Kyle Green, Jr., and if there is anything for which I can count on you, it is drawing small anxieties to their peaks.

Narcissism, thy name is Kyle Green, Jr., and you could pretend like writing about subjects other than yourself was also interesting, but let's be honest for a change.

I know she's right—Diamond—that I have to deal with my father's death. To actually go back through some of my formative years.

I don't want to.

I'm twenty-six. Twenty-six and still talking to myself. I'm so sick of the sound of my own voice. Diamond promises that, even if I don't necessarily feel better from this exercise, I'll feel better. I don't understand a lot of her methodology. Sometimes, after I talk with her for our weekly telephone call at nine thirty on Wednesday, I do feel moderately better, though. She keeps telling me to give myself more credit for my accomplishments. What those are, I don't really know. That's not true. I'm good at a lot of things…I think. Am I too hard on myself? Are the standards to which I hold myself and others impossibly high? Did I get that from my father?

Diamond promises me that she believes I'm doing my best. All the recollections I'm going to write down, I'm going to do my best to get them right. Or at least close to "right," whatever "right" actually means. Consistency. That's what I'm aiming for. It's never really been my strong suit.

I think it makes the most sense to me to write this thing out like a story. Since that's my job. I'm a "marketing narrative consultant" for brands. I'm making a decent living. It's such a fucking joke.

Sigh.

I don't want to do this.

Okay, so that's the backstory to the backstory. Now for the backstory.

Francine was from an "upscale" family. Her now-dead father got really rich from a patent on the glue for Post-it Notes, or some crap like that. Francine was always considered a beauty. A rich, lithe woman with unnatural burgundy hair and impeccable fashion sense. People said I looked like her.

Enter Kyle: broad-backed and rough-featured, from a single mother in Philadelphia. She was a paranoid schizophrenic who raised Kyle with a series of five or six stepfathers until he was old enough for early emancipation.

You can see where the familial conflict arose when Francine got knocked up at nineteen and refused to get rid of it. It, of course, being me.

I guess Francine's now-dead father gave her the ultimatum of Kyle or him. I don't know why she picked Kyle. It might have been a coin flip. Youth in revolt. Or love.

When Francine's now-dead father died, he had a ton of property and money. Francine had siblings who hadn't spurned him. They got the "good stuff." The three big houses and the lion's share of the cash. Francine got the runoff. Seventeen acres, plus the remains of her trust fund. The land came with a note from Francine's now-dead father that told her to take her garbage family to the landfill. She said it was her own fault—the way her now-dead father treated us—but she always looked straight at me when she said it.

Or maybe she didn't, at least not all the time? Maybe perception really transmutes into reality as you create meaning out of your unending fear of uncertainty. Maybe none of these ideas matter. Maybe consequences don't matter. Maybe superiority complexes are bred and not born. Maybe affection is just a natural byproduct of life, not something you can cultivate. Then again, if not every story wraps itself up neatly, if life is really that much messier than fiction, the above *maybes* are probably all true.

Kyle told Francine that she didn't have to worry about spending the rest of her life in her father's prison of a cabin. That was the word he initially used for the place. "Prison." Before it became "home." He said he was taking care of it. He promised her a new house, built with his bare hands. The day after we got to the cabin, Kyle took me to town in his rusty blue pickup. We drove down the mountain on which our property sat in search of the hardware store. It was early summer, with that weather where every gust of wind comes as a cool breeze and the sky is full of migrating birds in V formations. The road wound down from the leveled-off plane that comprised our property and out ten or twelve miles to the highway; the town was along the way and stood as a monument to mill communities everywhere clinging desperately to life. Population: twelve thousand. It had a Main Street, with a gas station that doubled as the grocery store, and with the other usual necessities: pharmacy, barber, ice cream shop, that sort of thing. The hardware store was situated in a long, low building stretching way back from the road, separated from it by a curbed and well-maintained parking lot.

Kyle and I got out of the truck and walked through the double doors. The store stretched out before us in neat aisles of metal shelving. Our immediate left was boxed off by the checkout counter, with a girl leaning her elbows on it, looking distant. I figured that was an act, given the way she clocked us in her peripheral vision before resuming the bored clerk routine. She wasn't in a uniform or anything, just a V-neck T-shirt and jeans. Dark hair. Makeup a touch too heavy on her eyes. She brushed her hair behind her ear and side-eyed us again. Scratch that. She side-eyed *me.*

I pegged her for sixteen, but thought, "Well, maybe a new face is just what she needs." Besides, I was tall for my age. Or at least that's what Kyle always said. I smiled at her. Her mouth twitched at the side.

Kyle stood next to me, looking bored in the entrance. Loud enough for the girl to hear, he said, "Are you gonna go ask that nice young lady her name or can we get going?"

She failed to hide a snort. All the blood in my body rushed to my ears. The store was suddenly two hundred degrees. Then my mind went to the scenario of introducing myself. I'd be suave, cool, tell her my name was Kyle Junior but that my friends called me K.J. She'd ask who my friends were. I'd say she was the only friend I needed.

And yes, I was fourteen and had never had a girlfriend, so *obviously* I didn't know how to talk her.

Even so, the thought of her enjoying conversation with me, maybe brushing my shaggy hair behind my ear the way she did it to her own, sent part of the blood gathering in my earlobes down south. It was a small blessing that I had jeans on.

Now, I don't remember most conversations from this time verbatim. I'm not that good. The interactions that stood out, though, the dialogue—I'll do my best to get the general wording right. Or at least the voices.

Anyway, I muttered that Kyle was an asshole, which he thankfully thought was funny. He rustled my hair. "Go find the lawnmowers," he said.

I went off looking. According to a guy stocking paints on shelves, who introduced himself to me as Mr. Turnton and the owner of the store, the riding mowers had to be special-ordered and delivered. Though his eyes were kind, Mr. Turnton had robust cheekbones and a weak jaw, making him look a little like a weasel. He asked how big our property was, if we couldn't make do with a push mower. I told him we'd just moved in up the mountain. He grumbled low in his throat and said, "Yeah, I suppose you can afford one of the riders then."

Kyle found us talking and walked up. He extended his hand to Mr. Turnton and introduced himself. They traded grips and looked one another in the eye. Mr. Turnton asked Kyle what he was looking to pick up. Before long the two were laughing aloud as they talked about housing projects.

I zoned out and wandered the store. My thoughts kept moving to the cashier and my feet followed. I meandered up to the counter, where she had opened a magazine and stood leaning over it, idly flipping pages, her V-neck T-shirt bright red.

For whatever reason, I remember this conversation very well.

"Hi," I said.

She looked up at me. She seemed familiar somehow. Her eyes were bright brown, almost orange. I realized they were close to the color of my own eyes, on which people liked to comment. The cashier and I locked gazes. The same kind of recognition lived in her unwavering stare.

"Mm," she said before looking back at the magazine.

"Good reading?"

"Yup."

I needed something witty to say. Something memorable to prove I was smart or funny or charismatic. I said, "You know, I'm reading a book about a world without gravity."

She looked up at me from under her brow. "Yeah?"

"Yeah. It's impossible to put down."

She groaned and lifted her head up. "That's really bad."

I lowered my voice. "You know, my father used to beat me with a camera."

Her face went blank.

"I still have flashbacks."

She snorted. "Wow. That is the worst joke I've ever heard."

"It's great, right?"

"It's okay. Are you gonna buy anything?"

"Just thought I'd come talk to a pretty girl."

She rolled her eyes, but some color rose in her cheeks. "How old are you, anyway?"

I prayed my voice wouldn't crack. "Seventeen."

She looked back at her magazine. "I don't like liars."

"Fourteen."

She looked up. "Me too. I'm Mary." She held her hand out.

I shook it, firm, with eye contact, like Kyle. "Kyle Junior, but my friends call me K.J."

She whistled through her teeth. "Just say 'K.J.' from now on."

Her breath smelled like peppermints. Her teeth were very straight, with small white stains at the front, suggesting the recent removal of braces. Again, I was thankful for the jeans.

"Noted."

Kyle walked up with Mr. Turnton, the pair chuckling the whole way. They had two pallets on rollers, each loaded with tools and materials. They dropped the pallets off by the door, nodded to us.

"Well, all right," Mr. Turnton said to Kyle. "But I'll tell you, you ever need something, you just let me know. That, or I'll buy you a beer."

Kyle grinned. "Not if I buy you one first."

"Mare Bear," Mr. Turnton said. "Please ring these nice folks up, with a ten percent discount."

Mary raised an eyebrow. "A discount?"

I said, "Mare Bear?"

She turned bright red, coughed into her hand. Mr. Turnton

laughed. "You think you gentlemen will need help loading up that truck?"

Kyle shook his head. "You've done plenty."

They shook again and Mr. Turnton went back to work. Kyle told Mare Bear to let him know if she needed him to pick anything up so she could reach it with the scanner. She waved him away and started looking at our items and punching the prices in from memory. During the long process she occasionally asked Kyle to move something so she could see behind it, at which time I'd cut in front of him and make a big show of moving whatever it was. I made a power drill look like it was as heavy as a table saw, flexing while I lifted. Mare Bear didn't seem to notice; she was focused on the numbers. At the end she took off ten percent. Kyle thanked her. I waved goodbye. She waved back, but cuter, waggling her fingers.

Kyle and I loaded the truck, me standing in the bed to slide things into position, him lifting and loading from the pallets. When we were done, the air filled with the smell of sweat from my pits and mixed with sweet vapors of gasoline drifting from the Exxon. I sat in the passenger seat. Kyle started the truck.

"So," he said, "did you get a phone number?"

I looked at him, eyes wide. "What? No. Should I have?"

He shrugged. "If you ask, the worst that'll happen is she'll say no."

This was Kyle's first real advice about how to advocate for myself. It wasn't a concept I knew how to name at the time, but it's something I took to heart. I find myself saying, "The worst that'll happen is they'll say no," more than I'd care to admit.

I started to open my door to go get Mare Bear's number.

Kyle said, "Don't panic, just be nice. She's pretty." He snapped his fingers. "She looks a lot like your mom, actually. Pretty doesn't do her justice. Beautiful. Especially those eyes."

I let the door hang half open, gripping the handle. I thought he might be right about the resemblance. I pulled the door shut.

"No?" Kyle asked.

I shook my head. "I'll get it next time."

God, I hated Francine. Still do, I guess.

June 4, 2019

Kyle and I went home with our provisions from the hardware store, and he brought in lumber over the next couple weeks to start on the house. He hired a guy with a backhoe for cheap, on the recommendation of Mr. Turnton, to dig out the foundation.

Francine didn't acknowledge all the hard work. Instead, she demanded Kyle build her a shoe rack for the several boxes of footwear she had brought. Kyle built it in a day. He showed me how to crosscut lumber on the new table saw and then made a box with a pivot door and attached shelves, doweled at the bottom so they opened forward from the top. Kyle explained each step to me, talked about safety measures for the saw, said he could have used a piano hinge for the door but doweling was simpler and wouldn't need WD-40 as often. He took an orbital sander to the wood, gave the shoe rack three coats of white spray paint, screwed a horizontal handle into the front door, and it was done.

Francine didn't say thank you. She asked Kyle what the fuck he was going to do for money out here, especially since he just spent

God-knows-how-much on tools and wood. She left out the fact that her trust fund remained intact.

Kyle sat with Nicholas and me at the kitchen table, teaching us Gin Rummy and mulling over Francine's question. An idea sparked. He got drunk enough to pitch it to our family.

Flashback: Kyle was sixteen, sitting at the desk in his bedroom. He and his mom were living with her husband of the moment in a two-bedroom apartment in South Philly. He was doing math homework, which had him stumped, but he was determined to figure out the equations.

He heard the apartment door bang open, followed by shouting. He was used to that, so he tried to zone in harder on his work. But on this particular night, his stomach empty, his heart not in the algebra, he couldn't ignore the fight. He moved from his desk to his twin mattress and listened through the wall.

His mom screamed about all the people on the street that were talking about them—her and her husband.

The husband was shouting back that there were barely even any people out there. That no one had said anything. That it was all in her head.

For Kyle, it was the usual. It had been the same with all the other husbands. Half had taken out their frustration on Kyle himself when he stepped in to protect his mother. He had scars of proof on his back. This husband, Derek, had not yet gotten to the point of physical violence, but it sounded like that was about to change. The voices rose. A glass shattered. Kyle got up and threw his door open.

He looked at the combatants in the kitchen. His mother, holding the window curtains to the side, with blood streaking her arm and a shard of broken glass clutched in her hand, was saying, "They're coming for us all," over and over. Derek, behind her, gripped his head with both hands, trying to get his voice loud enough to break through the ones in his wife's head.

Derek called Kyle's mom a crazy bitch.

That did it.

Kyle's mom spun on Derek, brandishing her glass fragment. Derek went about five-nine, 180 pounds and pudgy in the middle. Kyle's mom was all of five-four, 125 if she'd eaten a big dinner. It didn't take a lot for Derek to disarm her. He spun her into a chokehold and squeezed.

Kyle, already nearing six feet tall and eclipsing the 200-pound mark, moved fast. Derek had his back to Kyle. Kyle grabbed a chair from the kitchen table and swung it without breaking his momentum. There was a dull thud. Derek went down, limp arms releasing Kyle's mom.

Chairs don't break over people's heads like in movies. Not if they're made properly, anyway. Swinging a chair is the same as swinging a club. If you hit them hard enough to break a good wooden chair, you've hit them hard enough to kill them.

Kyle knelt beside his mom. She gasped for air and dragged herself toward the kitchen counter. Kyle got an arm beneath her arms and hoisted her up. She waved him away and stood there catching her breath. Derek moaned from the ground. Kyle's mom turned and saw him lying prone, facedown, the chair on its side next to him. She went back to the window, craning her neck to get a better view of the street. Kyle approached her cautiously.

"Mom," he said.

Nothing.

"Mom? Can you hear me?" He laid hands gently on her shoulder.

She whirled. "What?"

"We've gotta go, Mom. We can't stay here."

Her eyes tracked to Derek, then back to Kyle. She gasped. "What did you do?"

Kyle had known this might happen. One of the previous husbands, a doctor, had explained how Kyle's mom's condition could cause problems with short-term memory. It had taken a whole year for the doctor to lay a switch across Kyle's back.

"Mom," Kyle said. "We have to leave. Right now."

Kyle's mom rushed to her husband. She touched Derek's face with the back of her hand, asked, "Dear, who did this to you?" Her eyes came back to Kyle, didn't register recognition. She snarled at him and sprang from the room. Kyle followed to the door of her bedroom. She emerged from the closet with a stiletto heel in each hand.

The swings aimed at Kyle's eyes were clumsy and he shifted away from them in turn, begging his mom to please come with him. She kept trying to hit him. He batted the first shoe from her hand. She took a two-handed swing with the second. He caught it and ripped it away.

"You're one of *them*, aren't you?" she hissed, now backing away.

"Mom, you aren't thinking straight. It's okay. It's not your fault. You have to come with me."

Derek moaned from the kitchen.

Kyle reached for his mom. She caught his wrist, sunk her teeth into his hand. Kyle clenched his jaw, swallowed a cry of pain and wrenched his hand free. His mom ran into her closet and shut the door. Kyle stood in the hall, between his mother, locked away, and her husband, motionless on the kitchen floor.

He didn't know what to do.

He walked from their building into a humid May evening.

He didn't know if he would ever go back.

(Woof, okay, this would have been, like, 1990? I don't think the timeline is super important to my grieving process but I'll try anyway).

For the next three days Kyle wandered the city, sleeping in doorways, racking his brains for work, avoiding run-ins with junkies with a combination of sharp eyes and physical intimidation. Even though he was still just a kid, Kyle's stepfathers had forced him to grow up quick.

It had been a while since Kyle's last meal. He thought about panhandling but pride ran thick in his veins. He looked into windows and poked his head into shops and restaurants to see if they needed an extra pair of hands to work for cheap. He hadn't the foresight when leaving to bring anything along. By that third day, he was haggard and dirty from the streets. The job hunt proved fruitless.

That is, until he found himself on North 2nd Street, outside of the Animal Control offices. He didn't know what the building was, but the doors had flyers for lost animals tacked on them, and Kyle figured he fit that bill.

The entrance to the offices smelled rancid, but so did Kyle. He walked up to the front desk and asked about work. That was all it took. The woman at the front desk gave him soup. There was some bureaucratic stuff to tend to, but the department took care of everything, including an expedited emancipation and arranged housing.

In return, Kyle worked for them as a dogcatcher.

Philly was rife with underground dogfighting rings. Stray pitbulls hid throughout the city, getting tossed out of their homes if they were too small as puppies. If their owners didn't feel like dealing with them anymore. If they lost a fight and lived.

Kyle's first day out on the job was the one that taught him what he needed to know.

He was paired with a department veteran. A big German named Peter.

Peter was a kindred spirit with an unclear history and tender heart.

He showed Kyle the ropes. How to collar a stray without hurting it too much. The tones and grips needed to subdue or console, how to recognize which was needed and when.

Kyle was a natural. With his reflexes, brute strength, and determination, he caught and tamed the dogs to Peter's satisfaction, taking his mentor's tips to heart and picking up the German commands Peter snapped at the animals.

What seemed to impress Peter most was Kyle's patience.

One of the pits they caught together, a red nose with skin clinging to his ribs, served as Kyle's first real test, victory, and initiation. The two circled the beast, who spun, tracking both of them, teeth gnashing. Peter circled quickly to the dog's nine o'clock, Kyle impassable at the twelve. Without prompting, Kyle darted in. The dog leapt to meet him, aiming at his throat. Kyle dropped into a sideways roll as Peter intercepted the pit with his catch pole.

They hustled the dog into the van, where it rammed from side to side in the back, trying to break through the walls. Peter pulled the van into an empty parking lot so he could show Kyle how to settle the dog.

Kyle asked if he might take a shot at it on his own. Peter didn't like the idea but allowed it. Peter brought the dog out on the catch pole. Kyle approached, arms held out low, making clear eye contact with the dog.

"Hi, bud."

The dog snarled.

"I'm not here to hurt you, okay?"

The same response.

"We're gonna be friends, if you let us."

The dog lunged, pulled back by Peter.

Kyle waved his mentor away and got within striking distance of the dog, who was wary now, no longer snapping. Kyle dug in his pocket, came out with a piece of jerky.

"You hungry, bud? Can I give you this?"

The dog sniffed the air, keeping his attack posture, weight balanced on his back legs.

Kyle tossed the jerky. The dog caught it.

"See? Friends?"

The dog still snarled. Kyle tossed jerky to the dog until it settled onto the ground to eat. Kyle crept closer, palms up, showing he meant no harm, and knelt in front of the pit. He held the back of his hand out. The pit saw its opportunity and bit him.

Kyle had been more or less prepared for this but didn't expect it to hurt so much. On reflex, he punched the dog in the nose, eliciting a squeal of pain and the opening of jaws. Peter forced the dog into the van and got his first-aid kit.

"Looks bad," Peter said.

Kyle shook his head and looked at his hands. He thought the dog bite matched the marks from his mom's teeth. He told Peter he was fine.

The German shrugged, then disinfected and bandaged the hand.

"Bring him back out," Kyle said.

Peter did.

The pit couldn't make up his mind whether to be quelled or try to kill Kyle. In the end, after more jerky and two close calls, the dog chose Kyle over violence, settling down with a full belly, licking the back of Kyle's hand.

They rode back to the department with the pit in Kyle's lap, taking more jerky, learning to accept the food instead of snatching it. The command was, "*Sanft.*" Gentle.

Kyle pitched the idea with more candid enthusiasm than he had ever shown for anything. In no time, he'd sold Francine on giving it a try; I don't know if it was the story so much as the look in his eye while he told it. A brightness that coursed through him.

His idea was to start an open-air kennel and dog-training facility. It was the great business idea that would complete his American dream. This land, this opportunity, it was all Kyle had been waiting for.

People came from all over to drop their dogs off at our unbuilt house, using us sort of like a daycare service, sort of like surrogate parents. They came from Philly, from Central Jersey, even from up in New England. I don't know how my parents got the word out that far, but whatever they were doing, it seemed to be working. Rich patrons would roll up our gravel path in their Cadillacs and Mercedes and Porsches, hand Kyle the leash attached to their designer breeds, sometimes offer a quart of kibble. Francine would take their deposits and then the clients drove off.

I got the honor of greeting the dogs, since I was good at connecting with the more anxious breeds. One of these anxious little angel-babies, a blue-nosed pitbull—aka Staffordshire Bull Terrier—took to me especially. A one-year-old with a brindle coat and soulful eyes, he belonged to a pro baseball player or something who might have rescued the dog for good PR.

What people don't realize about Staffys is that they were originally nursing dogs. That might be apocryphal, but I believed it then and still choose to. Such sweet, sensitive, protective little monsters. But there was some Akita in that dog too. Akitas were bred as hunting dogs in Japan. They used to take down bears.

I renamed him Reptar. I don't feel ready to talk about Reptar.

But maybe I can write about his arrival. He was the first dog dropped off for the summer.

Kyle decided Reptar needed a house of his own, if our land was to be his home for the immediate future. Kyle decided we'd build the house using lumber meant for Francine's house. Meanwhile Reptar sat at the edge of the fence by the driveway, staring down the path by which his human had left.

It was hard seeing Reptar look so abandoned. I wanted to get the house made quickly for him. Slap it together and show the dog that he had a safe home here. Kyle had a different methodology. He was very much of the "measure twice, cut once" mindset in those days. It made me crazy. Probably because of the cognitive dissonance between his ability to construct a wooden object with infinite patience and his inability to apply the same skill anywhere else.

Kyle eyed Reptar up, framed the dog in a box made from his thumbs and forefingers, chewed on his upper lip. He drew blueprints. He calculated in some extra height and width, reminding me that animals don't necessarily love tight spaces. He told me that if the house was too big, we could throw blankets in there so Reptar could stay snug.

"Better to have space and not need it," Kyle said.

Kyle threw a weather-worn door over two saw horses and clamped his bench saw down. He took great pride in the fact that the saw was older than I was. He glowed with this pride when he told me the saw's age, disregarding the implication that his affection for it was somehow on par with his affection for his sons.

Anyway, we adhered to Kyle's plans. He cut a frame of two-by-fours about two feet taller than it was wide. He strode energetically to the cabin. He came out with a fifty-pound bag of Quikrete slung over his shoulder and a tall, white, plastic bucket in the other hand. He cursed at himself for being a dumbass and asked me to hook the hose up to the cabin's outdoor faucet. I obeyed without question. Kyle had a way, then, of disguising a demand as a gentle question. It was one of those things where he could bind his children to his will without trying or even necessarily knowing it.

I ran the hose over to Kyle. He took the hose head—an old metal gun with a black handle from which the paint was chipping—pointed it away from us, and squeezed the handle. No water flowed. He squinted towards the cabin.

"K.J.," he said, "what are you forgetting?"

I slapped a palm hard against my forehead, mimicking Kyle's way of punishing himself for small mistakes. Then I ran back to the spigot and opened the valve.

He tested the flow, then took an orange-handled box cutter from his back pocket and slit the concrete bag open. He asked if I could manage emptying the mix, maybe half of it, into the plastic bucket. I squatted down to wrap one arm around the bottom of the standing bag and balanced the top with my other arm. To Kyle's approval, I lifted with my legs, making sure the opening was pointing towards the bucket's mouth. Only a little of the powder missed the opening and puffed over the ground in a gentle plume. Kyle didn't say anything about the small waste of material, though he likely made a face when I wasn't looking.

Without further ceremony, Kyle pointed the hose at the bucket and let it rip, drilling the jet into the powder, sending fumes over the lip until the mixture filled the entirety of the bucket. He walked away and came back with a piece of scrap wood half as tall as I was.

"Churn the butter," he said.

He didn't stick around to make sure I stirred the mix properly. I watched him haul strips of vinyl siding over to the bench saw. He pressed a strip down with one hand to balance it against the ungainly length drooping off the edge of his makeshift table. After the first cut, he held it along the top strut of the dog house's frame, trimmed it, and then used that to measure the subsequent cuts.

This while I mixed concrete two-handed with a scrap of two-by-four and dumped sweat in from my forehead.

Kyle let Nicholas take a shot at digging the foundation holes where the vertical posts would go, then shooed him away, not wanting "concrete to get everywhere." Kyle went and inspected the holes once Nicholas begrudgingly departed. Our father shook his head with a small sound of disgust, went to where Nicholas had chucked the shovel, picked the tool up, and remade the holes the way he wanted them, digging out certain areas and packing others as he saw fit. I lugged the bucket over to Kyle, hoisting it by the handle with two hands, elbows bent, legs wide and waddling for balance.

Kyle looked into the mixed concrete and said, "Good."

Then he sent me to fetch the corner frame posts while he measured the foundation holes with his "thinker," aka tape measure. I dumped the frame pieces down in front of him. He said, "Pour slow," picked up a vertical post, and held it in place. I tipped the bucket so concrete flowed into the earth and surrounded the wood. We repeated this three times.

Once that was done, through exasperated breaths, I asked, "Okay, now what?"

"Go eat something," Kyle said.

I didn't want a break, but because Kyle said it, I did.

I ran past Francine, who said, ostensibly to herself, "This is such a waste of time."

I ate...something. Not important. Not relevant. You're grieving, K.J., don't get caught up on the semantics. Fuck, though, I love semantics. Thought loop, thought loop, okay, working through it, existential crisis over the nature of communication and my learned behavior of out-loud self-talk to express myself to others...and back to the story.

I ate something. I took my time. In my head, the Quikrete needed a lot more time to set and Kyle couldn't—wouldn't—keep going without me, even if I was a little tardy. I figured I had maybe an hour. I sat down. Actually, I did want a break.

By the time I went back outside, Kyle had finished nailing the dog house's frame together.

I wanted to say something like, "Why didn't you wait for me?" Or, "It was mean to send me away like that." Or, "I thought we were doing this together, and that was important to me."

I stood mute while he looked things over.

He told me to go get the vinyl from his bench saw. I did as I was told.

I asked, "What can I do now?"

Absently, he responded, "Nothing, I want to get this done."

Such were the moods of my father. He acted out of obligation or impatience. There was very little space in between. But he feigned patience well. I'm angry at myself for how long I let him trick me.

He attached the siding himself while I stood nearby, distracted and praying that he would need some sort of assistance. That he would need me.

I never learned to attach vinyl to a wooden frame or nail slate to a roof.

I want so badly to remember Kyle as a patient, kind, caring man. I'll never convince myself that somewhere in his core he was not those things. The fact of the matter, however, is that he typically set his needs higher than ours. It was always easier for me to see when he shirked fathering Nicholas, but he did it to me too. The problem is I loved him so much I wanted to absolve him of any and all possible wrongdoing, whereas he was an emotionally immature man and—while I do believe he often did his best—a shitty dad.

He finished the dog house without me and walked away.

Reptar hadn't strayed from his watch at the driveway's gate. I crept over eggshells behind him and softly said, "Hello."

The dog whined and gave a single, anxious wag of his tail. I sat cross-legged beside him and put my hand on his head. Reptar huffed air through his nose and lay down beside me.

I moved a little bit away from him and asked him to come.

No response.

I went with what I knew and let out a fabricated, excited little squeal. I found, deep within myself, an ability to create the reaction I wished my parents would show me. I rustled up all my unfulfilled excitements and hopes and joys.

I poured them into the words, "Come on!"

Reptar popped up in response to my high tone. I squatted on my haunches to play. The dog mirrored. Then I took off running. He gave chase across the wide expanse of grass, running with me until my lungs stung and calves tightened.

I fell down in the grass while Reptar trotted little excited circles.

I asked him if he wanted to see his new house. He matched my pace back the way we'd come. We arrived at the front of his new dog house. I told him to sit. He did. I pointed into the house and said, "Okay."

Reptar sniffed around the open threshold, decided he could give the ol' place a look-see, and sat down on his grass carpet. He needed proper flooring. I made my way to the cabin to get an old blanket. Reptar followed at my heels. I had him wait outside while I got it and he complied.

I arranged the blanket as his bed, told him, "Okay."

The dog sniffed furiously at the red and green weave, stomped and tugged at the fabric with his forepaws. He walked three precise circles to ensure comfort and dumped himself down.

Soon, hand-built dog houses dotted the lawn. Blue, red, and yellow houses with white, green, and black slate roofs. Kyle and I used the lumber from our own house to make our dog city.

This while Francine drank Mai Tais and read Philip Roth novels, muttering about how much work was going into the fucking dog houses instead of hers.

June 6, 2019

I'm out in the park today writing. DDP told me one of the reasons I'm experiencing so much writer's block, other than this whole not-processing-emotions thing, is inertia. I'm stuck, literally. She says a physical setting change could be "just what the me ordered." Since she's the doctor and all. Get it?

The park is actually quite cute. It's in the woods with a lot of mountain laurels and holly trees. There's a walking trail a little over a half-mile long that works its way in a meandering circle around the woods. There are a bunch of picnic tables at the beginning of the trail, set, I don't know, fifty feet from the edge of the bumpy dirt parking lot. None of this is important, I guess. But yeah, so I'm sitting at one of these picnic tables with my Airpods in and my computer open in front of me. I like it out here because there's no wifi, so distractions are fewer and farther between. I'm pumping Arctic Monkeys' first album *Whatever People Say I Am, That's What I'm Not* through my earbuds with enough volume to vibrate my brain. Now this Honda something-or-other—should I be embarrassed about how little I know about cars? Okay, so this Honda SUV pumps into the parking lot going, in my opinion, way too fucking fast, and hits the brakes closer to the picnic tables than the de facto line of other parked vehicles.

The back doors of the SUV fly open and out come two boys, one probably early teens, the other a couple years younger, I don't know, I'm not so good with kids or people's ages in general. Why am I inclined to ramble like this? Get. To. The. Point. K.J.

The two kids get out of the car with a Frisbee and start playing catch right there in the parking lot, displaying great accuracy with their throws and solid athleticism in their retrieval of the disc when it goes awry. After a few throws their mother gets out of the driver's seat. She leans against the side of her car with her hip, lights a cigarette, and admires her sons while they enjoy themselves. It brings up a strange memory for me.

When we were even younger, Nicholas and I—everyone in existence, aside from I guess Benjamin Button, was once younger, if you care for semantics—played a special pillow fight game with Kyle. This would have been, like, 2004 or 2005, I think. In our grey-walled, two-bedroom apartment in Randolph, NJ.

My memory of this time in my life isn't all that substantial. I can remember the apartment in which my family lived. It had grey shag carpet, lightish blue walls, and white trim. There were two bedrooms, one for me and Nicholas, the other for Kyle and Francine. There was a kitchenette that bordered the living room. The rooms were divided by a strip of metal that separated carpet from vinyl tiles in alternating black and white squares. I remember looking at those tiles from different angles and imagining they made Spider-Man's face in different versions of monotone.

For our game—Kyle's, Nicholas's, and mine—Kyle would storm out of his room, fluffy uncased pillows duct-taped around his arms and legs, torso, and neck, and sticking up from his head. He'd holler "Michelin Man!" as a war cry. Nicholas and I would pop up from our video games or doodling or writing in marble composition books to do battle with our greatest adversary.

We grabbed Francine's throw pillows from the two pea-green sofas and swung wildly at Kyle's armor. With the way he wore his pillow headband, his eyes, nose, and mouth remained exposed, but our father was too tall for us to get a good shot at his face. So Nicholas and I devised a strategy.

The Michelin Man broke out of his room with wild eyes. We grabbed our throw pillows.

Nicholas and I had planned and mapped out our new sneak attack. Kyle never fucking saw it coming, that *idiot.*

I threw my pillow on the ground in front of myself and knelt on it. Nicholas took three bounding steps from behind me and planted his right foot on the middle of my back, and I propelled him up and forward, springboarding him off my back, giving him all the momentum he needed to swing his throw-pillow club—eggshell white with a hunter-green floral pattern, why is that image so clear to me?—full force at Kyle's head.

We misjudged the distance pretty badly. We caught the Michelin Man off guard. Nicholas's head was what actually collided with the Michelin Man's face. Blood spurted from the Michelin Man's nose. Nicholas fell straight down. The Michelin Man reeled back, covering his face with cushioned arms, soaking blood into the pillows. His back hit the back wall. The Michelin Man sat down hard. Nicholas cried. I watched them both with wide, guilt-stricken eyes.

Then the Michelin Man laughed. A hearty, world-warming laugh. The Michelin Man unstrapped his helmet, transforming back into Kyle. Nicholas stopped crying, likely with a mild concussion but curious to observe our father's reaction.

This is when Francine walked through the front door, muttering about getting no help with bringing the groceries in, cradling two paper bags against her chest. She took in the scene and gasped. She dropped both bags, spilling tomatoes and chicken and cereal boxes and milk and everything else. She saw there was blood on the throw pillow Nicholas had wielded against the Michelin Man. She saw there was blood on her spare bedroom pillows. She saw blood.

She abandoned the groceries in front of her "This Home Is a Haven" welcome mat and stalked to the liquor cabinet in the kitchenette. She poured two shots of vodka into a tumbler and threw it back. She turned to look at us, leaning her waist against the counter.

She took a deep breath. "I want this place cleaned up. Now. And Kyle—" Her jaw clenched. "I want those pillows replaced. First thing tomorrow."

She turned to pour herself another shot. Then she took a deep, measured breath, accentuating the volume of her frustration, walked back to the front door, stepped over the mess of groceries on the floor, and left.

As soon as she was gone, Kyle grimaced and said, "Yikes," and then smiled at us. "You heard your mother. Let's get this place straightened up." He started unwrapping his armor. "No more Michelin Man for a while, I think."

Nicholas and I regained our feet and nodded.

"But," Kyle said, "that was pretty cool. I love to see my boys working as a team."

I can't pin down the moment yet when he gave up on the idea that we, as a family, were a team.

June 6, 2019 (cont.)

...I can't stop seeing the long, grey fibers of the carpet from the apartment in Randolph. There are so many memories attached to that carpet. I remember playing cards with Nicholas on it. We'd lay on our stomachs with our elbows propped on pillows, practicing Gin Rummy in a futile effort to dethrone Kyle.

I remember sitting on it with my back against the couch, reading at Francine's feet while she also read. I remember looking up at her to ask the definition of words and her absently telling me. I remember her handing me my first pocket dictionary in that very spot. I remember looking down at it, flipping to a random page, and deciding "iridescent" was my favorite word. The carpet backdropped all of it.

My memory of the last few years… few? Maybe the last decade? My memory isn't what it used to be. I feel like I used to remember everything. Every word said to me, every person's smile, every stupid injury or ignorant comment I made. Then puberty came. Then trauma came. Then life, I guess. And now I struggle to remember if I ate breakfast or took my discipline pills in the morning. Diamond hates when I call the stimulant she prescribes me "discipline pills." Tee hee.

Why does memory do that? Why does it come and go? Why don't we know anything?

Why am I like this?

June 7, 2019

Kyle, Nicholas, and I, in that summer of 2007: we were mostly still a team. In terms of governing our city of dogs. But Francine loathed what our land had become. (Or maybe her disdain was at being excluded. Isolated. Lonely.)

But as much as Francine hated the dog houses, she didn't hate them half as much as the dogs themselves. She was always bitching about the dead spots of grass killed by dog piss, the smell, the noise, etc.

Realistically, this was one of the tougher periods of Francine's adult life. We'll take a look at it on paper. Francine's father died. Her siblings informally disowned her based on her father's will. She moved to an area where she knew no one and had no neighbors close by. She was an introvert by nature. Her children didn't take her seriously. Scratch that, her husband and oldest son didn't take her seriously. Her emotions were tended to by a nine-year-old. She disassociated a lot. She drank a lot. She had a short temper. She could be mean. She didn't like that about herself. She didn't like herself.

Her childhood was full of alienation. Her current life was full of alienation. Add to that the dogs. The invalidation of her feelings. The smells and sounds and textures of the unknown swirling before her in a neverending kaleidoscope of discomfort. How in the actual fuck could any of us have expected consistency or support from her? How could I have not seen it? Did I not want to? I don't know those answers. What I do know, now, is that what she did wasn't about me. None of it was about me. Yet, I can't stop wishing some of it had been. That fact of the matter was that my mother had no spoons.

So, maybe a month after we moved up to our property, maybe two weeks into the dog business, Francine and Kyle went out dancing. They came home fighting, per usual. There was a lightness to the bickering, though, almost playful. Francine was at a level of drunkenness that Kyle loved. It was after she was looser with her speech but before belligerence. Francine was trying to explain to Kyle and us why she didn't want the dogs around (without mentioning the enjoyment she got from cashing the checks). The story she told was sad but patient and mixed with a nostalgic, melancholy tone that rarely took her. But when Francine told you a story, she was very good at it. Very descriptive, so that you wouldn't miss the pertinent subtexts. It was something I admired in her. Loved, probably.

Francine was a twelve-year-old girl—that would have been, like, 1986?—with no friends and a yearning for companionship. She'd understood from an early age that her family was not capable of being there for her and had decided she wanted a dog. Despite working on her father to allow a pet for several years, however, she could not get him to consider it.

Francine, headstrong and quick to anger, stood in her father's study and fought verbal battles over the merits of dog ownership. She even tried compromise, asking if she could start with a guinea pig. A fish, at least? By that point her father was done listening. She made the decision to separate herself permanently from her family as soon as she was old enough to live on her own.

The next day, which was in every aspect the epitome of spring's majesty apart from Francine's mindset, she tried to shun her chauffeur. (Only for the ride home, though, as the morning had been brisk and not the most comfortable.) At the end of the day, the sun was strong and weather pleasant, allowing Francine to stuff her sweatshirt in her backpack and walk the four miles home—the chauffeur in his Cadillac keeping an eye on her from a distance, of course.

Francine walked on the sidewalk, thumbs hooked in her backpack straps, brooding. Woods climbed toward the sky on her left, in contrast with the smooth pavement of the street to her right. She loved those woods, the same woods that filled and surrounded her father's property, but was tired of spending all her time in them alone. Halfway home she stopped walking and turned to face the Cadillac. She waved. The driver pulled up to the curb. Francine waited, hands folded, for him to get out and open her door. She got in and told him he was to take her to the nearest pet store.

"What for?" he asked.

"That is above your pay grade."

His earnest face darkened in the rearview mirror, but he acquiesced, taking her to a strip mall a few miles away. Francine checked her backpack for the long wallet she used to store the bills from her considerable weekly allowance. She thumbed through the

Franklins stored within, nodded, removed herself from the car, and stalked into the store.

She ignored the displays of amphibians, rodents, and reptiles, emanating disdain until she reached the glass-faced compartments that held puppies at the back. Francine's driver caught up to her.

"Miss," he said. "Your father has been very clear on this issue."

Francine barely heard him. The heavy, nebulous thing that lived in her sternum shifted. It was uncomfortable. Yet lighter. Her mood was slipping from her control. The sensation was something akin to hope. It was such a distant, unknown feeling. She could not name it.

In the center of the display, a Bernese mountain dog lay curled in a circle, detached from the hopping and yapping of the other puppies who vied for Francine's attention. The label taped to the cage said "male, large breed, $600." She stood on tiptoe, pressing her nose to the glass. The dog brought his head up, met Francine's gaze with melancholy eyes, stood and arched his back, balanced tenuously on paws three sizes too large for his body. He licked the glass once, tail swishing back and forth.

Francine's face tore itself into a smile.

She looked around for a store employee, ordered her driver to find one. While she waited, Francine named the dog Edgar after *Wuthering Heights* and cooed at him. The driver returned with a sales rep. He had bushy hair and a yellow polo shirt.

"I would like to play with this puppy," Francine told the rep.

He looked to the driver. The driver shrugged. The sales rep went through a door, reappearing in a hallway behind the cages, and slid Edgar's open, motioning Francine toward a play pen.

She paid cash for Edgar, bribed the salesman into asking no more questions, and threatened her driver into signing the papers. She purchased a royal blue leash and leather collar, refusing all the other upsells proposed to her, carried Edgar to the car, and watched him sleep in her lap for the short drive home.

They arrived at her father's opulent house—limestone, inspired by homes in Malibu that he had seen on a business trip. He never talked about the business he did on these trips, which made them seem not exactly on the up-and-up, so maybe the Post-it glue wasn't the real source of his income. Francine knew better than to ask questions to which she didn't want answers. She knew not to press issues that could destroy her share of the profits.

With a parting threat about the horrible things she would tell her father the driver did to her, should he spill the beans about the puppy, Francine hustled into the house and up to her room. Edgar explored the room in silence, trotting to each corner, stopping at each piece of furniture to sniff, looking up at Francine—making sure she was still with him—before acquainting himself with each new item in his new home. Then he squatted and peed square in the center of the carpet.

At first, Francine was aghast, mortified even. She thought her father had been right the whole time. That there was nothing good to come from having an animal in the house. Then Edgar looked up at her and the recognition passed between them again. She remembered soap and water existed, cleaned the piss, covered the floor in newspaper, and set a water bowl in the corner of the room. When she was all done, it was almost six o'clock and her father still wasn't home. She snuck down to the refrigerator, stole packages of turkey and muenster cheese, put them in a cooler, rushed back to her room, and locked herself in with Edgar. No one checked on her all night.

The next two days passed in companionable bliss. Francine filled her pockets with Ziploc bags full of raw bacon, grabbed water bottles from the cabinet. On Sunday, she packaged Edgar in her Jansport atop the water and a few books, praying he wouldn't have an accident, as she'd already had trouble disposing of so much soiled newspaper. She grabbed a lawn chair from the garage and snuck off into the woods with her dog.

There was a clearing under an ash tree of which Francine was fond. She set her chair up and freed Edgar. At first, she was terrified he would catch a whiff of something better and leave her, but the raw bacon kept him close. She taught him fetch. She rewarded him for relieving himself outside. She chased him. He chased her. When he got tired enough, Francine filled a Tupperware with water, then sat in her chair and took out a copy of *A Portrait of a Lady*. Edgar curled up at her feet in the grass and she read to him while he napped. Neither Francine's father nor her siblings thought anything of her being absent from the house, as she was prone to disappearing until well past the setting of the sun.

This blissful weekend, however, was finite. Monday came and she had to go to school. The unfortunate thing—though how could it have been unfortunate?—was that Edgar loved Francine as much as she loved him. He never wanted to be away from her again. His puppy anxiety was something Francine had never considered, what with her zero prior experience in dog management. Before she left for school, she kissed Edgar on his forehead, squeezed him tight to her chest, and told him to be a good boy, assuring him she'd be back soon. Edgar tried to follow her from her room, bouncing, wagging, hopping, and rustling the newspaper carpeting. Francine nudged him back into the room and closed her door.

Thirty seconds later, Edgar found his voice and let out a little yelp. Francine's eyes grew wide. Her father called up the steps to ask if everything was okay, to which Francine responded that she had stubbed her toe. Edgar's whining was barely audible as she continued downstairs. Francine's father, his hair cropped close and eyes semi-vacant, sat at the table in their marble-tiled kitchen, his coffee mug in hand. Edgar let out a sharp bark, followed by a loud cry.

Francine's father asked her what the sound was.

She had been so wrapped up in the euphoria of having the puppy that she hadn't thought of a good lie to use in such an emergency. Her voice caught before she asked, "What noise?"

Her father stood up with an air of calm. He walked past Francine to the steps, his brown leather shoes clacking against the floor. She followed, tugging at her father's sleeve, trying to distract him. She tried his favorite joke.

What do you call a deer with no eyes?

No-eyed deer.

What do you call a deer with no eyes and no legs?

Still no-eyed deer.

He absently answered the questions, single-mindedly moving towards Francine's bedroom. Edgar, barking his cute little face off, was not a laughing matter for Francine's father. He tried her doorknob—locked, but the lock had a tiny hole in the middle. The kind that can be unlocked with anything that'll fit the opening. Francine's father took a paperclip, hidden on the upper ledge of Francine's doorframe, and inserted it into the knob's central hole. Edgar's yelps were, by this point, continuous. Francine's father opened the door. Edgar rolled onto his back at the sight of humans and started kicking his hind legs in excitement. Then, as puppies are wont to do, he sprayed into the air, jettisoning his stream straight into Francine's father, soaking his shirt with urine. Francine watched in horror, holding her face, like Macaulay Culkin in *Home Alone* but without any of the fun traps in her house. If she'd been home alone, maybe the worst consequence of the morning would have been cleaning up the runs given to Edgar by the consumption of raw meat. Instead, she was watching the stream of pee that would seal his fate, knowing nothing would be okay.

Francine's father shouted for their maid. She arrived promptly. He looked up from his "ruined" shirt and stared at his daughter while addressing the maid. He said, "Selena, please call the pound."

Francine screamed and kicked and grabbed at her father's pants. He told her this was what happened when you lied. She said she hadn't technically lied to him.

His response was a shrug and the word, "Still."

Contrast that childhood experience with the actual interactions Francine had with the dogs on our land. Her story made it seem like she loved animals. Like she was capable of caring for another living creature. The story of Edgar was surely traumatic, but she always sounded wistful when she told it, as if it was a reminder to herself of who she could have been. Or wanted to be?

I could be projecting here. I think I am. Regret is such a fickle little monster. Also, the way she told a story—that wasn't what I *probably* loved about her. I did love it. Maybe I love resenting her more? Consistency is also a fickle little monster. For all her faults, she understood how to connect with her audience through a narrative. There are so many stories of hers that I remember down to their finest details even when I can't remember my own—memory is *such* a fickle little piece of shit. Rule of threes for the win, huzzah! Thanks for drilling that one into my brain, Francine.

Something also worth noting at this point, however, is Francine's propensity to lie. When she was sober, there was a sense of hypervigilance about her. She watched people so *carefully*. That's where I get it from. Genetics. Or learned behavior. Or the placebo effect. Oh, em, god, who cares?

Well, with Francine's keen powers of observation, she must have known how effective her stories were. How they lit up a room. How people always wanted that little bit more. She learned that the heavier or more outrageous a story became, the more engaged people were. She took that to heart. She had to. She had such difficulty connecting with other human beings. An avenue to that connection, I can't imagine it being anything other than addictive. (It also turned her into a horrible gossip. You could always hear her on the phone, talking with a girlfriend. Whichever ones weren't on her shit list or vice versa.)

So I wonder if the stories were ever utterly contrived. I wonder if the Edgar story was true. I'm going to take that for what it's worth. It's so hard to form a bond with someone when you can never be sure if they're telling you the truth. Especially if it's your mother and you *want* to trust her.

Did she even know she was doing it? All the lying and embellishing? Was it compulsive or pathological? Do these semantics matter? If someone believes themself hard enough, doesn't that make the story true for them? We're all just tripping our own realities, I suppose.

This is why I have decided that the Edgar story, in one way or another, even if it isn't "true," is true.

When the dog business was burgeoning, Francine did try to contribute. Why? To get the production of her own house sped up. To try and find the love she'd lost with Edgar. To feel like we were all a family working together. Maybe all of the above. She told Kyle she would give the dogs baths, if she could spray them with a hose from a distance; that maybe if she could ease her way in, she could carve out a place of comfort. Some exposure therapy, if you will.

Kyle beamed, almost sprinting to hook up the hose for her.

After that, Francine sent Nicholas into a literal dog pile, armed with a bottle of flea-and-tick shampoo. Nicholas soaped the dogs up and gave Francine the go-ahead. She stood about fifteen feet from the cabin, hose nozzle in one hand, a tumbler in the other, holding her pinky aloft so as to maintain her composure. Then she opened fire.

Some of the dogs tucked their tails and fled, Nicholas chasing after to soothe them. Most didn't seem to mind, though, playing with the gout of water or resigning themselves to the "bath."

There was a Rottweiler in the group. He was big, even for the breed, and looked insane with shampoo matting his fur down. He was accustomed to Nicholas, but Francine was a newcomer to this pack and the rotty didn't trust her. He growled. Francine thought he was playing. She focused the hose on him. The shampoo on the rotty's head washed into his eyes. His growl turned guttural and he bared his teeth.

I watched from the doorway of the cabin, seeing all the signs of his agitation. I did nothing. I didn't like that Francine was pretending to give a shit about the dogs. I didn't like how she couldn't set her cocktail down to give the animals some real attention. I didn't like the amount of effort her alcoholism took to maintain. I thought she used drinking to hide who she really was. I thought she was a cold, overindulged person who didn't take her responsibilities as a mother seriously.

And while it feels like there is merit to those accusations, I don't know. I want to give Francine the space she deserves. To see her as human. To find the links of consistency in her behaviors. The common thread of motivation that drove her clouded thoughts and murky relationship with reality. I'm really struggling to dredge up a positive emotion here. And hear-you-me, I have spent years now trying. It's so much…work.

Now, with shampoo in his eyes from someone he didn't trust, the rotty barreled, head down, into the water. Francine threw the hose away and ran towards the cabin, not looking for the door, nor at me guiding her to it. She put her back against the cabin wall, cornering herself. Part of me wanted to make her deal with the dog on her own. I would have, too, if she hadn't dropped the tumbler in her haste, and with it her armor. In that moment, all I saw was a terrified person facing something they didn't understand.

I sprinted from the door and jumped in front of Francine as the rotty pounced down in front of us. In the hierarchy of the pack, I was second only to Kyle and, while not necessarily a strict disciplinarian, was seen as firm and compassionate by the animals—holy overindulged, wistful emotional projection, Batman—until they had entirely crossed a line.

In my most commanding baritone I told the dog, "*Setzen*," Kyle's word driving up from my diaphragm. I don't know why I wasn't panicked, staring down a one-hundred-plus-pound dog with jaws strong enough to take my leg off.

I held the back of my hand up to the rotty, pinching my middle and index fingers against my thumb. "*Setzen*," I repeated, stepping deliberately towards the animal. The rotty looked into my eyes, his own bulging wide to reveal the white edges.

The third time I gave the command, the rotty grew uncertain. He put his teeth away. He sat down. I grabbed him by the muzzle and drove my stare into his. He broke first.

"Bad," I boomed, shaking his face. "Bad. We do not do that." He looked up at me, brow furrowed in shame. "Bad."

But he wasn't bad. He was a dog. Why do I feel so guilty about this memory? Should I have let things run their course? Why is being human so fucking hard?

I let go of the dog's face. He tucked his tail low and ran to the other dogs. I turned to Francine. She sat hugging her knees to her chest, back pressed into the wall, tears streaking her mascara.

I asked, "Are you okay?"

It might have been my arrogance, so young and male and self-sustained, that made it impossible for Francine to be honest. It might have been her own pride. It might have been any number of enigmatic lessons she learned growing up. Regardless, her face took on the demeanor of castle fortifications.

"I'm fine," she said. She stood up and went to collect her tumbler. "Get me a new drink."

I took the glass from her, filled it with rum from the cabin, and brought it back. Her strength restored, Francine took the cocktail from me with a nod. She couldn't cover the sound of the ice tinkling a haphazard rhythm via her shaking hand.

Kyle came back from somewhere on the property. Francine explained the incident to him, punctuating the story with, "I'm not sure I can handle all these animals being here all the time."

He said, "Well, K.J. took care of it. Relax. You're fine."

It was Kyle's voice, again, that stuck with me. "K.J. took care of it." He'd said it with a firm, final pride. My father took pride in my ability to stand on my own two feet—that is a sentence that will become so ironic that it's not even worth getting into here.

June 10, 2019

Back in the summer of 2007, even with the turmoil of change and the growing tension between Kyle and Francine, Nicholas and I found ourselves living in open air with limitless space to play. The dog houses made for excellent tiny jungle gyms, their ragged grid leaving plenty of space in which to run.

Normally, being isolated from other kids, no matter how pleasant the setting, would have driven Nicholas and me into constant conflict. But with a couple dozen canine playmates, we could stave off loneliness for a time.

On a particularly gorgeous Saturday, Nicholas climbed down from the top bunk, restless despite the early hour, awoken by his newfound alarm clock in the form of barking dogs. Kyle had made sure to plot the dog houses far away from the cabin, but the animals' voices carried through the still air as the beasties stirred and began their interactions.

Nicholas roused me from sleep by nudging my shoulder repeatedly with his palm, softly saying, "Hey, K.J., are you up?"

I rolled away, grumbling at him to leave me alone.

He pushed my back with both hands. "K.J., come on, get up."

"Ungh."

"I'm gonna belly flop you."

I rolled onto my stomach, side pressed against the wall, turned my head, and cracked one eye open.

"No belly flops."

"I'll belly flop."

"I want to go back to sleep."

He hopped onto the side of the bed in a crouch, his head shadowed by the planks of wood that held the upper mattress. "Wanna help me feed the dogs? Then we can play outside."

"Sleep."

I closed my eye and turned my head to the other side.

"Belly flop!"

Nicholas landed on my back, forcing the air from my lungs and depressing me further into the bed. I pretended not to notice. He sat on my back and bounced up and down, chanting, "Play—with—me" in rhythm to his movements.

After a few minutes it started to hurt. I timed my roll from underneath him with the upbeat of his bouncing and scooted off the bed. The wooden floor chilled my feet. Nicholas sat on the edge of the bed, looking up at me, trying to keep still despite the exuberance coursing through his muscles. I told him to let me put a shirt on, turned to the dresser, and then doubled back, calling, "Belly flop!" Then I dove sideways onto him, meeting his chest with my stomach and knocking him down. I lay perpendicular on him while he squirmed and giggled for me to get off.

"Can't," I said. "I'm sleeping."

I feigned big, deep snores.

Nicholas stopped laughing and tapped on my back. "I can't breathe, I can't breathe."

Sharing a bunk bed with Nicholas—I never thought I'd look back upon *that* fondly. It's wild, the things that can change from years of proximity and shared trauma.

I pushed up and got back out of bed. I grabbed a t-shirt from my drawer, pulled it over my head, and told Nicholas we could go outside after breakfast. Nicholas on my heels, I went into the cabin's long living room, which had a small TV against the wall, and next to it the stacked-high piles of boxes that housed Francine's immense collection of paperbacks. I crossed into the kitchen. The digital clock on the oven said it was seven thirty in the morning. I told Nicholas to grab whatever cereal he wanted from our cupboard while I retrieved milk from the fridge, spoons from a drawer, and bowls from a cabinet.

We ate Frosted Flakes at the kitchen table, an unspoken agreement between us to stay quiet. Waking Kyle and Francine early to their usual hangovers was not a pleasant way to start the day. One thing, however, that our parents had very much in common was the habit of heavy sleep.

Nicholas finished his food before me. His foot tapped in excitement.

"Go outside, already," I said. "I'll clean up and meet you."

A big smile opened on his face. Nicholas used to have the best fucking smile. His smile lit rooms so bright you'd think you were staring at the sun, but in a good way. He ran from the table without replacing his chair, threw the door open to the great outdoors, and disappeared.

I washed everything with soap and water in the kitchen sink, finished getting dressed, and left the cabin.

Why are these images so clear to me still? How do I know they even happened this way? I don't know how. I just *know*. Is this how some people feel about "God"? Like, even though they *know* they don't know God is real, they still somehow *know*. Objectivity is a total bust. We're all just tripping our own realities, like I said.

So outside the cabin, along with the dog houses, Kyle had built a mediocre storage shed, far enough away from them to be out of the way but close enough so that dragging supplies out wasn't a burden. Though Nicholas had asked me to "help" feed the dogs, I knew his share of the work was now off the proverbial table. Nicholas used the outermost dog house as cover, crouching halfway behind it, ready to spring. Two of the dogs—a Dalmatian and a Cockapoo—bum-rushed him. Nicholas bounded the other way and froze opposite them again. I didn't have the heart to break up the chase.

While Nicholas played with the dogs, I headed into the shed. We kept the fifty-pound bags of dog food on shelves, jugs of water on the floor, and the riding mower smack in the center of everything. I eyed up the nearest bag of food, remembered how much I hated lugging them out, and decided the dogs could wait to eat until Kyle was up—better anyway for them to eat with him around, to help manage any confrontations over what food belonged to which dog.

Three more dogs had joined Nicholas's fray. Arms spread wide, I ran towards them all, announcing myself with an elongated shout. The players in the chase took notice and froze in place. I leapt up and perched on the roof of a dog house, which they circled. The dogs hopped up on hind legs, tails wagging, eyes bright. Nicholas pointed at me and commanded the dogs, "Get him!" The dogs bounced at me, front paws scrabbling against the low roof.

Nicholas took an athletic stance. I cried out that the belly flop was imminent and sprang from the slate. Nicholas ran, leaving me to land in the grass on my hands and the balls of my feet. I took off after him. The dogs joined in.

And thus the morning went.

Remembering this part feels okay, if not good. Almost good. Maybe good.

Sometimes I get in this thought loop about spectrums. How, metaphysically, that's the only way we can measure things. Can something have value without a valuer? The spectrum is this: the value of a thing is on one end, and the one who values the thing on the other. So the sliding scale moves in both directions out from the center, meaning something can only have as much value as it is given by a valuer, and that the correlation is a positive one. Horizontal spectrum thinking. Scientific graph thinking. Direction and ideas and the directions of ideas. Holy fucking poop balls this is confusing. The value of a thing increases only as the value of that thing increases to someone or thing who assigns the initial item value in the first place. Woof, I'm steaming my brain out on this.

I'm using the value thing as an entry into the more common thought that pleasure cannot exist without pain. In my mind, any amount of pain has to come with a direct correlation to that exact amount of pleasure. That's, like, the whole human experience in a nutshell, maybe. For as much immense emotional suffering as I've endured, I do also believe I have experienced equally intense spurts of happiness. They seem much fewer and farther between. But if I could be happy once, or at least experience happiness in such a high degree for a moment, that means I can do it again.

It's weird. Some days, I feel like I experience the entire range of human emotions. Others, like I feel nothing at all.

Why can't I find the healthy in-between?

There is only one thing of which I'm certain. Well, technically, two things.

Life is weird.

People are weirder.

So: this summer of 2007, we were happy. At least Nicholas and I were, at the start.

We had sanctuary. That's what the dogs gave my brother and me. We were never alone unless we wanted to be. We were mostly free of manipulation and confinement, physical or otherwise.

I learned so much about individual personalities. That no two of any one thing are the same. I learned a lot about communication. I learned about love languages, in a weird way.

For instance, there were three Shiba Inus on our property from a single client. The first—black and brown, like the traditional coloring of a German Shepherd—would not approach people under any circumstances except to accept treats. His name was Shi. This dog never stopped trotting circles. Sometimes around open space, but usually around objects. When he was excited or wanted to play, he'd loop the entire cabin. When he was anxious or cranky, he circled his own home with shortened steps. His love language was chase. He accepted no pets or belly rubs or ear ruffles. The way to make him happiest was to follow after him while he circled, letting him bound around, curly tail pressed way up against his back. He was a fun little weirdo.

The second Shiba was named Ba, her coat orange around her back and fluffy snow white on her chest, belly, and paws. Her love language was play. She loved tug of war with a long woven rope her human had left. She clamped down on one of the frayed ends and jolted straight backwards, trying to wrench the toy from your hands. You could swing her in a circle in the air, with her jaws closed so tight on that rope that she arced through the air, paws inches from the ground, tail furiously swishing. "Play dead" was her favorite. You made a little gun out of your thumb and forefinger and shouted, "Bang!" Ba rolled over onto her back, let her tongue loll from the side of her mouth, and clutched her heart with her little forepaws until Shi inevitably trotted up and circled her to come chase him.

A twin to Ba, Shiba number three—Inu; apparently the humans had gotten all three dogs at the same time and either thought themselves clever or were too lazy to give their dogs actual names—connected through physical affection. He needed pets and ear scratches and to occasionally ball up in someone's lap or nuzzle in with his siblings.

I learned the dogs. I learned all of them. I learned their personalities and their wants and needs. I trained myself just as much as them. I practiced paying attention, nurturing, and caring about other living creatures more than myself. I learned, without necessarily knowing it, how to behave in a one-eighty direction from Francine and Kyle.

Maybe that's not fair to them. Lol. "Fair." What if *that* concept were realistic?

The work I did around the property, I did because I enjoyed it, not as an obligation, though it certainly would have become one eventually. If the work didn't get done there would have been an avalanche of complaints from Francine about "the shit that needed doing." There would have been frustrated shouting from Kyle to get all the chores done. There would have been constant stress and conflict that my parents would never address as inappropriate despite just how unbelievably inappropriate and developmentally stunting those things were.

This was a time without that. I miss it terribly.

June 10, 2019 (cont.)

...the physical proximity between Nicholas and me isn't what turned things so drastically around in our relationship. Sure, brothers fight or whatever, but we didn't all the time back when we shared a room. The emotional neglect from our parents was the turbine that turned our adversarial engines. And then, Kyle liked that we both had deep-rooted competitive streaks. In Gin Rummy. When we would wrestle or have foot races. In frivolous little debates or the rhyming games we invented.

Nicholas and I weren't too close in age, but close enough. Maybe that made it all harder. Nicholas had to look up to me for certain things that he couldn't ever hope to receive from Francine or Kyle, whether Nicholas knew that or not. Which meant that I failed him like our parents did. At least I have the excuse of also being a child at the time, though it doesn't make me feel much better about things.

We're grown up now. I've mumbled apologies to him about when we were kids. He's waved them away and assured me that it was what it was, and that he's over it, and that I should get over it too. He's never technically accepted the apology. It would probably make me sad if he did.

Deep breath. It was what it was and no one can change it, and at the end of the day it's not even anyone's fault. Or it's all of ours. There's our spectrum for this thought loop. It's almost midnight. I have a big day at work tomorrow. I need to try and get some sleep.

June 11, 2019

The Valkyrie warrior women charge over a dark hill. Their swords are held aloft and their war cry is guttural. The moon hangs abnormally large and low in the night sky. A constant wind blows the hill's grass in violent waves. The winged helmets of the women reflect the wan lighting.

They reach the bottom of the hill and come upon a swift, red river. They stop their charge. On the horizon rises a massive, crimson dragon covered in dripping blood. The dragon circles over the women, blasting flames down upon their heads.

The warriors raise their shields to protect themselves from the fire.

The dragon lands on the opposite bank of the river and laughs a malicious laugh. The prime Valkyrie looks back at the other women. They are scared, several showing scorch marks on their arms. The leader nods to the wind, hoists her sword high and calls out a wordless challenge to the dragon. The dragon laughs again.

The leader takes several steps back, runs forward, and leaps high into the air, defying physics. She soars over the river. The dragon watches her flight, stunned. She descends upon the dragon and with one stroke of her sword beheads the monster. The dragon's head falls to the ground, eyes wide in death.

The Valkyrie pins the head to the ground with her sword and stands beside it. She looks straight ahead.

She says, "Vagylenol. Slay the red dragon."

I pitched this at work today. Our creative director, Brad, huge fat prick with a fauxhawk like he wishes he was in Good Charlotte or some shit, didn't even look over the pitch deck before the meeting. I do at least half of his job so he can leave at three o'clock every day. I hate him so much.

Anyway, I pitched it to our client today for a commercial and they loved it. Genuinely. It's the direction in which they're looking. Then idiot fuckwad Brad, utterly incapable of reading a room, turns beet red and literally yells at me in front of the client, who'd laughed and clapped at the little table reading.

So now the client is on edge, kind of looking back and forth between me and Brad with a lot of noticeable concern. Now Brad and I look like neither of us know what the fuck is going on. Super unprofessional.

Before Brad blowing up at me while simultaneously proving he knows exactly nothing about women or how brutal menstruation cycles can be, I was loving life. This commercial pitch is probably the first thing I've written that I actually like in, I don't know, eight months? I think this journal is helping with my creativity again. Just writing. Writing is good for me. Sometimes I forget that. Or actively work against it. I'm not sure which is true or both or neither. Certainty, amirite?

So anyway, today was shitty for me. The client was very polite in telling us they'd be in touch. Without Fatty McFauxhawk, I'm eighty-five percent sure I could have gotten an agreement made in the room.

Now I'll most likely see a version of my very same idea on TV in six-ish months, tweaked just enough to avoid any legal disputes. Some other agency will produce it and get credit for my idea.

This has happened before.

Do I have to grieve my dignity along with all this other shit? I think I'll be sick tomorrow.

June 11, 2019 (cont.)

Alright. I took my little bubble bath with my book and now I'm ready to get back to work on the summer of 2007. At least my brain is firing for a change.

Francine had officially had it with the dogs. She demanded Kyle go back to work as an electrician. Or maybe start a business in which he built furniture. She mentioned how much she loved her shoe rack. She asked him to please, if he loved her, stop exposing her to open wounds. Kyle couldn't—fuck that, wouldn't—hear it.

Behind their bedroom door, she said things like, "I just don't know how to deal with them, is there some way to keep them away from me?" and, "I'm starting to shake whenever a big one comes near me, should I see a psychiatrist about it do you think?" and "I've just had my third panic attack. You need to get rid of the dogs."

Kyle said, "You're making mountains out of molehills. The dogs are harmless."

She reminded him about the Rottweiler.

"That was one time. And the dogs listen to Junior. Just keep him around if you get nervous. This is what we were meant to do—the family, that is. All our lives' hardships, escaping our shitty families and coming together, it's all led up to this. We can build our own house and raise our kids right. Teach them the lessons that we learned too late."

What a fucking roflcopter that shit was.

Francine said, "It's not *one* time. They don't respect me. None of you respect me."

Ugh. Here's the thing with Francine: I'm not entirely without sympathy for her. Thinking back on moments like this, I could see the how and why of what she was. Why I can't seem to put a good effort into absolving her the way I'm so desperately trying to forgive Kyle…no idea.

Then they'd both have a few more drinks and discussion inevitably turned to shouting. At the end, the shouts always changed, became wordless, breathy and hurried, mixed with slapping flesh and moans. The noises were violent but also not. I had no frame of reference for makeup sex. After, Francine would leave their bedroom, heavy on her feet. A thunk would come from the kitchen table. Then the clacking of keys on an old-fashioned typewriter. Francine started writing her memoirs this way, the story that would "free her," or so she said.

Nicholas and I listened to it all from our bunk beds. He'd climb down his ladder, sit across from me, and look into my eyes. Neither of us would say anything. It was all understood without speaking. Our parents were driven out of love with each other by animals. They never recognized that's all they were themselves.

June 13, 2019

...one of the big things that caused problems was how Kyle constantly invalidated Francine's needs. The woman was nothing if not communicative. She was raised by a money-motivated father and a mother from dirt-poor roots—neither of whom I'd ever met, so I'm taking Francine's word for these things, which is a distinctly uncomfortable experience w/r/t one's grandparents. According to her loose, inconsistent, drunken stories, she was raised by a father who essentially had children to bolster optics, to appear more human while not bothering to behave as such with his family. Her mother had married this cruel and emotionally oblivious man as a financial lifeline to escape the monotony of hopelessness. The details of my maternal grandparents' lives are mostly a mystery to me, my only knowledge derived from Francine's loose, inconsistent, drunken stories about them.

And then there were her siblings. Her older brother, born in 1970(?), was the "golden child," Michael. He only went by "Michael," never Mike or Mick or Mack or anything, and was groomed by Francine's father to meet a standard that no human being could ever hope to meet. That didn't stop Michael, whom I've never met, from "against all odds almost doing it." Michael was a star athlete. An honor roll student and eventually Ph.D. of something or other. A beautiful man without obvious flaw, but "the EQ of a bearded dragon on Xanax." Francine's words, obviously.

Michael had received all of Francine's father's attention. He was encouraged and driven to compete. Francine had once heard her father tell Michael he was proud of him. Francine's father even gave a nice speech at Michael's high-school graduation party, saying how he couldn't have been more fortunate in his firstborn son. Francine's father said his dream had come true when Michael was accepted and decided to matriculate at the University of Pennsylvania with a measurable plan to become great at "whatever-the-fuck-it-was he was going to study."

Francine was born four years after Michael, and only about a year and a half after that her mother was pregnant again with her younger brother, David. David always went by David. Never Dave or Davy or Dewey. Francine's mother—according to Francine, and this part seems completely inferred, because there's no way Francine could have remembered it—didn't do a proper job with Francine's development as an infant. Francine's father was too wrapped up in work and molding Michael to pay her any attention. When Francine was a year and a half old, along came David.

Francine's father took an active role in David's upbringing. David, however, lived in Michael's shadow with Francine. The two of them were close in age and felt a lot of the same pressures growing up, though in distinctly different ways. David was beaten down emotionally by Francine's father. Francine and David had their most basic emotional needs utterly neglected. This, I do believe to be true.

But so three years after David was born, Francine's parents had another child: Francine's baby sister, Natalie. Natalie went by Nat. Sometimes referring to herself as the Nat Attack. She was "headstrong and spoiled all the way down to her soul in every context." She was gorgeous and tended to hand and foot by Francine's mother. Nat got her way when she stated her needs. Her emotions were taken seriously. She was never accused of being dramatic when things didn't go her way or when she expressed displeasure. This while Francine was left to the untrained, detached staff her parents hired to help out since four kids was "too many." Which begged the question: why have so many fucking kids in the first place? That definitely ate at Francine.

I think she passed some of that baggage down to me. If epigenetic trauma is your bag, call it that. If nature's not for you, we can call it "nurture." Learning by osmosis. Whatever works, I guess. I've always felt sort of…wrong, in the depths of my being. This feeling that whenever I experience intense emotions, or suicidal ideation, or loss, or grief…it feels like I was cheated by having been born. Maybe. I don't understand things the way I once thought. The complexities of existence are stupid and unbelievably complicated. Human foresight and perception are so limited. It's all overwhelming. And Francine wasn't, isn't, and never could be immune to that. And yet, I can't bring myself to stop hating her for it.

David hanged himself, drunk, in his closet, when he was sixteen years old and Francine was seventeen. Francine never went into much detail about that. Or talked about how lonely it was to lose the only person in her immediate family who made her feel safe.

I kind of understand her inconsistencies. The emotional ones, certainly. Also her behaviors. I sometimes remember her as this bristled, hard-edged thing who only wanted her way, but that's not…fair? We'll see.

I'm realizing now that Francine probably has some pretty bad PTSD and never learned how to mourn her childhood. Relatable content. Is that why my therapist recommended this? Is that what I'm doing? Mourning my childhood? Not just my now-dead father?

I understand Francine, on paper at least. I don't know why the fuck she can't try to extend me the same courtesy.

June 14, 2019

I'm glad it's Friday. I feel sort of good today. Work wasn't too bad. They instated "Summer Fridays" so we get let off at two. I'm going out with this woman named Madison in the city tonight. We met on Hinge. She's cute and a solid texter, which, it seems, is the most you can ask for as a start from any of these dating apps. I want to get some writing done before we meet up. Clear out the ol' noggin, if you will.

Still in the summer of 2007 with the dog business in full swing. On average days, in the mornings, Kyle stood at the front of the dog houses while the animals sat at attention in neat rows. He drilled the dogs in German, like he'd learned from Peter. He said it was a harsher language. That the dogs responded better to it. Kyle treasured those few words he knew. He drilled the dogs to *setzen*, *hier*, *bleib*, *fuss*, *git laub*, and all the other basic commands people wanted from their "good dogs."

Reptar—I think maybe now I can go into more detail about Reptar, that sweet Staffy/Akita mix who I came to love more than I thought it possible to love another thing. He was the only dog exempt from training. He walked back and forth behind the rows of sitting poodles and golden retrievers, watching for disobedience. He was a watchful but kind drill sergeant. Whereas I was General and we both knew Kyle was Commander-in-Chief. Between the three of us, order was imposed on our seventeen acres. This despite Nicholas's wrestling and playing with and otherwise distracting the dogs. Francine watched with a distant disdain as her children "devolved into filthy little creatures themselves."

When the dogs got distracted or broke from formation to play, it was up to Nicholas and me to wrangle them back into their ranks, an activity we mostly loved but sometimes hated. Apart from that there was shoveling pounds of dog shit, getting used to smelling it without gagging, and, on Mondays, unloading the heavy water jugs and bags of dog food Kyle brought up from town. On Tuesdays, I rode the mower around the property, surrounded by burning fumes, occasionally hitting an overlooked pile of poop, spraying it through the air. One time, Nicholas was standing too close to the mower. He got his face covered in shit. Francine was furious. She blamed me to my face. I rode away.

Another weird thing about that summer: I never remember it raining, although it must have. From June to August, usually between ten and one o'clock, I sat at Francine's feet and read through a Norton Anthology of American Literature from which she insisted I study. Most of the stories didn't make complete sense to me, but I liked the characters written by Joyce Carol Oates and Eugene O'Neill. Francine, after questioning me about my reading, told me I had terrible taste.

Francine lectured from the throne of her lawn chair, gaze bearing down on where I sat in half lotus before her. Francine had no interest in math or science, foreign languages or sports. She preached that we needed to understand the human condition to understand the world. That we all inherently thought in narratives.

But she also said the social sciences were for the meek to delude themselves into thinking the earth would be theirs because they didn't have the gall to take it for themselves. Interestingly enough, she taught us nothing about business or government. Or reality.

I still don't know much about those things. The basics, I guess. Nothing world-shaking. I know that reality is created by the one who perceives it as such. But then, does that mean reality is relative? Thought loop, thought loop, existential dread, do I even exist, is this all just a deep-rooted solipsism in which I am my own god and false idol…

As Francine taught me literature, she taught Nicholas philosophy. Primarily the likes of Sartre and Kierkegaard. Nicholas blatantly didn't understand the materials, the dense rhetoric or the principles. But Francine was patient, chugging along, unpacking the more complex bits for him, though the existentialism made her sad. That's what Nicholas really learned. That existence was sad. That our mother was sad. That he, a nine-year-old boy with a birthday coming up, had no choice but to be sad.

Francine's patience with Nicholas became a seed of something dark in me. Instead of treating me as a pupil, she spent our time berating me about "intellectual frivolities." To Francine these were things like magic and psychosis in "Young Goodman Brown" or vengeance in "The Cask of Amontillado." Both were stories I loved. Francine only wanted me to consider serious themes. She wanted neat, inevitable structures. She didn't have the time or imagination for suspension of disbelief. Maybe she didn't "berate" me? Maybe she taught in the ways that worked best for her? I think I'm being too hard on her and I also don't.

Oh boy, here comes an unlocked memory.

Sitting on the lawn in the summer of 2007, she told me, about Poe, "He was a sick man, with sick ideas. You absorb what you read, whether you want to or not. If you want to live in your little fantasy worlds, you'll never be able to understand the complexities of realism."

"Says the alcoholic."

Francine offered a condescending smile and sipped her drink. "That's the kind of acute perception you'll want to develop." She sighed and pulled a thick laminated paperback from beneath her chair. "If you're going to read nonsense, it might as well be good."

She dropped the book down in front of me: volume one in the complete collection of Theodore Sturgeon's short stories, *The Ultimate Egoist*.

"Written about you?" I asked.

"Such a sharp tongue on a child with such a dim wit."

I scowled. "This is science fiction."

"A paradox if ever one existed. The gospel of empiricism mixed with the infinite nature of the human psyche."

"Do you like contradicting yourself?"

"Does the Pope cover it up when his priests fuck little boys?" I for sure loved Francine's wicked sense of humor. She was never one to pull a punchline.

"Why do you answer so many of my questions with questions?"

Francine sighed. "Because that way my responses demand consideration. Hopefully, someday, it will rein in the stunning arrogance you've inherited from your father." There was a slight mischevious twinkle that arrived in her eyes, then. "I can maybe even drive home the invariable fact that I am more intelligent than you."

"Do you really think I'm stupid?"

I know now that she didn't. It doesn't make me feel any better.

Francine looked down on me with her leonine stare. "Do you?"

She refocused on the stack of pages that comprised her in-progress memoirs sitting in her lap. I picked up the Sturgeon book. I couldn't focus. I started thinking I didn't understand any of it anyway. I glanced up at Francine, absorbed in editing her manuscript pages and sipping her rum cocktail.

"Am I dumb?" I asked her.

Francine arched an eyebrow and said, not unkindly, "I'm trying to read."

"Really, though."

She looked gently up from her pages. "Of course you're dumb. You're fourteen. If you read more you'll get less dumb, but you'll never be 'smart.' There's no such thing."

"Do you think you're smart?"

Her gaze drifted down. "If I were smart I'd have picked a real career, married a man who listened to my feelings, and gotten away from these fucking dogs by now."

At the mention of the dogs, my jaw clenched until the roots of my teeth were driven deeper in the gums. I breathed through my nose, let go of the tension.

I'd been wanting to share something with Francine for a long time, now. I didn't know how to have an honest, non-contentious conversation with her, so I just blurted it out. "I started writing something."

The edges of her mouth pulled back into a thoughtful line. "Well," she said, "pitch me your story."

"What?"

Her eyes rolled. "What is the story about?"

"So, like—"

"Like."

I ground my teeth. "It's the origin story of the Grim Reaper."

"What do you know about the origins of the Grim Reaper?"

I shrugged. "Nothing, I guess. I made it up."

Her silence permeated the afternoon.

I told her it was about a human cult whose members all acted communally as "the Grim Reaper," so the position was a title, not an immortal bringer of death. To be initiated into this death cult, one had to sacrifice the thing they loved most, but the protagonist didn't really understand what that meant, nor how once he began initiation there was no going back. So this protagonist, Thaddeus, thought the sacrifice was going to be something material or whatever. But actually they killed his fiancée. He goes on a psycho rampage and kills all the other Grim Reapers until he's the only one left. Then maybe he would meet death or something and become what we know today as *the* Grim Reaper? I didn't have all the details hammered out yet. Only a rough beginning.

"And what do you know about death and fiancées?" Francine asked.

"..."

She muttered, "Write what you know."

"Does that mean I should only write increasingly frustrating patterned arguments?"

Francine smirked. It was somehow an expression of admiration. A fencing instructor acknowledging a point well struck from a promising student.

"Give it here," Francine said.

"It's obviously really rough, like—"

"Like."

"It's not good yet."

"Give it here."

I handed her my notebook with the beginning of my handwritten story.

She read slowly while I stared at her, trying to read her expression, finding nothing in the shape of her mouth or the shifting of her eyes. She finished what was there and handed me the notebook.

I asked her what she thought.

"Purple," she said.

"What?"

The gentility of her voice belied her sharp words. "Overwritten," she said. "Too gaudy, not enough substance. Think *Bartelby the Scrivener* as your goal, not *House of the Seven Gables.*"

"What about the story?"

"What about it? There's no discernable structure, and the characters are cartoonish. Plot and character. Those are the essence of story."

I decided I hated plot. Still do.

"Well, can we maybe go through it together?" I asked.

"Learn by doing," she said. "Try again."

Red clouds floated behind my eyes.

If there was one thing I respected about Francine it was her command of language. It was the area in which she presented as an expert and I'd always felt she could back it up. I craved that approval. That I was valuable in the sector from which Francine derived her own value.

I'd been denied that.

I whistled through the gaps in my teeth, long and shrill.

Reptar trotted up, fat lines of drool hanging from the corners of his mouth. He stood next to me, panting in the heat. Looking at Francine, watching the uncertain twitch of her eyebrows, I patted Reptar's flank. He circled, lay down beside me in the grass, and rolled onto his side, requesting a tummy rub. Francine asked me to please lay with the dog somewhere else. I ignored her. I swiveled to use Reptar as a pillow. He stretched long and grazed Francine's shin with a forepaw. She stood up. She made a disgusted sound, a note too high to mask her fear, and stalked into the cabin. Reptar put his ears back and looked up at me.

"Don't worry, buddy," I said. "She's just like that."

I dropped onto my back in the grass, absently scratching the dog, until Kyle clapped his hands and shouted, "All right, let's go!"

I popped up and turned to him. Reptar let out a grunt of complaint and went back to sleep. Kyle dropped a six-foot door over two saw horses. Nicholas ran up to him.

"Go wash the dogs, Nicky."

"Can I help with the house today?"

Kyle knelt down. "You're still too young, just like every other day you've asked."

"But I'm older today than I was yesterday."

"Go wash the dogs, Nicky."

Nicholas turned his back and stomped away as I arrived at Kyle's side. Kyle unrolled a scroll of blueprints for our house, pursed his lips, squinted, and measured the scale of the plans with his thumb and forefinger. He tucked a pencil behind his ear and told me it was time to get to work.

This is where I learned about values.

I learned the rewards of a day spent working with your hands.

I learned the rights ways to measure and add and subtract.

Kyle, without knowing it himself, knew quite a bit about engineering and architecture and basic physics, shown by the way he made flush butt joints, by his explanations for why we drilled pilots before driving screws. When he'd point to the blueprints, marking subtle changes, he'd have me calculate the length of the cuts and tell him the answer he'd already figured out. When I got it wrong and challenged him, he'd hand me a tiny calculator from his tool belt and make me ask him any problem. He never failed to solve them. He said multiplication and division were quicker ways to add and subtract big numbers, and he didn't need to memorize tables. He said advanced mathematics were okay in theory, but that I'd never need them in the real world. Throughout the day, Nicholas ran up and asked to help in any way he could.

Kyle said things like, "Not now," and "Nicky, enough, go play with your mom," and "Damn it, how many times do I have to tell you no? Go clean up the dog shit or something."

It was amazing how much calculation went into the details of the house. I started to wonder how anyone could build an entire city. People can make anything once they set their minds to it. A house could be a metaphor for a marriage. Or the antithesis to one. I thought houses were like people and cities were families. They took forever to build and minutes to ruin...

June 15, 2019

...We worked until sweat from the relentless sun beaded my skin and pasted the T-shirt to my back. Kyle's energy seemed unlimited. He sawed and planed and sanded, never stopping except to sip from the flask in his tool belt. June of 2007 smelled of sawdust. It sounded like the perfect ratio of play and hard work. It felt how life should feel, even if it was never perfect.

Because nothing is ever perfect, and there's nothing wrong with that. Or at least that's what Kyle told me when I fucked up.

Working on the frame for the foundation, I missed a cut. Short. Kyle showed me that we could use the short piece for a different part of the house but taught me that it was better to leave a board long for leeway. He made me sign my name to the mistake and put it in a pile of the other wrong-cut pieces. He told me I was doing fine as long as the pile had less wood added to it each day.

When it was almost dinnertime and Kyle was satisfied with our work for the day, he returned his attention to the dogs: reinforcing their earlier lessons; tossing sticks and seeing who came back a winner from the ensuing pile of dogs. Reptar was usually victorious, except when he deemed it beneath himself to consort with the others.

All throughout the day, while Kyle taught basic carpentry to me and "*holen*" to the dogs, Francine taught Nicholas "fetch."

During their talks on the basics of nihilism, whenever Francine's Mai Tai was finished, she'd hold the glass up, pinky extended, and tinkle the ice around. Nicholas would pop straight up to grab it from her. He was the youngest mixologist you'd ever seen. The change that took place in him was exactly like the dogs as they learned to "behave." The difference was startling, what with how quickly Francine was able to condition his behavior. She morphed him from a soft, playful thing into an obedient pet. He existed for no reason but to serve her. Or, at least, that became his filial role. While Kyle and I worked, Nicholas hovered about Francine. She said she couldn't be confined to the cabin all day and used Nicholas to run interference on the dogs, shooing them away or distracting them by throwing tennis balls. All while Francine sat in her literary bubble and tried to pretend her husband hadn't trapped her in the land of her greatest discomfort.

For Nicholas's birthday that year, on July 9, Francine got him a book of cocktail recipes and told him it was important that he read literature like his older brother. She quizzed him on the ingredients in a Tom Collins. What goes into a Mint Julep. The exact ratio of lemon juice in a Hurricane. When Nicholas got an answer wrong he had to go make the drink until it was committed to memory. With all the different brands of alcohol our parents brought in and went through, it was only a month before he could pick out the type of rum you had by the scent. By the viscosity. By how many sips made his mother black out.

Kyle must have known Nicholas was doomed. I did. But Kyle didn't care and I only wanted what he wanted. So, while Nicholas facilitated Francine's alcoholism, circling a long drain of his own, we remained complicit through silence.

Kyle was so one-track-minded that I don't think it ever really occurred to him to take Nicholas seriously. I don't think that was Kyle hating his younger son or anything, more just that Nicholas was the baby of the family, and to Kyle, babies belonged with their mothers and shouldn't get in a man's way. And so Nicholas did his best not to. That could have been why Nicholas became so devoted to his mother's happiness. Maybe he thought that if Francine could be made happy, then we all could. Nicholas started off as the kind of kid who couldn't stand pain in other people. Whenever he brought Francine a new cocktail, made properly, maybe even with his own creative twist, Francine smiled. That was his first drug. His mother's smile.

Okay, guess I needed to get that out. Lost track of time and was almost late to meet Madison. It was a good date. I think I like her. She didn't ask me about the way I walked, which was chill. It's almost four in the morning. I need sleep.

June 17, 2019

Took a couple days off from you, oh grief journal, mine. I slept in on Sunday. Got about six hours of sleep. That's about an hour, hour-and-a-half longer than I'm accustomed to. I woke up pretty groggy but feeling okay. Madison had sent me a good-morning text. I thought about seeing if she wanted to grab coffee but then figured that was *way* too eager. We made little jokes to one another every hour or so throughout the day.

Then it was Monday, and Mondays are meetings all day at work, and my brain was too drained and steamed out to even think about writing in you, journal. Now, however, I have made my glorious return. I hope you didn't miss me and my mental and emotional masturbatory style of writing too much. Is that me being too hard on myself? Too critical? Or was it kind of funny and self-aware? Okay, I cannot get into that right now.

One especially hot July day—still 2007, early afternoon—Francine passed out in her lawn chair. Nicholas tried to rouse her, couldn't, and ran up to Kyle, who was working the chop saw.

"Dad, I think something's wrong with Francine."

Kyle sighed. He stopped the saw. He turned to Nicholas and wiped sweat from his brow.

"What's up, Nicky?"

"Francine's sleeping and won't get up."

"So she's sleeping. What's the issue?"

"She won't wake up."

Kyle grunted in frustration, told me to hold tight, and walked the two-hundred-some feet of grass to Francine. He stood by her for a few seconds, held his index finger under her nose, felt the pulse in her wrist, and walked back.

He said, "She's just napping, Nicky. She'll be up in a couple hours. Let me and your brother get back to work, okay?"

I looked at Kyle sideways but he had already returned his attention to the saw. Nicholas scurried back to Francine. He held his finger under her nose to check her breathing and then sat down next to her. I positioned myself to keep an eye on them while Kyle and I worked. Nicholas kept clapping to keep the dogs away, checking Francine's breathing every minute or so.

"Is Francine okay?" I asked Kyle.

He looked over his shoulder at her, shrugged. "She'll be fine."

"Well, should we do something about Nicholas?"

"He'll be fine too. Besides, he likes being around your mom more than us anyway. Now hand me that one-by and I'll show you how to cross-cut on the table saw."

Francine turned out to be fine after all. I sometimes wonder what life would have been like if she hadn't. She woke up about fifteen minutes later, leaned over her armrest to vomit, and shielded her eyes from the sun. She stood up on uncertain legs and made her way into the cabin, Nicholas running interference on the dogs that tried to follow.

***

While Nicholas was having the clear beginnings of his full-fledged Oedipal obsession, I began to think about a woman of my own. Mare Bear Turnton. It had been a little over a month since I'd met her. The problem was that whenever I thought of her I could vaguely hear Kyle saying she looked like Francine. It was an issue. But as I thought about it more, it became less and less bothersome.

She was a girl.

She'd smiled at me.

I don't know why I'm writing about Mare Bear. I don't think or know if she's even very relevant to the grieving process here. But I guess I'll roll with it? My therapist says this works best if I do what feels natural. If I were to take that to heart I'd make a fire in a metal barrel and toss you right in there, journal.

But anyway, Mare Bear. We'd had some kind of rapport, but since I'd chickened out and never gotten her number, I was stuck staring at WWE magazines with the pictures of the divas. With their flat stomachs, heavy makeup, and fake boobs high on their chests. All of them wore latex outfits or bikinis, or went topless covering their nipples with their hands.

I spent a good amount of time looking at the men in the magazines, too. Reading their boneheaded profiles, growing more and more envious of their oiled muscles and chiseled features. I worked outside almost all day and had none of that bulk. I was gawky with adolescence. I'd never be able to put on that kind of muscle. I'd never be able to score a girl like Mare Bear Turnton.

The sun was burning strong the morning Kyle asked me to go into town with him for lunch.

I know the timeline in which I'm writing this is not totally linear. Things come and go. Ebb and flow. M'fuckers know. Rule of threes! Weeeeee!

I sat on the lawn with my Norton Anthology. "Why?"

He looked at me sideways. "Do I need an excuse to get lunch

with my kid?"

"We've got food here."

"You remember Mary Turnton, from the hardware store?"

I blushed. "Yeah, I think so."

"Well, I ran into Mr. Turnton and her the other day. They wanted to know how you were. I thought we could all sit down to lunch. So you can make some friends."

Panic set in. "And you're telling me this *now*?"

Kyle's smirk widened to a smile and his eyes brightened. "I didn't want you to get all worked up."

I slammed the book shut and bit my lips. "Okay."

He laughed. "Okay."

I stood up and ran towards the cabin.

"Where are you going?" Kyle asked.

"I've gotta get ready!" I called back.

"We've got two hours until we have to go!"

I stopped in the doorway of the cabin, turned to face him, and gripped the doorframe with both hands. "That's barely enough time."

The diner at which we met the Turntons was practically a set piece, with aluminum siding and red vinyl seats. The Turntons sat at a booth next to a long window. Mare Bear had her elbow on the table, chin in her hand, idly flipping through a tableside jukebox. She was in a black tank top; I couldn't see her lower half but I assumed jeans or maybe a denim skirt. Her hair was down and styled to appear wet and curly. It made her hair much darker, darker than Francine's. My heartbeat hammered in my chest. Kyle led us past the host to meet the Turntons at their table. Mr. Turnton stood and shook hands with Kyle, then me.

"Good grip," he said.

Mare Bear looked up, smiled, blushed, and went back to the jukebox. I slid in across from her.

I'm writing about Mare Bear because she was my first friend who felt like a friend. My first love. The first person around whom I felt safe in the real emotional sense of the word. Even if it didn't last, because nothing lasts forever. And now I'm doing that loathsome thing my therapist calls "black-and-white thinking." Thought loop, thought loop. Fuck, I'm cycling and I can't get out.

In the diner with Mare Bear, Kyle, and Mr. Turnton, I said, "Hey."

Mare Bear looked back up, said, "Hi."

"Anything good on the jukebox?"

"You like David Bowie?"

"Sure."

"Bowie?" Kyle said.

Mr. Turnton said, "What's wrong with Bowie?"

Mr. Turnton gave Mare Bear a quarter and started a debate with Kyle. Mare Bear put on "Rebel, Rebel." It played quietly next to us. We didn't say anything for a bit.

"This is good," I said.

"Yeah, classic."

"Is he your favorite?"

Mare Bear shrugged. "I don't really have a favorite. How about you?"

"I like Iggy Pop and the Stooges."

"Who's that?"

Kyle leaned over. "Who's Iggy Pop?" Then to Mr. Turnton. "She doesn't know Iggy Pop? It's all I let K.J. listen to when he was a kid. Iggy Pop rocks."

Mr. Turnton said, "Bowie lived for something like three years off nothing but raw peppers, milk, cigarettes, and cocaine. There's nothing more rock and roll than that."

Mare Bear told me there wasn't any Iggy Pop on the jukebox. The waitress brought us waters and took our food orders. Mare Bear got a chicken Caesar salad and a Coke. I asked for chocolate chip pancakes. She laughed at me.

"What are you, five?"

My cheeks burned. "Chocolate chip pancakes are good."

"If you're a child."

"We're the same age."

She shrugged. It was the kind of response Francine would have given. I stared at my folded hands on the table.

Talking under the louder conversation of our fathers, Mare Bear asked, "So what do you like to do?"

"Um, I like to read."

"What do you like to read?"

"I like Herman Melville right now."

"Call me Ishmael."

I snorted. "Okay, Ishmael. I'm K.J., nice to meet you."

Mare Bear rolled her eyes. Kyle and Mr. Turnton looked over at us. Mare Bear's cheeks flushed red. She retreated to the jukebox. Once the dads' conversation picked back up, she and I talked about books. I was the only other kid she knew who liked to read classic stuff. She liked Sylvia Plath and Emily Dickinson. Mr. Turnton made a comment about how amazing it was that two kids could read like old folks. The food came. We all ate in a half silence. Mare Bear finished her soda, making that horrible slurping sound at the end. Then she lifted the plastic cup and clicked the ice cubes around, for no apparent reason other than the sound.

That little motion—Francine's motion—made me sick to my stomach. The nausea was made much worse by the fact that I knew I'd masturbate to the thought of Mare Bear Turnton at the earliest opportunity once Kyle and I returned home. I pushed my plate away and sulked through the rest of the day, thinking how people in Oedipal houses shouldn't throw stones.

June 19, 2019

Still the summer of 2007. Why has it taken me so fucking long to deal with the summer of 2007? Why do I have to give myself credit? What if I just don't want to and that's actually the healthier option? Lol.

The conflict between my parents over the dogs, fueled by Francine's never-ending guilt about the puppy her father had doomed, wound up losing Kyle his left ring finger.

By late July, we had set the foundation and were ready to frame the house. Before we got started, Kyle stressed the proper way to assist on the table saw. He said not to push the board against the blade. To hold it tight—but not too tight—up against the fence and let him guide it through.

I was supporting the back side of a stud, with Kyle standing to the side of the blade, running the length through. That's when Francine let out an ear-piercing shriek. It startled me, snapping my attention toward the sound. Francine had toppled her chair over to run away from Reptar, who stood wagging his tail and drooling over a loose stack of her manuscript pages, one sheet stuck to his lower lip. Meanwhile, my body weight shifted and I pulled the wood we were cutting off the fence, towards the blade. Kyle didn't react fast enough. He held onto the board. The saw nipped his ring finger off right under his wedding band. When I looked back, the stump sprayed blood in my face.

Kyle looked at where his finger used to be and time stood still in my mind's eye. He looked so calm—curious even—before the injury registered and he jammed the stump in his mouth.

He drank his own blood to protect himself.

His shock spread to the rest of us. No one had thought something like this would happen to Kyle. We still saw him as capable and independent. Someone who rarely made mistakes and was always able to fix the ones he did.

But that was never the truth. It's so fucked up how perception shapes reality. How distance clarifies. How if you hold anything under a magnifying glass long enough, the truth—if that's even real—rears it's petty little head.

Then a shared reality set in. Francine screamed and time reset. A stuffed-sausage of a dachshund—we called him Jimmy Dean—ran up, grabbed Kyle's severed finger in his mouth, and sprinted away.

I called for Nicholas, who ran from the cabin to help me corner the dog and wrestle the finger out of his mouth. It took another minute of standing around on the lawn for Francine to realize that I wasn't old enough to drive and Kyle was losing a lot of blood. Kyle took his hand out of his mouth, dripping blood into his pale beard, that look of strange calm still pasted on his face. He removed his T-shirt, revealing the hard planes of muscle on his chest and stomach. He clamped the sleeve between his teeth and ripped it free from the rest of the shirt. He wrapped the fabric tightly around the nub that used to be his finger. He turned the saw off.

“Francine, love, get the car ready. Boys, follow me.”

We marched behind him, past the dogs sitting at attention in front of their houses. Reptar was back to business, pacing the front of the line, making sure no one broke rank.

In the cabin, Kyle told Nicholas, “Fill the cooler with ice, it’s in the cabinet next to the freezer. Put my finger in there.” He led me to his bedroom. Francine’s ever-growing manuscript dominated the space. Stacks of paper littered the chest of drawers and bureau; loose sheets scattered the floor; crumpled pages filled the waste bin and crowded the corners.

Kyle shuffled through these papers without comment and pulled a roll of duct tape from his nightstand. He peeled cloth—soaked with blood, sweat, and salt—off his stump. He talked me through wrapping the tape around, covering the opening at the top with adhesive. He cringed but never complained. When he was bandaged up, he took the roll of tape from me, ripped a strip clear with his teeth, and secured the loose end to his hand. He thumped me on the shoulder.

“Can you stay here?” he asked. “Take care of Nicky and the dogs for a bit?”

I nodded.

Kyle kissed me on the forehead and left.

He walked unhurriedly across the grass, past Francine’s lawn chair, and up to the pickup where she stood shaking. Kyle said something to her. She shook her head and wiped the blood from his mouth. He placed the keys in her hand, held the door for her, and got into the passenger seat. Reptar came to me and, with a low moan, lay down next to my feet, chin resting on his front paws.

What I can’t quite figure is how, given how Kyle held the boards, his ring finger was the one that came off. Maybe he was adjusting his grip. Maybe he needed to stretch a stiff finger. Maybe his pinky was tucked, an opposing force to the little finger Francine held out when she drank, and the ring finger happened to be next in line.

Nicholas and I ate a bag of potato rolls with butter for dinner and slept with the cabin door open so the dogs could come in and out. Kyle and Francine were just getting back when we woke up the next morning. Kyle's finger was still a stump. Jimmy Dean had mangled the digit too badly for it to be reattached. Kyle wore a scrubs top with a deep V-neck, revealing a length of twine with his wedding ring dangling at the end. He looked at me but showed no recognition. His eyes were glassy and unfocused, bloodshot. Their blue was duller. His feet seemed too heavy for his legs, the way he shuffled past Nicholas and me on the way to his bedroom.

The drifting way he said, "Hey, boys," his voice coming as wisps of vapor instead of resonant waves, alarmed us both. Nicholas looked concerned for a second, then shrugged and went to ask Francine how the hospital visit went. I stuck my head into Kyle's bedroom to ask if he needed anything. He was already asleep.

I didn't see him again until the next day. He sat at the kitchen table, swaying and turning scrambled eggs over with his fork. An orange prescription bottle with a white cap rested beside his plate. Francine sat across from him with a cup of coffee, scanning papers laid out before her.

"Hey, Dad," I said. "How are you feeling?"

"Junior. Your mother made eggs. Want some?"

I looked at Francine. She met my eyes and waited for a response.

"I'm good," I said.

Francine returned her attention to her pages.

Kyle arranged his eggs into a smiley face.

I asked him what I should do with the dogs.

"Can you take care of it for today?" Francine asked.

I stuck my tongue out at her. Nicholas came out of our bedroom, stretched, and stood beside me. Francine got up and set a plate of eggs down for him. Nicholas pulled out the chair I was standing behind, forcing me out of the way, and dug into the food without ceremony. I looked at the three of them: Kyle staring into space, Francine at her writing, Nicholas at his plate. I walked out of the cabin.

The dogs sat in lines, waiting for Kyle to come drill them. I stood in my father's usual spot, scratching my neck. Reptar trotted up to me. I knelt down and offered him the back of my hand, which he dutifully licked before having his ears ruffled. I looked past him to the other dogs, stood up straight again.

"Okay," I said. "Let's get to it."

But that son-of-a-bitch puberty cracked my voice. The dogs took right off at the sign of weakness. I tried to corral them, using my command voice, calling them by name. Nicholas heard the commotion and came outside. He took the situation in and, before I could give him any directions, was off and running along with them. I went back into the cabin to enlist Kyle's help.

He had migrated to the couch and was staring at his gauze-wrapped stump. Francine sat next to him, reading aloud from her manuscript. They either didn't feel my presence or paid me no mind. Francine's writing was purple and preachy, two things she supposedly loathed in the work of others. While Francine had a knack for words, no one's writing is perfect the first time. She was working towards something. For all her faults, her inconsistencies, her ineptitudes...she applied a stick-to-it-iveness to her writing that was singular. (Well, maybe not quite singular. She was also really good at drinking.)

I stood behind them and listened. Francine read Kyle a section about when they eloped and married in a church, just as a fuck-you to Francine's then-alive father, who played at Judaism but was described by Francine as Jew-*ish*. Francine lied to the priest through her teeth to arrange the ceremony, which Kyle had taken as both endearing and hilarious.

She told Kyle, "I took some poetic license with this next part, but I think you'll find it funny." She cleared her throat to read, "The thing they don't say out loud to young girls married in churches—engines of the indoctrination of youth, overwrought artistic structures with reinforced, barrel-vaulted ceilings and windows worth more than small houses in nice neighborhoods—is what the church wedding teaches you. The first thing I saw was the aisle. Then the altar. Then, Kyle, I saw you. And there is the formula the Church teaches their brides. Aisle altar you. Not a winning direction for the institution of marriage."

I will credit Francine here. I remember her reading this to Kyle so vividly. The writing was just so utterly fucking bad. The prose making an already terrible joke almost incomprehensible. That was who she was as a writer at that time. She was driving for narrative complexity through convoluted sentence structure. She was swinging and, I think, being gentle with herself when she missed. It was something I could have learned from her in that moment. Even when she whiffed, she always got back in the batter's box. I guess that's the silver lining of textbook narcissism.

From behind my parents in the cabin, I cleared my throat. Francine jumped in her seat. Kyle moved a slow half-turn to look at me.

"Christ," Francine said. "You scared the shit out of me."

"I need a little help with the dogs."

I said this entirely to Kyle. The words passed straight through him without purchase. He eyed me with an insubstantial gaze and said nothing. Francine took charge. "Your father cannot attend to those beasts right now, K.J. You'll have to figure it out."

"And just how do you propose I do that?"

She squared pages on her thigh. "I don't know and therefore cannot tell you. Please get it done."

I ground my teeth. "How about you try helping, then? Pull your weight a little bit."

"K.J., please. I'm taking care of your father."

"Or—I know. You could stop hiding in this cabin and try taking care of your kids for once."

Her shoulders set, her jaw clenched, and her neck rolled. "How about you earn your keep and give your father a fucking break."

My fists coiled in on themselves. I stormed out into the bedlam of animals, began a search for Nicholas around the property. I found him sitting by Jimmy Dean, who lay on his side, panting so hard his chest looked fit to burst.

Nicholas was trying to explain syllogisms to the gasping sausage.

"See, Jimmy Dean, dogs need water to live. You're a dog. Therefore, you need water to live." He took a half-empty bottle from beside him, rolled Jimmy Dean onto his back, and dribbled water into the dog's mouth.

"Hey, Nicholas," I said. "I need some help getting things in order around here."

He looked up at me. "Where's Dad?"

"He can't do much right now."

"I'm busy."

"Doing what?"

"I'm teaching Jimmy Dean about logical rhetoric."

"He's a dog."

Nicholas scowled. "So?"

"So I'm telling you to get up and help me with the dogs."

"You're not the boss of me."

I ground a knuckle into my forehead. "How about this for a syllogism. Older brothers can kick the shit out of their little brothers whenever they'd like. I'm your older brother. Follow the logic."

Nicholas's face darkened. He looked back at Jimmy Dean and rubbed the dog's belly.

I stalked closer. "Get up."

He stuck his tongue out at me.

Sometimes, now, I lie to myself about my temper and patience threshold. I tell myself I'm someone people like to be around because I'm an active listener and give them space and try to not to control others. Like on my date with Madison. She said something about how she's always late to everything and I laughed and told her that didn't bother me. But here's the rub: it bothers the utter fuck out of me when people are late. Even more when I'm late because of someone else. In a relationship with someone who takes forever to get ready and is rarely on time, I get so anxious when I have to be somewhere. I get angry whenever external factors stop me from being early to things. I lie and mask and tell people it's no biggie. In truth, it makes me feel like they don't think my time is valuable. Time is the one thing we can *never* get back.

So, Madison said she was always late and my brain instantly told me it could never work out between us. Then I got angry at my brain for being impatient and negative. I kept it all off my face. I know I did. I had a nice time with Madison. Why am I poking holes now? I'm angry at myself again. This temper of mine, it's never been "good." That's why I don't want to write about what I did to Nicholas next, while he spoke to Jimmy Dean. It makes me so fucking mad at myself.

Standing over Nicholas on a grassy expanse of land in the Poconos, I slapped my brother in the face. His head jolted sideways. He covered his eyes with his hands and cried.

I told him to get up.

"I'm telling Francine!"

I knelt down and grabbed his shoulders. He took his hands off his eyes and tried to wriggle free. I grabbed him by the face. He started to scream but I pressed his cheeks together. "You tell Francine and I'll fucking kill you."

His expression sobered. "You're a jerk."

Maybe this is why I don't go back to this time. Maybe it forces away the emotional dampening I've been doing ever since. Nicholas said *jerk*, but even with his advanced vocabulary, he couldn't conceptualize what a real monster I was. Maybe I don't like reminding myself that, underneath all the masks I wear, I've always been a monster.

I stood up straight. "Yeah, whatever. Start picking up all the shit around here while I get the hose out."

But Nicholas didn't do that. The slap I gave him faded into the ether and he spent the day chasing the dogs until he and they were exhausted, retiring to the shade of ash trees in the depths of our land. Throughout the rest of the week, I bit my tongue and did what needed doing. This while Francine hid in the cabin under the pretense of caring for Kyle, typing at a fitful pace and drinking herself into stupors.

I don't remember exactly what it said, but I do remember picking up a potential opening page of her manuscript and reading it. I remember my only thoughts being, "This is actually quite good," and, "Fuck her."

The dogs mostly laid around or played with Nicholas in the summer sun. There were moments when I wanted to beat Nicholas to a pulp but instead wound up watching him at intervals between doing chores and making us grilled cheeses.

Nicholas, without Francine for that small time, was without responsibility or direction, but he seemed relaxed. He had an incredible ability to seem unaffected by things, though I know better now. He was almost like a normal kid, that August. He ran around constantly, the dogs chasing him until he turned around to chase them back.

They didn't take him for granted like the rest of us.

I'd occasionally run up to him and shove him over. He'd stare up at me from his elbows, eyes watering, jaw set. He didn't fight back, even with the dogs backed off to watch. They listened to me a little more after they saw me push my brother around, though I knew I'd never recover full control.

In a lucid moment during this hazy week, Kyle made his way out into the yard. I wandered the property with him.

He flexed his maimed hand and told me, "Phantom pain is a hell of a lot worse than the real thing."

He said I should keep that in mind when dealing with Francine.

That she'd led a more complex and painful life than I could understand.

June 20, 2019

Still that same summer. When Kyle did get back to his routine, a week or so later, things returned mostly to normal. But we weren't getting as much done each day, and it bothered me. That kind of thing still bothers me. I think it's why I can't stop thinking about this journal while I'm doing other things. I want to get it done with. Diamond assures me that there isn't ever a real "done" in terms of what I need to put down in this journal. I didn't write in it Wednesday, as a little bit of a you-can't-tell-me-what-to-do to her. She is a really good therapist. This journal has become increasingly important to me. I did randomly start crying at work and hustled out of an impromptu meeting with our director of PR. I was thinking about this next part I want to go through. I feel like I "need" to do it, not that I "want" to. Diamond tells me that the word "need" is a little bit of a trap. Quicksand, kind of.

John Mulaney ruined the image or metaphor of quicksand for me. I want to change *quicksand* now.

I'm overthinking words to avoid getting into this. Onward and upward, as they say.

Summer 2007, Kyle incrementally getting back to things as they were before his finger, but with our progress significantly slowed down. I looked longingly at the house we were supposed to build. A deep hole in the ground with a skeleton frame and thick posts sticking up from the corners. I asked Kyle when we could really get going again.

Francine overheard. She said, "Your father will return to work when he is good and ready."

I said, "I wasn't talking to you."

Francine bared her teeth. It was a new response. She was used to my backtalk by then, which usually came in the form of academic discourse, veiled as a battle of wits between student and master. This time, she was defending her husband in earnest.

She asked, "Kyle Junior, may I please speak to you inside?" Kyle nodded at me. I followed her into the cabin, stood face-to-face with her inside the threshold. "How dare you speak to me that way. I'm your mother. You had damn well better start acting like it."

"I don't know what the title *mother* has to do with anything. Not when you stay inside all day relying on a fourteen-year-old to raise himself and your other son."

She rocked on her heels like I'd hit her. "I have been taking care of your father." The way she slurred the "th" in father was almost comical.

I remember having the next thing I said so *very* locked and loaded. I snorted. "Do you think having Kyle's ring around his neck will make it easier to strangle him to death?"

Reptar stepped through the open door, tongue bouncing with the rhythm of his panting breaths. He walked tiredly up to me, circled, and flopped down on his side at my feet.

"Get your dog out of my house this instant," Francine snapped.

Never breaking eye contact with her, I knelt down, pressed my hand into Reptar's blocky head, and scratched behind his ears. He stretched long, eyes closed, little grunts of pleasure escaping through his nose. His paws pressed against Francine's legs. I suppose this was the straw too heavy for her back.

Francine didn't know how to teach me *setzen* with words. She couldn't find a command that worked.

I started to stand, knees bent, weight forward, not looking at Francine.

She shoved me.

My left temple hit the corner of her shoe rack. The impact was sharp and abrupt, followed by shots of electricity through my back and limbs. The impulses stood every nerve I had on end. After that, most of the feeling left my body, leaving me prone on the wooden floor, too stunned to cry, unable to move my head, staring at the shoe rack.

Francine's shoe rack was just like her. It judged you. Watched from the corner and agreed when Francine snapped *Chew with your mouth closed* or *Don't laugh at the dinner table* because she didn't like to see people's teeth. *Turn down the TV* in the morning because she was hungover. Either *make yourself useful or get the fuck away* from her.

Kyle had done a flawless job on the shoe rack. It was the work of an expert, lovingly crafted. There was no doubt in my mind that Kyle loved me, but he didn't love me like that. Not so extensively, at least. He loved that shoe rack because of how much his wife loved it. Unlike me.

And that was the main difference between the shoe rack and me. Francine loved it. I thought about the marred boards Kyle insisted we use for the house. Those boards became me. Kyle didn't care how poorly formed I was. He didn't care if my life came out sturdy and supported or slapped-together and ready to topple. He wanted things to be perfect for Francine and nothing else.

I don't know how long Francine stood over me or whether or not she thought I was okay. I don't know when she decided to get help or if Reptar was still there or if I'd tripped on him and he was hurt too. I didn't know how much time passed before Kyle rushed into the cabin and knelt beside me. The following eighteen hours turned out to be the most uncertain of my life.

My memory of them…I'm trying. Really hard. It's giving me a headache.

I'm starting to see it again…

Kyle asked, "Junior, are you okay? Can you get up for me? Kyle Junior? Can you hear me?" The pitch of his voice went higher with each question. The final note, almost hysterical, irrevocably pierced my brain.

My voice was as steady and unmoving as the rest of me. "I can't move."

"Okay. We're going to the hospital. Tell me what happened."

I couldn't find the words. He rolled me onto my back and held my head between his hands, forcing me to look at him. He asked me to please, if I could, to please just move.

I tried to tell him again that I couldn't, but my thoughts scattered.

Reptar walked up from wherever he'd been after the shove and stood over me. He licked me between the eyebrows. Kyle, with intense care, placed my head on the floor and gripped my wrist to lift my arm. He let go. The limb dropped straight down. Kyle lifted me up and carried me to the pickup truck, Reptar moving in and out of view, whining the whole time. Francine was nowhere in my limited field of vision. I closed my eyes, listened to Reptar's concern, and smelled the whiskey on Kyle's breath. He put me in the cab, adjusting my body to a sitting position, taking a couple extra tries to stop my body from slumping over, and buckled me in.

Nicholas came up to the open passenger door. He stepped up on the pickup's foot railing and leaned in. "Where are you and Dad going?"

The response was my voice, but it didn't feel like me speaking. It was more like being a ghost trying to possess myself. "Hospital."

Nicholas asked, "Why?"

"I'm hurt."

"You're faking."

Kyle opened the driver door. "He's not faking, Nicky. Come on, you can make sure nothing goes bad on the drive."

"He's *faking*. What's even wrong?"

"Can't move."

"You can too." Nicholas pushed my shoulder. The seatbelt caught me, but my head rolled to the side. "You can move," he said. "Just move."

Kyle adjusted my head against the headrest. "Nicky, go open the damn gate."

I can't help but think about luck here. Variance, more precisely. What if my neck had been broken? Kyle could have killed me when he picked me up. Why wouldn't he have called an ambulance? Why wouldn't he have thought to have medical professionals come and immobilize me for transport? I guess panic will do that: make someone act outside the realm of good sense. Luck or variance or what-have-you is what kept me alive. Well, no…variance kept me alive. Whether or not that was "good" or "bad" luck is a different thing.

In Kyle's pickup truck waiting to go to the hospital, Nicholas's voice got high, moving from petulant to panicked. He gripped my shoulders and shook. "K.J., *move*."

"Nicky," Kyle snapped. "Knock that shit off and go open the gate."

Nicholas hopped down from the truck, ran to the gate, opened it, and waited there. Kyle fixed my head again and rolled the truck onto the driveway. Through the open window he told Nicholas to get in the car. Tears rolled from Nicholas's eyes. He climbed up and over me to sit in the middle of the cab's bench.

"Where's Francine?" he asked.

Kyle pulled onto the winding road beyond our driveway. The truck bounced and shook down the mountain.

Until this time, I hadn't been off the property much, nor had I been particularly curious about the surrounding woods. Now I watched the tall sugar maples zip past, their foliage rich and dense and green. Every few minutes the truck took a big hop and bounced my head around. Each time, Nicholas said I'd moved on my own, but you could tell he was trying to speak it into existence.

"I know," Nicholas said, snapping his fingers the way Francine did when she had an idea. He reached down and pulled my sneakers off. He tickled my feet. It was my lack of reaction that set him sobbing. He sat there, my foot in his hand, bawling and running his fingernails back and forth over my skin.

I used to be very ticklish.

Kyle wanted to know exactly what had happened to me. He said it, "ex-*act*-ly."

I told him what happened as best I could, speaking through the haze swirling inside my skull. I said Francine and I were talking and she pushed me. I repeated that it wasn't Reptar's fault, again and again.

Kyle told me he knew it wasn't.

I can't be sure, but I think, when I said how Reptar touching Francine was what sent her over the edge, Kyle blamed himself. He didn't say it. He never said it. But for that fraction of a second, it was there in his voice.

Really, I don't think it was any one thing in particular that broke my mother. I don't even think it's fair to call her broken. She was just so...lonely. No one listened to her. Or no one heard her? I don't recall the exact semantic difference but I know there technically is one.

I'm avoiding again. Or processing? I'm starting to lose sight of the important differences. Look hard at yourself every once in a while. It sucks, but it's overall probably a good thing?

Anyway, that look on Kyle's face, it made me think back to his and Francine's constant shouting matches. His insistence that she'd get used to the dogs. His begging her to give it a few more months.

It's possible that's my flimsy way of trying to excuse Kyle for what he did next.

He told me and Nicholas over and over not to say anything about what really happened and ran through story options. He decided that what we should say is that I was running around the property, not wearing a hard hat like he always demanded, and a stray board from our housing project fell on my head. He said that would be believable. He told himself a bunch of times.

"Am I going to die?" I asked.

He shook his head.

Three times, he made me repeat the story he'd concocted. Well, not the whole thing. I wasn't there enough at that moment to get it all down. Kyle reached across Nicholas and gripped my shoulder. He said, "Construction accident. Say it, K.J."

I did.

"Again."

"Construction accident."

Kyle nodded.

Then he made Nicholas say it too. He told us that if we were good, we'd all be able to sit down and play a couple hands of Gin that night. Neither of us asked any more questions.

At one point—I don't remember exactly when—I tried to remember these events happening exactly the way Kyle said we should tell people they did. Tried to overwrite my own memories. It warped things. I can call to mind clear snapshots of life before the head injury. Really damn good ones, sometimes. Later things come and go in waves, in and out of focus: sometimes so distinct that I'm back there again; other times, hidden in black clouds of obscurity.

In the truck, in the summer of 2007, we hit the highway. Kyle gassed it. The engine fluttered.

June 20, 2019 (cont.)

Can't sleep.

I was in the hospital for a couple weeks after the accident. It wasn't very eventful or interesting. When I reach back in my brain for the details, they're fuzzy and the timeline may or may not be exactly right. I keep trying to pin down moments in time. Time is something I want so badly to subjugate. Life in only three dimensions is ass.

The medical staff ran a bunch of tests: MRIs and CT scans and such. After the first eighteen hours, I felt a tingling in my right hand. I moved my index finger. Feeling gradually returned to my arms, shoulders, neck, head, chest, back, and navel. Two days later, my legs came back. A lot of different doctors and nurses and other professional types came into my room and asked what happened. They weren't certain about the type of injury and used the word *psychosomatic* a decent amount. That didn't stop my legs from feeling atrophied and weak. I was promised they'd get better over time, but I'd need crutches until my legs caught up with the rest of my body.

Whenever someone asked what happened, I recited Kyle's story word for word.

Francine never visited. The closest she got was calling Kyle on his new flip phone. He'd yank my curtains closed to have a terse, whispered conversation with her. There were three of these calls, that I knew of. Kyle came back after each one, produced a prescription bottle from his pocket, and ate several pills with no water.

The hospital stay wasn't the worst time in my life. The staff was really nice, at least. Apparently, as it was explained to me, my brain was failing to relay signals to my legs despite the physical health of the limbs. A nurse elevated my bed and wheeled in a television on which I could watch *Austin Powers* and other silly comedies that Francine called "dreck." I got to watch Adam Sandler fight Bob Barker or Will Smith and Tommy Lee Jones deny aliens sugar water. I didn't laugh out loud, but these moments made me feel *some*thing.

There was a very real solace in that.

I also thought about the stories I wanted to write. About Francine telling me over and over that writers who stray from their base of knowledge, experiential or studied, are destined for folly.

I thought about what I knew. I thought about what I felt certain of.

I realized the answer was nothing.

The Grim Reaper story returned to mind. But this time, the content was not fiancées or ritual sacrifice. This time the story came to me in dark cabins and only cared for the consequences of disobedience.

Nicholas wanted to stay and watch movies with me, but Kyle said Francine needed him at home. Nicholas threw a temper tantrum, screaming that I needed him, mixing that argument with one where it wasn't *fair* that he had to go back to work with the dogs, if I got to watch movies. Kyle smacked his younger son on the back of the head and dragged him from the hospital by the armpit. Once, after that, I overheard a nurse talking about criminal negligence in the hallway when she thought I was sleeping.

There must have been nothing to it—legally speaking.

June 21, 2019

It's all coming back. I keep crying at random intervals throughout the day. I might finally take my bereavement time from work. I'm sure they'll try to say something about the applicable time period of bereavement having passed. I'll still maybe say something. If they push back, I can always quit.

The nurse in charge of me at the hospital in 2007 was a Baywatch-type beauty in her mid-twenties, blonde hair receding to dark roots, with a natural smoldering expression. She was nice to me.

I asked if I could tell her a joke.

"Sure."

I don't remember the exact joke, but here's one I lowkey like as a placeholder.

"Okay, so there's this guy at a party, and he's been there for about an hour, and he finds the host to say goodbye. The host asks why he's leaving. The guy says, 'Oh, you know, I need to use the bathroom.' And so the host tells him, 'There are four bathrooms here, why not just use one of those?' The guy says he needs to use salts. The host is confused but tells the guy to do whatever he needs to. The guy says, 'No, no, I really need my salts.' They go back and forth like this for a bit until the guy who needs to shit relents and agrees to stay and use one of the host's bathrooms."

We'll say the nurse nodded and humored me with a smile.

I went on, "And so after a while, the host comes upon a line for the first-floor bathroom. People are coming out looking totally green. The host cuts the line to see what's going on. When he opens the door he is absolutely appalled and confronted by the foulest odor he's ever come across, because there's shit *everywhere.* I'm talking, on the walls, the side of the sink, even a little on the ceiling."

We'll say the nurse said, "Ew," but had grown more invested in the story at this point.

"Now the host goes to find the salt guy to ask him what the hell happened. He asks the guy 'What kind of goddam salts did you use in there?' The guy gives him kind of a blank look. He says, 'Somersaults.'"

The nurse probably snorted and shook her head. I vaguely recall her saying something like, "So gross. But I'm glad you've found your sense of humor. You have a nice smile."

I fell in love with her while she took my vitals.

I remember Kyle arriving just as she departed. I remember how he stared after her as she left the room.

He said, "What a gorgeous girl. She looks a little bit like your mother."

That's when it occurred to me: Kyle thought anyone who attracted him looked like Francine. She was his epitome of beauty. It didn't matter who the person was. Jenny McCarthy looked like Francine. Halle Berry looked like Francine. Jennifer Lopez looked like Francine. Hell, Taye Diggs looked like Francine.

My mind turned to Mare Bear Turnton. I brought her image up in my mind's eye. Her hair wasn't the same color as Francine's. Nor were her eyes similar, nor the shape of her face, the tilt of her mouth. She didn't look much like Francine at all.

I wanted so badly to talk to Mare Bear Turnton. For her to hold me and tell me everything was okay. I wanted that from anyone. I still do. I think I have to get comfortable with the fact that I may never get that. It doesn't mean things will never be okay, because sometimes they are. And sometimes they aren't or won't be. And that's okay too.

June 22, 2019

I'm meeting Madison at the park today. Our texting has felt more distant lately. I think we're probably running our course. It's worth a try to meet her again, though, I think.

June 22, 2019 (cont.)

The date was fine. Madison was twenty-two minutes late. She texted me a bunch to update me on her ETA. It didn't make things feel better. We ate lunch at a cute little coffee shop and kissed goodbye after walking to her car. She texted me to let me know she got home, which I reciprocated. I thanked her for a nice day. She didn't answer. I don't think it feels important to me whether she ever replies. It's been nice to meet a new person, even if we didn't quite connect. Maybe I'll swipe on the apps a little more this week. Diamond tells me it's important to listen to what my body is telling me. I guess we'll wait and see how lonely I feel in the coming days.

June 24, 2019

I don't know how long it was before the doctors reluctantly discharged me back into Kyle's care in the summer of 2007. Hospital policy required that I leave the facility in a wheelchair. They gave me the kind of crutches that band around your forearms and have perpendicular handles to grip. They told me to use the wheelchair if my arms got tired and to avoid too much stress on my weak legs. Before I left, the nurse warned me about potential weight gain. She warned me about bloating. She told me to be on the lookout for shooting pains in my legs. I nodded and lied that I'd be sure to pay close attention. She gave me a laminated sheet of paper with exercise diagrams, as I'd opted out of coming back for physical therapy. She said that if I started to feel depressed, which was common with this kind of injury, I needed to tell someone.

She wrote her phone number down on a scrap of paper for me. I didn't bother telling her that I'd be ecstatic if depression rolled around, that it might mean I wasn't already. I threw her phone number away as Kyle wheeled me from the hospital.

At home, the lawn was studded with dog shit. The air stunk of turds baking in the sun. Francine was waiting in her lawn chair with a scotch and soda, the legs of the chair pressed deep into the grass. The dogs rushed around the property but gave her a wide berth. Every time one got too close, Francine gave it a look that sent the animal running away, tail dropping down beneath its butt. I guess the dogs had maybe had a conversation amongst themselves about who was the new alpha, what with Kyle missing his finger and me gone for a while.

Francine finished her drink and shook the ice against the glass. Nicholas appeared from the cabin to fetch her a refill.

Kyle parked inside our gate and Reptar rushed up to the car, tail wagging so hard his entire body wiggled. He saw me in the window and jumped up, front paws scrabbling at the door, then ran excited circles around the truck. Kyle got out to wrestle my new wheelchair from the truck bed. He opened my door and lifted me into it.

Reptar jumped into my lap, almost knocking me over backwards.

Intimacy…

Not sure why, but this is the first time during the whole ordeal when I sat and bawled my eyes out. I remember crying so hard I thought I would choke.

Reptar, like I said, belonged to a misunderstood breed—pitties are in fact very sensitive. He looked at me with his head tilted, questioning. I still don't know what triggered him to act. Maybe I looked the answer at Francine. Maybe he smelled it on me. Maybe he understood consequences better than Francine or I ever could.

Anyway, Reptar leapt from my lap and let out a bone-deep snarl. All the other dogs stopped in their sporadic, distracted tracks before scattering in all directions.

Reptar and Francine stared one another down. Reptar bent his legs, lip curling way up. Francine knew from watching Kyle that it was time to get the hell out of Dodge. She raised herself to stand and considered her options. She locked eyes with Reptar. She bolted for the cabin.

If you know anything about dogs, you'll know this wasn't the best move.

Francine was a lot closer to the cabin and beat Reptar through the open door. Kyle took off after them. I managed to roll my wheelchair over the grass an eternity later and stopped at the threshold to the cabin. Francine stood on the kitchen table, shrieking, the tendons in her neck bulging. She must have knocked her manuscript over when she got up. Pages of her writing cluttered the table and floor. Nicholas was between her and Reptar, holding a copy of Kant's *Critique of Pure Reason* like a shield.

That's when the Michelin Man came rocketing from Kyle and Francine's bedroom to tackle the dog. They rolled once before the Michelin Man established his weight atop Reptar and pinned the dog.

Reptar snapped and whined, the Michelin Man keeping his throat well away from the dog's mouth. Reptar, realizing the futility of his escape attempts, went limp.

"Collar and leash," the Michelin Man panted to Nicholas.

And then there was no more Michelin Man. Just Kyle wrapped in cushions, sweating in the heat of summer and his makeshift armor, the illusion shattered forever.

My younger brother attached a chain collar and matching leash to my dog. Kyle, maintaining his position with pillow- and duct-tape-laden belly firmly pinning Reptar, took the leash in his right hand. The second Kyle lifted the pressure of his weight, the dog was on his feet. He lunged for Francine, who screamed again.

Kyle yanked on the chain leash. Reptar, with no footing, was pulled backwards and landed on the floor with a hard thud. Reptar got up, this time more slowly. Kyle began dragging him outside, towards me and my wheelchair at the open door. Reptar tried to brace against the leash but his paws couldn't find purchase on the hardwood flooring.

Reptar kept whining and fighting the tension of the leash as Kyle pulled him to the truck.

I looked back into the cabin. Nicholas stood frozen, eyes wide. Francine had pissed herself at some point during all of this. She lowered herself from the table, shoulders trembling.

The pickup truck's ignition rumbled in the background.

I couldn't cry. I was done crying.

I was never ticklish again, either.

I remember what Francine said next. It hurts to write it here. It all hurts. I don't think I trust my therapist anymore. God, I fucking hate my mother.

"Look at this mess," Francine said, trying to regain her composure. "All these pages, ruined."

June 25, 2019

Intimacy…

Oh yeah, baby. Ya boy has got some *issues* here.

I talk about them with Diamond once in a while. She seems to think that my emotional and physical intimacy issues stem from my relationship with Francine. The whole "generally withholding" thing. I think that's too nice of a way to put it, but I'm not the one with the psychology degree so what the fuck do I know?

Diamond sometimes softens her criticisms of my behavior and thoughts too much, I think. She describes my intimacy issues as stemming from some "cracks in attachment with Francine." I think of it in much simpler, more direct terms. Francine was physically and emotionally abusive and it's hard for me to trust that other humans won't be those things. Why beat around the bush?

Isn't this journal supposed to be about my now-dead dad?

Ok, then: It's clear to me now that Kyle didn't know how to feel safe in a relationship unless he could comfortably sit in judgment of the other person. He cut us down in smaller, subtler ways than Francine did. The dismissive *You'll figure it out* when a problem seemed simple to him. The condescending tone attached to *Everything is fine. Stop complaining.* The flares of temper that accompanied *I don't have time for this* whenever he was confronted with someone else's feelings.

I don't talk to Diamond about Kyle's emotional neglect nearly as much as Francine's. Maybe because she's so focused on the attachment of a child to their mother. Residency in the womb and all that gross shit. I don't get it. I don't want to put any more thought into the differences. They were both shitty parents. End of that part of this entry, thanks for listening.

What do my own intimacy issues look like?

Well, I hate being touched. That's a big one. I've read a lot of different studies about the importance of physical touch and its relationship to emotional stability. Still don't fucking like it.

I had a girlfriend in college, Valerie, who was super "my love language is physical touch." I loved her. We held hands. She put her arms around my waist from behind me in public. We enacted some light PDA in kissing one another hello and goodbye, which, honestly, made my skin crawl a bit. It was really important to her to be comfortable touching her partner and feel a reciprocity there. So I made myself participate. It helped me, I think. I became more comfortable with human contact. I stopped jumping as much when someone would put their hand on my shoulder in congratulations or to get my attention. I stopped having extreme muscular tension if someone grazed me as they passed by. Valerie was a truly lovely woman. Raised Roman Catholic—eat my ass, Jew-ish parents—and pretty staunch on the "no sex before marriage" part of things. This worked out wonderfully for yours truly.

When it comes to sex, I think of myself as an archetypal Victorian lady. Not how they would have existed in reality. More in the repressed, Jane Austen sense, where I think about sex a lot but I'm too concerned with potential fallout to make it a primary pursuit like so many of my cis-hetero-male peers. My general feeling about sex (back then and still now) is that I am happy to participate if and when it is something my partner wants. It's never felt… necessary? I don't want kids. I know that for sure, despite everyone who has children insisting I'll feel differently one day. Sure, maybe I will, but just shut the fuck up about it when I say I don't want kids, okay?

Maybe the biological imperative to procreate is missing from my brain and that's why I take so little interest in sex.

Lol. I know it's the intimacy issues, Diamond. Fuck off and let me work through this.

The physical intimacy issues are obviously tied to the emotional ones. The fact that I was comfortable touching and being touched by Valerie brought us emotionally closer. There was an overall closeness there. A connection. And again, she was verbally pretty gung-ho on the whole no sex without a ring on it stuff, so there wasn't as much pressure attached to the romantic touch for me.

Then it turned out that, like most nineteen-year-olds, Valerie wasn't actually quite so into the wait-until-marriage thing. The statements were for optics, I guess. Whenever things would get hot and heavy at night, I'd stop, generally with some amount of relief, because I had the out that her moral compass pointed to waiting. Then we'd do some mouth stuff or whatever and go to bed. Valerie dumped me over winter break without us having a real conversation. It was just…over. Like that. I never got a second chance.

That's unfair. I never looked for one.

I learned later from a mutual friend that she broke up with me because I wouldn't pull the proverbial trigger when it came to sex.

I think that made for a big step back in my intimacy journey. I sometimes regret never having sex with Valerie. Mostly not, though. We weren't right for one another. Our communication and moods were seldom in harmony. Some days I miss the way she'd rub my shoulder and kiss my cheek. I miss doing those things for her. But it's obviously not her fault. It's no one's fault. It is what it is.

Diamond tells me that intimacy looks different for everyone. I want to figure out what healthy intimacy might look like in my life, but I don't even know where to start. Maybe it's as simple as having someone care—really care—about whether I'm happy or safe from day to day. And to feel comfortable caring about whether that person is happy and safe.

Reptar cared.

I'm suddenly very lonely.

June 25, 2019 (cont.)

I've been thinking about what school was like for me before we moved to the Poconos in 2007. I had a couple decent friends. Kids who would come over for playdates so Francine and Kyle could bank on sending me to one of their houses later. Get that good good free time away from the kids you don't pay much attention to anyway. Tight.

I was a smart kid. I knew it. I liked the positive attention from teachers. Craved it, really. It filled the cup that ran empty at home. I also had undiagnosed ADHD and paid not a huge amount of attention in class. Some teachers found it charming, the way I'd be not quite listening but somehow still comprehending the information around me. Other teachers seemed to find it obnoxious. With those teachers, I liked to drum fingers on my desk when they asked me questions. Sometimes I'd whistle to myself, too. One of those hateful teachers sent me to the principal for drumming and singing and then mouthing off to her about how that was my thinking process. The teacher "knew" it wasn't—even though it was.

After that I bottled it inside my skull out of consideration for my classmates, but there was always music and shit in my head. Some of my classmates liked me. But then there were other kids. One, Ryan Freehold, only wanted to be my friend to cheat off my tests and homework, which worked for me because of his "cool kid" status. Some of my classmates resented my presentation of not giving a fuck while simultaneously outpacing them in academics. I did give a fuck, though. I gave a thousand big ol' fucks. The glowing faces of my teachers—the ones who found me charming when I answered a difficult history question or explained covalent bonds long before we were supposed to get into them—it made my cold little heart beat.

School wasn't the most interesting thing to me. It did, however, bring me external validation. Papa loves him some external validation. I'm very withholding from myself, Diamond. Anyway, I've been thinking about this a lot because I want to get a little further into the weeds with this whole grief thing. I was low-key hoping I could be done after finally writing about the accident. Not so lucky, it seems. I'm going to have to get into the high school years, at least a little bit. That sounds like a job for the me who will exist tomorrow. And fuck if I know who that'll be.

June 26, 2019

Summer of 2007, nine days left before my first day of high school. Kyle put a new puppy in my lap. A rat terrier/chihuahua mix named Paws. I remember the way I would wobble around on my crutches, Paws trotting sleepily along behind me, while Francine read or wrote, always drinking. I slung the strap of my own collapsible lawn chair over my back and set it up seven or ten feet from Francine in lush green grass the dogs hadn't killed yet and leaned my crutches against the armrest. Paws and I stared at Francine while she read about the repressed sexual exploits of a kid from a Jewish ghetto and drank Nicholas's craft cocktails.

I read from my Norton Anthology out of habit, but Francine didn't have any questions for me anymore. Every hour or so she looked at me over the rims of her sunglasses. She never said, "Stop looking at me like that." Or, "I wish things had gone differently." Or, "I'm sorry."

How did this feel? It was fucking weird. That's how it felt. I wanted something from her. Not from Francine, but from my mother. I needed her to speak first, but to tell her that would have utterly contradicted the need. I wanted her to admit to being shitty. To being selfish. To not caring about her family in the slightest. I wanted her to call the police and admit to what she did and have to go to jail. I wanted her to say sorry so I could reject it and scream in her face and tell her how much I hated her. I think she sensed that. And dissociated. Found a sanctuary inside herself where she wouldn't have to look at who she'd become.

Her eyes, wandering up over the glasses to observe me—I can't actually remember what they looked like. I can't remember if they brimmed with tears, if they were ice cold, if they tried to communicate anything at all.

Diamond tells me I can't expect people to read my mind. That I need to communicate my feelings when they're important. She reminds me that it's okay to ask for help. Maybe that's what I wanted from Francine. A need as simple as some help.

I do remember creating doom scenarios for her. I dreamed of digging a huge pit and shoving her into it. Of going and finding Reptar and training him to tear her throat out. Of her giving me a hug and me pushing her away.

Neither of us could swallow our pride and speak. Neither of us knew how to handle the situation. Neither of us had the emotional stability or confidence to do any more work.

I think back to this setting a lot these days, thanks to you, Journal.

I think back to before Francine pushed me.

I think back to asking Kyle for help in some spat with Francine and his answer: "One of you has to be the adult."

I'll never understand why it had to be me.

June 27, 2019

I asked for additional bereavement time today. I'd forgotten I had taken three days off immediately after Kyle's suey. I was denied more time but told I could use sick days or any of the two-and-a-half weeks of PTO I've accrued. I'm taking all of it. Then I'll be unemployed. I can't do it anymore. I can't listen to Brad jerk himself off taking credit for other people's ideas. I can't listen to our CEO remind the team that we're "lean" when what she really means is that the company doesn't treat employees well enough to retain talent. I can't write another Twitter calendar for a "quirky" noodle brand.

With the end of summer in 2007 came the end of the dog business. Back from their trips to the Hamptons or Aspen or wherever, the rich folks who paid through the nose to house their dogs with us took them back. Even a lot of the ones we'd thought would never return. They paid what was owed, and more for those who hadn't properly arranged their pick-up times, a rule Francine swore she'd mentioned. Kyle and Francine found themselves wealthier than they'd ever been. Francine used the payments to cover up a six-figure periodic disbursement from her trust fund, adding to the large sum accumulating in their bank account—an account which Francine managed in totality. By this time, Kyle was almost always drifiting on opiates and blindly signing off on anything she wanted. The baseball player who returned for Reptar was sent down the mountain to the house now fostering him and given a partial refund. He had some choice words for Kyle and Francine, but it was all posturing.

Kyle hired contractors to finish building our house, which was still as it had been since "the accident," which is what we were calling that thing where Francine pushed me. There was nothing more than a hole in the ground with some sad beams sticking up. Francine took control of the project. She directed the builders like Kyle did the dogs. She pointed and snapped and shouted, keeping strict order over the work, making sure it was done "right."

When Kyle asked how much it was all costing, Francine waved him off, told him this was the house she wanted. Having grown meek, having lost control of himself and his family, Kyle backed down. He started smoking cigarettes and playing a lot of solitaire. He refilled his flask more than he used to.

There were a few times when Francine asked if he'd read the memoir pages she'd given him. He'd make a slow nod. He'd tell her he wasn't sure what to think, but that he wasn't a good reader. He'd say the whole thing was over his head. He'd look dejection into Francine's frown, sitting without the words she wanted and ashamed of that fact.

Kyle was now the dog whose only trick was play dead.

I want to end this entry here. Because, you know, I'm thinking, "Oh, me likey that sentence," but I don't feel finished for the day. Sometimes I wonder why Francine never asked me to read any of her writing. It makes me think she actually hated me. I wonder if she ever asked Nicholas to read any of it? Maybe I'll ask him later, if I remember.

The thing that's eating at me today is how easily I fell in line with everyone in calling Francine's assault of me "the accident." I think about that a lot. What my life would have looked like if I'd had the fortitude to tell the truth. To scream to the heavens that the only accident was actually me.

June 28, 2019

So now we're finally moving past the summer of 2007 and into fall of the same year. The start of the school year, my freshman year of high school. Nicholas was starting the fifth grade.

Without dogs on the property—Francine was refusing any new kennel clients as she focused on the house—and Kyle grown solitary, Nicholas and I got too uncomfortable with human interaction to make many new friends at school. I was the new kid with crutches and he was the boy who didn't talk much and cried a lot. We didn't have each other, even. Our schools were on opposite sides of town. Kindergarten through eighth grade on the south side, ninth through twelfth on the north.

The buildings both had Cold War–era architecture. Long, squat lines with small windows and green awnings over the front doors. The fortresses were painted beige with trim in azure and lemon (the colors of the school teams). Both schools were small, and most families had more than one kid. It took no time at all for word to get out that we were related.

Kids called me names when they thought I couldn't hear but didn't bully me physically. My only consistent company was a fellow freshman named Glen Sanders. He got assigned as my "buddy." We had all the same classes based on our aptitude tests. Glen didn't talk a ton, for which I was thankful, but he still managed to project this weird, cocky self-assurance that made me subtly hate him.

He did his best to walk slowly with me. He asked too often if I needed help.

"I don't need any help, Glen. I've got it, okay? Stop fucking asking."

I remember the look on his face when I told him that. I think I was so scared of getting bullied that I became a bully myself, at least in how I talked to people. Smack 'em first and you'll be prepared for the counterpunch. Something Kyle used to say. I don't remember the context.

Glen wasn't used to swearing, what with his wholesome family that sat down to dinner together every night and sent out yearly Christmas cards.

That first time I cursed at him, he stopped dead in his tracks, like my words were a force field more solid than any wall. That was when we both knew we weren't going to be friends.

Why am I still harboring so much resentment for Glen fucking Sanders, of all people? Oh, right.

At the start of high school, I thought Mare Bear Turnton might be my friend. I sometimes dreamt of her standing up for me. That maybe someone would make fun of my legs and she would come to my defense in a blaze of righteous fury, stand beside me against the other kids and say it didn't matter what they thought of me, that I was a good person and that was all that counted. But my life wasn't a John Hughes movie. Mare Bear Turnton was an average high-school girl with bigger concerns than potentially alienating herself for the sake of the new kid.

When Mare Bear and I passed one another in the hall, Glen beside me, Mare Bear clutching books and chatting with friends she'd known her entire life, I'd nod. She'd smile and give a small wave as I wobbled past.

I pretended it didn't bother me when she didn't stop what she was doing to come have a real conversation. (Why did I think it was her responsibility to start one?)

There were days when I saw Mare Bear talking to some boy and grew livid with envious hate. That quickly turned to shame. Even if Mare Bear didn't look like Francine, even if she could be genuinely interested in someone like me, I could never be enough for her. We could never even do something as simple as take a comfortable walk together.

Sometimes I thought about, you know, stopping to say hello and ask what she was doing. The fear was too much. Even when she slowed down and made faces of consideration. Even though we had classes together. My shame over what I'd become forced silence upon me for the first few weeks of school.

The start of the school year wasn't easy for Nicholas either. He didn't make friends for different reasons. He was big for his age, with Kyle's genes running through him. Turns out, all the turmoil at home affected him more than I'd thought—scratch that, more than I'd been willing to see. I saw it. I just shoved it away.

All the beatings I'd given him, Francine's drinking, Kyle's neglect, it all added up to quite the little anger issue.

In the first three days at his new school, Nicholas was sent to the principal's office four times, twice for verbal outbursts at teachers, once for cornering another kid in a hallway and threatening him, and the fourth for pummeling the same kid, who'd asked Nicholas why his brother couldn't walk and if I was retarded.

This fight led to Nicholas's first suspension from school. I came home and found him at Francine's feet, where she stood in front of the contractors working on her house, now with an almost-complete frame of vertical boards and angled supports. Nicholas sulked, answering the questions Francine pointed at him about Aristotle's enthymemes.

"It's a syllogism with an unspoken premise," he mumbled.

"And?"

"And is often thought to be incomplete, for it assumes knowledge held in common by both parties?"

"Keep going."

"But that's not always the case, making enthymemes a tricky rhetorical device."

Francine drained her glass and held it out. Nicholas took it and stumped to the cabin.

Francine shouted at the contractors for a time before checking her watch. She turned towards the cabin to see Nicholas standing in the doorframe, sniffing her drink.

"Don't you dare!" she shouted.

Nicholas walked up, handed her the drink, and resumed his seat by her feet.

She asked, "And what was the unstated premise of the enthymeme that you forgot today?"

"That we use our words to solve problems, not our fists."

"And who forgot to state that premise?"

"Me."

"Wrong." She looked down at Nicholas. He looked up. Their eyes met. Voice soft, Francine said, "It was my fault, sweetie. I haven't done a good job teaching you how to solve problems."

I crutched over and snorted. "Not one to lead by example, are you?"

She ignored me and shouted at one of the builders to get back to work. Paws ran up from deeper in the property and hopped around on her hind legs. She bounced after me on the way to the cabin. I sat down on the sofa and opened a book, surrounded by the permeating stink of Kyle's cigarettes. Paws whimpered and curled into a tight ball, burying her eyes under her tail.

Kyle came home, having heard about Nicholas's altercation, and locked him in our room. The kid he'd beaten up was Robby Turnton. Kyle was furious. All evening, Nicholas's sobbing could be heard through the door, but we all ignored it. Francine typed, Kyle smoked on the couch, and I read. Francine occasionally sent Kyle a yearning glance. He either didn't notice or wouldn't acknowledge the plea. He only freed Nicholas once Francine had finished making dinner. I sat in a small rocking chair next to the sofa, reading Chaim Potok's *The Chosen* and worrying over the thematic value of fate. Nicholas stalked past me across the gaudy blue-and-white area rug.

"Hey, psycho," I said.

He stopped a few feet away from me. "What?"

I looked up from my book. "Sup, psycho?"

Nicholas clenched his fists. "Don't call me that."

"Why not, ya little psycho?"

He rushed forward and shoved my shoulder. My chair tipped up onto one rocker, but I shifted my weight and forced it down. Nicholas grabbed me and wrenched me from my seat onto the hardwood floor. He sat on my chest, got his hands around my throat. Kyle and Francine finally took notice. Francine didn't intervene directly, opting to call Kyle into action.

He said, "Let them work it out. Boys need to settle their differences this way sometimes."

Air had trouble getting past Nicholas's grip and into my lungs.

This is the moment I realized, proper legs or no, I wasn't going to get anything more handed to me.

I anchored my elbow against the floor, bent my arm, shoved down and twisted my shoulders, using the momentum to punch Nicholas in the face. My fist connected right where his jaw met his cheek. He fell off of me. I rolled onto him, using my weight to pin him. I wanted to hit him again, even though he barely seemed conscious. I would have, too, if I didn't slide to the floor and twist onto my back. I hardly felt it when Francine grabbed me by the ankles and pulled me off Nicholas. She crouched over me, eyes wild. She raised her hand up, palm open. Kyle wrapped his arms around her waist and lifted her away from me.

This established our familial power structure without the need for words. I was stronger than Nicholas. Nicholas was protected by Francine, but Kyle wouldn't let her do any more physical damage to me. Other than that, there were no holds barred.

Kyle set Francine down in the corner, where she stood panting. Then he came and held my crutches out to me while I pulled myself up, levering my weight against the sofa. He checked on Nicholas, who was sitting up and crying. Kyle told him, "You're fine. It's time for dinner."

I limped to the table on my crutches. Kyle went to the kitchen counter and ate two painkillers. We all ate overcooked spaghetti with canned marinara, each with our own proverbial Sword of Damocles dangling above.

June 30, 2019

Nicholas learned at an almost preternatural rate. It took away any chance for him to be an ordinary kid. His intellectual aptitude mixed poorly with the daily existential crises forced upon him by his alcoholic mother, aided by an equally addicted father who wanted nothing to do with him and a brother who was too absorbed by his own anger to extend him a little kindness. Then, with all these nightmarish, complicated relationships boiling in his developing brain, he had to learn responsibility. For himself, certainly. Often for Francine, what with his constant visions of her choking to death on her own vomit. If he hadn't been so intelligent, maybe he would have kept fist-fighting at school until they kicked him out for good and he joined the army or something.

Instead, Nicholas became a forty-year-old mind in a ten-year-old body.

There's no cure for that.

People have always told me I'm an "old soul." I've heard people say it to Nicholas, too. I think about what that means. "Old soul."

The way it makes the most sense in my brain is that people say that when they recognize a person is placed out of time. I had a friend in college named Taylor. She was another "old soul." She and I connected over feeling more mature or advanced or tired than most of our peers seemed. She had a bunch of people over at her house in New York one summer. Her parents were older than I'd expected. She was twenty-two but her father was sixty-seven and her mother was sixty-five. For her, that's what placed her out of time. Her old parents. They were raised too long before the culture in which their daughter existed. It made Taylor feel as though she'd been born too late.

What placed me and Nicholas out of time? Trauma? Isolation? Those are contributing factors, but I think the real issue is we had to learn to take care of ourselves the way adults do when we were still children. We didn't have caretakers. We didn't have each other. Sometimes, it felt like we didn't have ourselves.

Nicholas, if you ever decide to snoop in this journal to find out what's in my head, I'm not mad at you, but fuck off. It's my journal and I can speak for you in here all I want.

Anyway, Nicholas took Francine's words about problem-solving to heart at school. He didn't fight. But he also didn't need to. The bruises on Robby Turnton's face established Nicholas's reputation. Word was out that Nicholas was not to be fucked with. This, combined with his need to please Francine, taught Nicholas that a sharp tongue was a better way to make friends than a closed fist.

The reason for my leg issue was not known to the public. It was never spoken of by my family, but we were asked about it tactlessly and often. This became Nicholas's avenue to revenge. He had absorbed some of Francine's creative streak, and he used it to lead an ad hominem campaign against me.

He started by telling everyone I was gay, which in 2007, in a small, conservative-leaning town, was a real bullet. Then he said I was born with no real spine. Then he told everyone we had to close the dog business because I was molesting the animals.

Word reached the high school in bits and pieces, but these first rumors didn't bother me. It wasn't like they could tarnish my image, given that there was nothing shiny about it to begin with. But Nicholas was the smartest, most articulate kid in his class. His philosophical training gave him a different way of thinking than your average ten-year-old. And, to kick a dead horse, his physical dominance freed him to focus on psychological warfare. It was only a matter of weeks until he figured out how to hurt me.

After the fight, Robby Turnton avoided Nicholas like Robert Blake avoided jail. Then my younger brother figured out who Robby was. I don't know if Kyle drinking with Mr. Turnton rang the bell, or if Nicholas was slow to learn Robby's last name, or if I raved about Mare Bear in my sleep, but soon Nicholas and Robby were best friends. Robby, as sidekick, became the engine through which Nicholas spread his rumors. This is how his lies got to the ears of Mare Bear Turnton.

I was on my way past Mare Bear, where she stood by her locker, surrounded by her girlfriends. I gave Mare Bear my customary nod, making deliberant eye contact to show confidence. She turned bright red and all her friends broke out laughing.

One of them pointed and called, "Fiveskin!"

Ugh, I still remember all their faces. Right now, when I blink, it's like they're mocking me from the insides of my eyelids.

Glen laughed along with them. I looked over at him. He winked at Mare Bear, who shook her head and started to say something to me. All I heard was buzzing in my ears from sheer adolescent embarrassment.

I wanted to ask what the fuck was going on, but their laughter cut deep in my chest. I limped on, leaving Glen and the girls behind, feeling ashamed and overwhelmed with confusion.

In mine and Nicholas's bedroom in the cabin—a wooden box with floral wallpaper, bunk beds, and two dressers with a mirror between them—I pulled myself up onto the top bunk. This was where Nicholas hid his journal, thinking there was no way for me to get up there. I flipped through to the last page with markings. It had some notes in it about logical empiricism, quotes from Francine, and a lot of question marks, annotations to look into something later. I backtracked until a note caught my eye, pressed down hard in Nicholas's spiky handwriting. It read, "When people ask about ass face's legs." Beneath was the story he'd been telling, burned into my brain regardless of time's passing.

I'll tell you, but it's a secret, and you have to promise not to say anything. K. J. has a really rare disease. It only happens to one in like a hundred million kids. There's some stupid long name for it that the doctors use, but they call it "fiveskin" to save time. Basically, even though we're Jewish, my brother couldn't get circumcised because his fourskin—

Idiot! How could a kid who read Immanuel Kant not know how to spell foreskin?

—was too thick to cut off. They broke the little penis guillotine trying to get it or something, but it's not cool armor like Colossus from X-Men. His fiveskin keeps getting thicker and thicker and now it's so heavy and fat that it weighed his legs down and that's why he can't walk straight. Someday he'll be in a wheelchair because his fiveskin keeps growing until both his legs'll break forever and he'll just be a big penis. Even though he's already a dick.

If I hadn't been the subject of the story, I might have laughed. I might have defended it as objectively hilarious. But I was the subject. And Mare Bear's sad eyes, mixed with the mocking faces of her friends and Glen, swam through my vision over and over.

And, okay, one more thing: if a fiveskin is, like, a huge overgrown foreskin, then wouldn't it stand to reason there would also be a threeskin? What would that be? Just a headless shaft? Hmmm,

I'm not a weinerologist. Would it be like an M&M in some PVC pipe? Or a skinless tip that leaves the bearer in endless penile agony? Should it be weinerologist or dicktrician?

My school day ended at 2:15, but I never got home until around 3:30, what with waiting for my bus and being the last one dropped off. Nicholas didn't get dismissed until 3:20 and it took substantially less time for him to get back on the bicycle Francine had bought him. I figured I had about twenty minutes to set up.

The bus driver, Ms. Jane, was happy to let me off the bus early, since it allowed her to eschew navigating up our driveway and back. I struggled up the hill on my crutches and hid behind a tree, a quarter of a mile from our gate. I thought about how irresponsible it was to let a ten-year-old travel so far by himself on a bicycle. It compounded my hatred for Francine. Nicholas could have suffered an accident or been abducted or had any number of unspeakable things befall him at any moment.

Live long enough to become the things you hate, right? The thing that was going to happen to Nicholas that day was me. I can't stop thinking about how I'm all the things that are wrong with me. My therapist talks a lot about self-compassion. About how to train myself to talk to myself like I'm my own good friend. She had me write out my internal narrative once, when I started seeing her, like, two years ago or so. I read it aloud to myself and thought, "Fuck, if I saw a stranger talking to another stranger on the street this way, I would have a moral obligation to intervene." And then I think of the things I've done and it makes me want to throw up.

Anyway, I hid behind a tree and waited for Nicholas. The snapping of a Jimmy Rollins baseball card echoed on the deserted, winding roads. I took my left crutch in hand and waited. Nicholas rode up from around a bend, appearing out of the low foliage, weaving back and forth across a double yellow line while the sun cast long, skeletal shadows of the overhanging branches.

Nicholas came near me, tired by this point in his uphill ride. I pivoted out from my cover, shoved the crutch between the spokes of his front wheel, and let go. The bike's momentum came to a violent halt. Nicholas flew forward over his handlebars.

I hobbled from my hiding place and looked at him for a minute, lying on his back on the road, dutifully wearing wrist braces, knee and elbow pads, and his helmet, since Francine demanded it. His arms were spread in a T, legs straight out below him. I wondered whether his luck was good or bad for surviving, not that I thought he'd actually die, but projection is weird. I wondered why I didn't really care. I got beside him and looked down.

"Remember this," I said. "Remember that you pay what you owe. Remember that you'll never be safe. If you tell Francine the real reason you're limping when you get home, I'll kill you."

Then I picked up the other crutch and pushed my way up the hill, the effort and strain on my arms never fully registering.

I wish I'd died when my head hit that shoe rack.

July 1, 2019

I should write about my legs. I've spent such an ungodly amount of time talking about them in therapy over the years, but I guess I've never processed them on paper for myself this way. Right after Francine knocked my head against the shoe rack, in the hospital, I was sad and thought I was going to die; I've told therapists this stuff ad nauseum; etc., etc. The busted legs were the lingering remnant of what she'd done. They wobbled and hurt and didn't respond to things the way I wanted. They were such a direct and distinct reflection of how I felt inside.

When I choose to remember the slow, painful recovery of my legs this way, it makes the whole process feel less…I don't know… bleak? Because over time, my legs got stronger. The less I obsessed over what other people thought about them, the stronger they got. It took practice and hard work and perseverance, but within a year, I didn't need the crutches anymore. Looking back on it now, it feels simple to find the metaphor. "As I grow strong and stable, so do my legs." Hindsight, blah, blah, blah. Now, I'm a little bow-legged, shorter than I might otherwise have been, and a slow runner;

otherwise, it's tough to tell that anything so severe happened to me so early in life.

But the sad fact is that my injury did come at the onset of puberty. A time rife with insecurity, uncertainty, and social anxiety. When I got to high school on my crutches, I decided that no one would ever like me and that the only way to gain acceptance was to hide and see who would take pity on me. I never quite stuck to that plan. My mouth was too big when I wasn't utterly distracted or detached from the world around me. And fuck if I didn't have a mean streak from the misplaced rage of my home life.

None of that's important at this exact moment, though. I'll get into all of that in more detail. What even is important? Why can I only think via using so many words? Why can't I collect my thoughts first and then say whatever it is I want to say? Why is this whole damn process difficult? Do other people struggle with this sort of thing? Am I broken?

Those are not useful thoughts.

I know Diamond would have a nicer way of saying that.

Refocus.

The legs.

What did the injury mean to me at the time when I was dealing with it most acutely?

The legs were inconvenient. They were an emblem of my brokenness. They were proof that Francine hated me, even though I'd never present them in the court of public opinion. Maybe I should have. Ruminating on that isn't going to get me anywhere.

My injury made me an outcast, but not as much as *I* made me an outcast. It's hard to make friends when you're scared of human attention and refuse eye contact with any and all passersby. Sometimes, I overheard schoolmates talking in low voices about what was wrong with my legs. Or they'd murmur, "That's Fiveskin."

Or maybe I imagined those things. It's tough to tell, now.

Gym class was annoying. Even though I wasn't required to participate in physical activity, I still had to put on the stupid little blue and yellow uniform and sit in the bleachers while the other kids played basketball or ran ridiculous relay races or learned badminton. I always showed up late, the legs an easy excuse. That way, I didn't have to change in the locker room at the same time as all the other kids. I sat on one of the little benches and got the uniform on as fast as possible, then allocated my brain space to creating story concepts in my notebook. I remember a couple that I liked, but nothing ever happened with them.

One was about military snipers with PTSD who become hitmen. To entertain themselves, they play horse with literal trick shots.

Another was wearwolves, about the secret cabal of werewolves that control the fashion industry and start trends in materials based on what they feel like eating.

Then there was one in which the protagonist solves every conflict and minor inconvenience by Shawn-Michaels-superkicking people. That one was always imagined based on my aggravating interactions with Glen Sanders.

Anyway: I was a high school boy in a landscape where community standing was based primarily on athletic aptitude, so you can see why being the kid with the "disability crutches" wouldn't lend itself to immense popularity. Some days that bothered me more than others. It irritated me most when it came to the topic of girls. My self-esteem spiraled every time I thought about what I could even potentially bring to a romantic relationship.

Then, of course, there was the problem of physical autonomy. The indignity of feeling out of control with respect to one's own physical body.

Diamond would say that the subtle switch to "one's" instead of "my" is a defense mechanism here. She would ask, "Is that serving you?"

Ugh.

There are an infinite number of things that just I flat-out don't, and can't, know. It's infuriating. Diamond would say that radical acceptance is key to overcoming control issues.

Ugh.

She'd say that control, in and of itself, is a myth. Diamond would tell me that awareness is half the battle—and then admit that it's realistically more like five percent of the battle.

Ugh.

Feeling like I didn't have command of my own legs was supremely difficult, obviously. It made me think a lot about the things we all take for granted. For me, running water. Knowing my next meal is secure as long as humanity continues to stall inevitable fallout and mass destruction. Healthcare because I'm thankfully employed and not unaware of what a hand variance had in that.

But not having my legs as my own. Sheesh.

I thought a lot about whether it would have been easier if I was born with the condition I wound up in. So that I wouldn't have ever known anything else. I thought that maybe that would have staved off some of the resentment that overwhelmed me and sent my anxious depression spiraling for days or weeks or months at a time. Then I would get so *angry* with myself. Then I'd use that anger as motivation. That was the sole thing that drove me through my teens. Nothing but raw, unabated anger. I'm still angry.

Diamond would ask, "Is this serving you?"

I don't know.

Nah, scratch that. The answer is no.

Words words words words words. These are all nothing but stupid words.

The legs.

What the legs stopped me from doing—I'm dancing around it. The legs didn't quite stop me from "doing" anything. I stopped me from doing things. Sure, I couldn't, like, go hiking or play golf or baseball or anything, but I also had no interest in those things, independent of the legs. My interests were more sedentary. I guess, sure, I couldn't work outside with Kyle anymore, and that was a bit of a bummer, but after the accident, I didn't want to be around that fucking guy anyway.

Or I'm telling myself that to minimize the impact the injury did, in fact, have on me.

I can't figure this shit out.

Long story short, having fucked-up legs was super inconvenient and I used it as a way to avoid my life. But they got better over time. I could go for runs now, if I wanted to. Madison goes on runs every morning. She asked me on our second date if I wanted to go with her sometime. I told her I'd take a pass because of my stride. I was embarrassed about how I might look. So yeah, the legs still affect me in a lot of ways. They don't feel like they belong to me some days. They're something else entirely. What that thing is or was or could be is alien. They hurt my self-esteem when I think about them. Sometimes I think they have a life and voice of their own. They behave how I want, but always at a cost. Always with the remembrance of who or what I was or could have been before Francine's shoe rack. That fucking shoe rack. So stable. So unyielding. So opposite of me.

The worst part was the dreams. I developed a recurring nightmare.

I'm on my crutches in an abandoned parking garage, minding my own business, hobbling towards the exit under flickering ceiling bulbs. In the distance behind me, I hear an odd scuttling sound. I look over my shoulder and there's nothing. Only red-lined parking spaces, nary a car nor life form in sight. I pick up the pace on my crutches, but my top speed is too low to feel safe. The exit booth comes into view, the striped bar down. The volume of the scuttling behind me grows. I look over my shoulder again. A looming, indistinct shadow stretches around the corner. I stumble and fall on my stomach. I lose the crutches and frantically army crawl towards the exit. My fingers scrabble at the smooth concrete floor until I somehow regain my feet. I check behind myself again. Coming towards me is a centaur, except instead of a horse's body, it's a spider. The face of the spidertaur is always shifting, the edges blurred, the center in motion, morphing between sharp and rounded expressions and shapes. It's wearing a tall, rectangular hat, black with a red diamond on the front, and a loose white shirt and black cape. I turn back to the exit and try to run. The exit bar comes closer. The scuttling picks up pace. When I look behind me for the last time, the spidertaurs have multiplied. I'm only a yard from the bar. I feel pressure on my back and I wake up.

This nightmare comes to me every night.

July 2, 2019

During the fall of 2007, I met an English teacher at school who I actually rather liked. His name was, and I'm not making this up, Martin Short. To add to the absurdity of him—or the predictability, depending on your intuition—Mr. Short was about six-foot-five.

He was maybe the first adult who I felt really treated me like a person of value. Or made me feel valued in the way I wanted to be. *Saw* me. I never had to tell him I was sad or angry and why. That man could read the room.

He wore his hair shoulder-length and had kind, good-humored eyes. He was also my homeroom teacher. I arrived earlier to school than ninety-five percent of other students, so I was able to claim the back corner of the room, furthest from the door, as my seat. Mr. Short didn't mind. He tried to engage me in conversation anyway, at least some mornings. He didn't press when the attempts went unreciprocated. But he always tried again, a day or a week later.

Mare Bear and Glen were also in Mr. Short's homeroom English class. Glen sat next to me but we largely ignored one another, me inside my solitude and him obnoxiously laughing at inside jokes from three guys he'd been friends with since elementary school. Mare Bear sat front and center but rarely participated, keeping her head bent over her notebook and pen, working furiously throughout class.

Somewhere around three weeks into the school year, when our class was discussing *A Separate Peace*—a novel about two boys in boarding school, with a very strong subtextual gay relationship, which I found to be slowly paced and simply written—Mr. Short dismissed class five minutes early.

It was my habit to let the class empty out before taking up my crutches and working my way into the hallway where Glen dutifully waited with a scowl. Mr. Short asked if I'd stay behind and chat for a couple minutes, said his prep period was next and he'd write me a note for my next class if I was late. He dismissed Glen, who took his job as my chaperone much more seriously than he publicly let on, whether from being trained to take his responsibilities as full commitments or so he could write all about it on a college application. Probably a combination of the two.

It was a relief to be away from him.

Mr. Short asked me how I was doing.

I probably said, "Good."

He probably rolled his eyes and said, "What is it with teenagers and one-word answers?"

"What's with teachers and inquisitions?"

A gleam in his eyes. "Is that wit I detect?"

I sighed. "What's up, Mr. Short?"

He mimicked my sigh. "The way kids talk to teachers is wild to me. 'What's up?' you ask me. When I was a kid it was, 'How may I help you?'"

"How may I help you, Mr. Short?"

"I wanted to check in. You haven't said a single thing in class, yet. I see you every day back there, scribbling or poorly hiding the book you're actually reading under your desk."

"I'd hardly call it a desk."

"..."

"I don't know, man. I don't find what we're talking about to be particularly interesting."

"Let me see what you're reading, then."

Why do I remember this conversation so well? I wonder if I'm actually recording it verbatim. Something tells me I mostly am. The way memory works...thought loop, thought loop, reality is what we make it. In college I ran into this guy who I think had fried his brains, probably on LSD. Anyway, he was pretty insufferable for most people. I kind of liked him when he wasn't subtly condescending to me about topics I empirically knew way more about. He used to talk about how we're all just tripping our own reality. What he meant was we can't possibly understand another person, really. Our experiences can only be known to ourselves. It makes me think about invisible diseases. My struggles with anxiety and depression and anger. Present day, my best friends are the ones who struggle with those same things in more serious degrees. I'm tired of saying how shitty I feel. It might be a little easier for me to express this because, you know, the whole leg situation. There's something there people can look at and think, "Oh, that's hard." But most people don't get it. They don't understand the debilitating weight of something like, let's say, Borderline Personality Disorder. A disorder that turns your own brain into your greatest enemy. On one hand, I'm glad more people can't entirely comprehend what that's like. It means they haven't gone through it. Even if they take it for granted, that's such a fucking blessing.

But anyway, that's more or less what this guy I knew with the French fry brains meant. We're all just tripping our own reality. Creating it in our minds and living it however we can. With whatever capacities. However feels authentic? Thought loop...thought loop...mindful breathing...weeeeeeee! Tangents!

"Let me see what you're reading, then."

Out of the backpack beside my desk I took a copy of DFW's *The Broom of the System.*

Mr. Short made a pained expression, looked into my eyes, didn't find the answer there for which he had been looking.

He definitely asked, "You know Wittgenstein?"

I most likely said, "Not personally, no."

Mr. Short scoffed, his eyes crinkling. "This book makes sense to you?"

"Some of it. I'll probably read it a couple more times to figure it all the way out. Or at least the timeline and actions and stuff."

"Do you like to write?"

I swallowed. My voice lost confidence. "Yeah, sometimes."

"What's your next class?"

"Physical Science. With Ms. Towson."

"Let me give her a call. I'd like for you to stay and chat for a while."

"This isn't a Neverland Ranch thing, is it?"

He blinked; said, "Jesus Christ."

"Was that in poor taste?" I asked.

"Maybe I *don't* want you to open up."

"O Captain, my Captain?"

"Are you about finished?"

"Well, I can't jump up on a desk like in the movies."

His lips vanished inwards against one another. "You're quick."

I shrugged.

He said, “Have you thought about extracurricular activities? You don’t seem interested in talking to other students much.”

“No, I haven’t, and no, I’m not.”

“What do you do in your free time?”

Our eyes met, and again I was struck by the bright, genuine nature of Mr. Short’s gaze.

“Are you a Medusa?” I asked.

“What—wait…what? K.J., can you work with me here a little?” Before I could speak, Mr. Short held up a finger and paused me. “If you’re about to try and sidetrack me with a question, joke, or sarcasm, get out.”

There was no animosity in the words.

“Okay,” I said. “Extracurriculars. What do you have in mind?”

“Your in-class writing assignments so far have been exceptional.”

Color rose to my cheeks. It had been a very long time since I’d experienced the pleasure of an earnest compliment. Feeling dumbstruck, I said, “Thanks.”

“Do you ever like to write in your spare time?”

“Yeah, sometimes.”

“What do you like to write about?”

“I’ve tried my hand at a couple stories, I guess.”

“You guess?” he asked.

I nodded.

“What do you like to write?”

And before I knew what was happening, I was blurting out my stupid Grim Reaper story in which Francine, accurately, had seen an utter lack of substance. It had been retooled many times and looked at only by me since. The changes had been in the vein of Francine’s advice. “Write what you know.” So now the main character was the son of the Grim Reaper. His goal was to inherit his mother's title, the only way to do so being to murder her after she mutilated his legs.

Mr. Short listened with intent. "Could I read what you have? I'd be happy to give you notes. If you want them, that is."

A lump rose to my throat. All I could do was nod.

"But," he said, "there is one condition."

I croaked out an "Mm-hmm."

"You have to come to the meeting for the school paper tomorrow."

With this one little ultimatum, Mr. Short punched a hole in the iron maiden I was slowly but surely building for my brain. I owe him a great deal for that.

That next morning after the chat, before homeroom officially started, I brought Mr. Short a printed packet, stapled at the top left corner: five pages, double-spaced, double-sided.

Mr. Short scanned the first page of my Grim Reaper story, sitting on the edge of his desk, and smirked at something he saw.

"What?" I asked.

He gave an absent, "Hm?" He looked up at me. "Oh, it's a good thing. I can hear you in these first couple paragraphs."

I blushed hard and cared not at all.

He told me he'd read the whole thing during his prep period and have comments for me when we met for the school paper.

I nodded. The other early kids filtered into class and I crutched urgently back to my corner.

The rest of the day passed in an anxious blur. I had printed a second copy of the story for myself. Every free or distracted moment, I slipped the pages out and went back over them. The words were typo-free. The sentences were mostly clean. I found a few passages in which I could have given the characters more room to breathe. Overall, I thought the whole thing was garbage. A pit opened in my stomach. Staying after school was a terrible idea.

I'd left Francine a note on her kitchen counter, saying I was going to be home late. I'd had a fantasy of just letting her freak out. Me failing to show up when I usually did; her screaming, "Where is my son? What happened to my son?" But I decided that was dumb, because the reality was she probably wouldn't notice.

Is that black-and-white thinking? Why have I always had to think so hard? Is ignorance bliss? Gah.

Mr. Short seemed to care if I showed up. That was enough motivation to follow through.

The final bell rang. The Algebra 2 class I shared with only two other freshman—Glen Sanders and Mare Bear Turnton, the rest of our classmates being sophomores through seniors—emptied out.

I told Glen to go get ready for baseball—that he didn't have to escort me to the bus today, since the newspaper meeting was in Mr. Short's class, right across the hallway. He made an uncertain face, then shrugged and waved goodbye to Mare Bear, who smiled at him and waved back.

Mare Bear walked directly into Mr. Short's classroom.

My mouth beat my brain and, out loud, I said, "Oh, fuck."

The Algebra 2 teacher, Ms. Howitzer, was behind me.

"Excuse me?" she probably said, aghast.

Without looking over my shoulder, I probably shouted, "Nothing," and hurried across the hall to escape.

My entrance put the room population at three. Me, Mr. Short, and Mare Bear Turnton. Ms. Howitzer followed me to scold me about my language. Mr. Short told her he'd take care of it. She left with a huff.

The stare I gave Mr. Short was desperate. My whole day had been leading up to this: I'd hear his comments and be crushed as a terrible writer with a hopeless future.

He told me he'd give me his comments after the meeting so I could focus on the task at hand. He said it with great humor. If Mare Bear hadn't been there, I might have screamed at him. I navigated to my corner.

Mr. Short said we'd get started once everyone else arrived. Mare Bear, from her customary seat at the front of the room, twisted towards me, draping her elbow over the back of her chair.

She said, "Sup, Fiveskin," her tone conspiratorial. She said it in a way I'd read and heard that friends can talk to each other but outsiders can't.

I rolled my eyes. "Yo, Mare Bear."

She grunted. "What brings you here?"

"I told that guy—" lifting my chin towards Mr. Short "—that I couldn't read and he's making me come here to learn."

"Meh," said Mare Bear, "three out of ten."

Two chatting juniors walked in. Mare Bear's eyes widened and she turned back around. I looked over at two girls. The first was short with rigid features and a part shaved into the side of her short hair. She had a hawkish nose and bright teeth. The other girl was taller, with flowing honey-brown hair and a maroon, long-sleeved dress. I'd seen her in the hallways and always averted my eyes. She seemed so…cool. Not in the way that high-school jocks considered themselves cool. But, like, *cool*. She carried herself with confidence in her identity. I don't know. I was in awe of her, I guess.

The first girl's name was Rhiannon, and the second's was Sheila Shinebock. I was instantly in love with Sheila.

They both said hi to me. I nodded and averted my eyes. They went and sat at the front of the room, Sheila next to Mare Bear, Rhiannon next to Sheila. Sheila wrapped an arm around Mare Bear's shoulders and gave her a noogie. They were apparently old family friends, practically sisters.

They talked about politics, a conversation in which I had exactly no interest. I flipped my armrest table up and opened a notebook, bent my neck down to stare at the pages.

Sheila's voice came from the front row. "Hey," it said.

I moved my eyes up without moving my head.

Sheila laughed a silver laugh. "Yeah," she said. "You, in the back."

I couldn't find my voice.

"Why don't you join us up here?" she asked.

Rhiannon got up and pulled the chair out next to Mare Bear. "Look at that," she said. "An open space, just for you."

Panic set in.

Mr. Short said, "Rhiannon, Sheila, that's K.J. K.J., these two fine young people are Sheila and Rhiannon. K.J. is going to be writing fiction for our paper this year. Add some flare to it."

"That's awesome," said Rhiannon.

"You don't have to join us up here if you don't want to," Sheila told me. "But it would be super cool." She smiled, her left canine slightly askew. There was nothing inside me that even considered saying no to that smile. I flipped my notebook shut, stuffed it into my backpack, took up my crutches, and went to the front of the room. Three more kids filtered in a few minutes later.

The meeting started with your typical icebreakers, fun facts, interests, whatever. There turned out to be seven of us who would run the paper under Mr. Short's supervision.

We talked as a group—I contributed nothing—about the goals for the paper. What we all wanted it to look like. Proposed roles for each person. Workshopped those a little. Things ran for about an hour.

Desperation to get Mr. Short's notes on my story grew and grew. I found myself staring expectantly at his desk, having to pull myself back to reality. Negative attribution appeared in the form of Francine's voice. He hated the story. I knew that. My questions were about how much he hated it and why. Those were the things I *needed* to know.

The meeting wrapped. Yawning, the students who weren't me, Sheila, Rhiannon, or Mare Bear stood to depart. Mr. Short stood facing his desk, his back to me.

Mare Bear said, "Hey, K.J.?"

I snapped from my reverie. "Mm?"

"I asked if you wanted a ride home. My mom is picking me up."

The way she said *mom* made my toes hurt.

I didn't know how I was getting home. I was suddenly unsure whether I should have arranged it with my bus driver or something.

So when Mare Bear said her mom could drive me home, I sat without words.

Sheila asked, "Where do you live?"

"Up the mountain."

"We can give you a ride back," she said—*we* being her and Rhiannon. "If you don't mind hanging out for maybe fifteen minutes while I finish some things up."

Rhiannon, standing behind Sheila and formerly unaware of the "things" in need of finishing, grimaced. She said, "Uh, Sheels, I was really hoping to get going."

Without turning her head, Sheila said, "You know, once I'm done with this stuff, I'm done with everything, and there's a spot somewhere up there I've been meaning to show you."

With great haste, Rhiannon said, "Yeah, K.J., we could give you a ride home."

I told them, with more earnestness than I thought I had left in me, that I'd really appreciate it.

Then Mr. Short turned around, the small packet of my Grim Reaper story in hand. He scanned it, flipped the front page, and looked up at me. He favored me with a small smile. He handed me the pages, sparsely annotated with red pen.

He said, "You have a real knack for voice. We do need to work a little bit on conventions, though. This is a really good start, K.J."

"A good start?"

The fantasy department of my brain, despite its nagging that I was the worst writer ever to write, was doing double duty with thoughts of, "It's perfect, K.J. You are the best writer in the history of writers. No notes. I'm going to call literary agents on your behalf starting right now."

"Yes," Mr. Short said. "One thing to keep in mind with stories is suspension of disbelief. As well as ebb and flow. This is sort of…a spiral down."

"Art imitates life."

"Sure. But life is messy; fiction needs to make sense." Then, after an uncomfortable pause: "K.J., how are things at home?"

"Peachy," I probably said.

July 6, 2019

I went camping with some friends over the holiday. I was *super* hesitant. It turned out to be a nice time, though. We stayed on my friend Vingh's property in New York right by Binghamton. Everyone mostly sat around drinking and dipping into the creek at the bottom of the property. The whole place is an enormous hill. I walked up and down it a few times, just to stretch the legs and gauge where they're at these days. They held up nicely.

Everyone there knew my stance on drinking and didn't try to peer-pressure me. Except for one guy who had no idea and kept offering me beers when he was good and wasted. It didn't feel triggering. That kind of thing used to be triggering. In the words of blink-182, I guess this is growing up.

I spent most of the weekend whittling a wizard staff from a cracked maple branch, which was tight. It's still unfinished, but I think I'll sand, stain, and wax it sometime this week. I'm thinking Brazilian Rosewood might give it a nice color.

Okay, enough pleasantries.

Kyle and Francine. Their marriage. Me. Nicholas. Our family. It should never have happened. I should never have been born. Then Nicholas wouldn't have been. Francine and Kyle wouldn't have kept trying to force their square marriage into circular lives. Francine could have had the entirety of her inheritance and lived in Miami sipping Mai Tais on the beach. Kyle could have met a nice Italian girl from South Philly with whom he could breed pitbulls and live a simple, pleasurable life. Instead, with Francine's kibosh on reopening the kennel business, Kyle went back to work as an electrician. He managed to find steady work. He didn't acknowledge how many Oxys he ate daily—if he even knew—or how his voice had lost all trace of its former gravitas. He didn't acknowledge that he had failed as a father, nor did he make any apparent plans to do better. Instead, he told me that as long as he could be home for dinner and to play a hand or two of cards with his boys, the days could never get that bad.

Per usual, he was wrong.

The land had become desolate. Still lush but no longer booming with the ambient cacophony of barking. The dog houses sat in empty, dirty rows. No one bothered to hose them off once they were free of occupants. The land was quiet all the time, but never with that serene feeling you sometimes find in nature.

There was one clearing on the east side of the property that held a semblance of tranquility. It was home to a gorgeous old white pine. Whatever elements shaped its growth left it with a wide base and seven thick trunks rising in tight angles to one another. When we'd first arrived at the property and toured the land—Kyle and me—we'd stared in wonder at its gnarled majesty. Over time, after the accident, it grew painful for me to be around it. It felt like the tree thought me weak for not branching through hardship the way it always had.

Between Francine's house and the cabin, the dog houses seemed smaller than they had when we built them. A ghost town that, if visited by a tourist, would haunt them for years. Upon completion of Francine's house, finished three days before Thanksgiving 2007—*way* ahead of schedule, according to Francine and her biblical-Egyptian style of oversight—she asked the builders if they had sledgehammers. They didn't but could easily obtain them. She inquired whether or not they could use some free lumber and slate, which they said they could. She told them that if they'd like to, they were welcome to demolish all the dog houses and take the remaining materials, which they did.

The builders came and destroyed the ruined city Kyle and I had built. I got home from school while the builders were halfway through sacking the city for materials. I watched and said nothing, knowing that Kyle would come home and somehow make everything right. The structures were gone before he was home from work. He pulled up in the truck and saw the grass, marred with the impressions of the dog houses, the foundation holes with bits of concrete strewn about, the old urine stains. Francine lounged in her lawn chair, reading the latest pages of her manuscript, a pen jutting from the corner of her mouth. Kyle threw the truck door open and jumped out. He stormed right up to her. He opened his mouth to speak. Francine held a finger up to him and kept reading.

Kyle snatched the pages from her hand.

"What the fuck?" she snarled. "You gave me a fucking papercut. Are you out of your mind?"

His powerful gaze returned; the fog that had crept into his eyes vanished. "What did you do?"

Francine looked back into his face and crossed her arms over her chest. In a sweet voice she said, "Whatever do you mean?"

Kyle threw her pages aside, sending them flapping through the air. This was the first time it occurred to me how much physically larger Kyle was than Francine. He had at least a full head's height on her and was twice as broad. And yet Francine looked up at him without an ounce of fear.

"I was sick of looking at those disgusting dog houses," she said.

"You couldn't have talked to me about it?"

"Talked to you about it? When have we *not* been talking about it? I told you how much I hated them. I told you I wanted them gone. What did you think was going to happen?"

"K.J. and I worked hard on those."

"What's that got to do with anything?"

Kyle ground his teeth and took a deep breath. "What about next summer?"

"What about it?"

He balled his fists. "*Stop* answering my questions with questions. It drives me goddamned insane, Francine. Now I'll have to build new houses for the dogs when we open again."

Francine's voice gained an edge. "We will not be opening that business again."

Kyle tilted his head.

"No, we will not."

Kyle flushed. He drew his hand back, palm open.

Francine stood and threw a scornful laugh in his face. "Good. Finally do it. Become just like one of your stepfathers. Cross that line. We all know you're no different deep down."

Kyle screwed his eyes shut, lowered his hand, and inhaled through his nose.

Francine said, "I will not spend another second, let alone another summer, dealing with those monsters. Look at what they did to our son."

"What they did?" I screamed. "What *they* did?" I raced over the fifty feet of grass, my crutches barely in use. "The dogs never did anything to me or you. They never did anything wrong. Why can't you take responsibility for yourself?" Paws barked twice and ran off. I planted myself inches from Francine. "*You* did this."

She looked away.

"You're the one who did this," I snapped. "You forced all of this. It's all because of you. You bitch."

Kyle slapped me so hard I almost fell. I stood stunned for a few seconds before looking at him, his face red, breath seething. Francine hid her face in her hands. I rubbed the spot where Kyle had hit me. It was hot to the touch.

I looked from Kyle to Francine and back. "Why do you both hate me so much? What did I do to deserve this?"

My voice was too much for Kyle. He gripped his hair between his knuckles, looked to the sky, turned around, and went into the cabin. His cries forced themselves through the door and must have reverberated for miles.

Francine stood in front of me. She opened her mouth to speak but no words came out.

I stared at her through eyelids brimming with tears. But I didn't cry. I couldn't.

She asked me if I wanted an apology.

Which, let's be honest, is just about the craziest fucking thing anyone has ever said.

I told her to fuck off because I didn't know how to tell her an apology wasn't enough. That I needed her to change. Or at least *try* to change. To take some of the onus off me and be a parent. If I could do it over, I want to say I'd handle it differently. I don't think I would. Things were so bleak in that moment. So heavy. So hard.

I spat on Francine's Sketchers. She disconnected from reality then. I remember watching it happen. Her face going from soft to blank. She was in as much pain as the rest of us. The difference, I think, is that the rest of us—lol, actually not me, I'm so much more like her than I'd ever say out loud—tried not to make our bullshit everyone else's problem. And maybe she did try to do that. Maybe she just wasn't equipped for it. She didn't have any spoons left.

So Francine kind of...vanished. To protect herself, certainly. Also, maybe, in her mind, to protect the rest of us. She announced dinner would be ready in twenty minutes and walked straight past me. I turned in time to see her go up the ramp of her new house and through the front door, leaving it open behind her.

Nicholas came up and stood awkwardly by my side. By this time, new rumors about me had stopped surfacing. We had settled into a mutual understanding that our interactions would be kept to the essential and nothing more. It felt like he wanted to say something. I think he wanted to say, "Goodbye," but was still too young to realize it.

He followed Francine into the newly constructed house.

I sat down on the ground in the brisk November wind, my face burning with Kyle's slap. My eyes watered from the wind. Paws hopped onto me, moaned, stood on her thin hind legs, and nuzzled her wet nose into my neck. I patted her head and kissed her cheek. I held her face between my hands, promised I would never leave her. I reminded her how much I loved her. I swore that I would never unduly transfer my pain onto her. I kissed her on the nose. She licked my forehead, stepped a tight circle on my lap, and burrowed into herself.

Eventually it got too cold for me. Paws grumbled as I lifted her off my lap. I got up without the help of my crutches. I stood on The Legs, their uncertainty wobbling beneath my torso. I bent and took up only the left crutch. Paws walked slowly behind me as I moved lopsidedly towards Francine's house.

July 7, 2019

The day in the fall of 2007 when Kyle slapped me was the last he came home for dinner. He started staying out late after work. I stayed in Francine's house to avoid the cabin's cigarette stench. I didn't sleep much. Every night Kyle's truck crunched up the gravel drive between two and three in the morning. I would watch from my first-floor window as he stood in front of Francine's house, swaying in the light of the moon.

It was a beautiful two-story English country house with a brick façade and lots of white-shuttered windows. Brown slate roof, chimney at the back. Five bedrooms and three baths. The front lawn had landscaped topiaries, sculpted into the heads of Francine's idols: monuments to Dickens and Hemingway and Queen Elizabeth. I imagined that, to Kyle, the house's façade was made of dead dogs, their organs as the mortar. The windows were the mouths of screaming stepfathers, the ramp was his mother's body in seizure, the front door his missing finger. When he got back from wherever he'd spent his night, he'd look at the house for a long time before making his unsteady turn to the cabin.

I thought I still loved him. I didn't recognize him anymore, but I still loved him. Maybe out of habit. A bad habit, surely, but I'd heard those were hard to break. When I watched him flex his maimed hand, the connection between us was more than filial. We were both slowly but inevitably falling apart. Still, as I watched him walk into the cabin that had helped take my legs, my first thought was always, "Good riddance." The guilt that followed was so extreme it sent spasms of pain down my legs. I told myself this loathing for Kyle was an intrusive thought. That I didn't really mean it. I tried blaming the brain injury for the inconsistency. Really, I was a fourteen-year-old with unstable mental, emotional, and physical foundations. One who knew deep down not to blame himself but couldn't stop.

Francine's installation of the ramp to her front door was interesting. It still is. The gesture of it. It's not something I've thought about for many years. I probably took it for granted at the time. Never thought of what it meant. That Francine still was a mother, or trying to be. The ramp could have been an invitation back into her life, or maybe a half-assed apology. Maybe she actually cared about how hard things had become for me.

Or maybe she was every bit the narcissist I believed her to be and the ramp was all about optics. Whatever the case may be, my allowance into her home became an opportunity I wasn't willing to waste. My injuries made it more difficult to play sports (not that I had any interest in them), and I could only read so much in a day before my eyes grew sore. So I needed something to occupy my time.

My greatest hobby became fucking with Francine's house.

I started small, moving things in the kitchen cabinets and drawers, stuffing the TV remote down inside the couch cushions, tearing random pages out of whatever she was reading when she wasn't around. The most gratifying parts came when she had a slip-up concealing her anger. Usually a rough exhale or grunt escaping from deep within her. She didn't punish me. She had to have known it was me, but what was she supposed to do? What could she have done to make my life worse?

Enacting these minor inconveniences grew tiresome and unfulfilling. I took gardening shears and decapitated her lawn sculptures. I would have put the heads in her bed like Luca Brasi, but I couldn't get them up the stairs. I laid the heads in a neat row on the lawn, arranging them to face the front door as a greeting to Francine.

She said nothing.

I plastic-wrapped the downstairs toilet between the bowl and seat, making sure no folds showed or visible edges remained. Francine sat to "take a tinkle" and the urine rebounded right back up on her.

She said nothing.

I finally got her at Chanukah time, which Francine observed by lighting candles, though she didn't make us say or memorize the prayers. She laid a Chanukiah out on top of a metal tray from the toaster oven to catch the wax drippings and protect her dining room table. She made Nicholas read the English translations of the prayers from the back of the candle box before he could have his gift. I told them I wanted to skip the candles and wasn't met with any resistance. While they were occupied in their little play world, which they would be for fifteen-or-so minutes, I pulled myself up the steps, grip tight on the bannister. At the top of the steps, immediately to the right, was Francine's home office: a mahogany room with floor to ceiling bookshelves, a bay window, and a double-pedestal desk. I walked in on one crutch and closed the door behind me.

The desk's surface was immaculate, decorated with three framed photos. The first was of Francine and Nicholas from before we moved, during a trip to the Jersey Shore: Francine crouched behind Nicholas on the beach with both hands on his shoulders, the ocean waves standing frozen in arcs behind them, desperate to crash. The second was of Kyle and Francine on their wedding day, younger and thinner and happier than I'd ever seen them, beaming into one another's faces in contrived ignorance of the cameras. Third was a family portrait of the four of us, taken at one of those Sears studios two years prior. Nicholas and me on the wings, Francine sitting in the foreground, Kyle standing erect behind her. We all wore white button-down shirts and jeans. Francine's smile was the only one that looked genuine. The whole family had spent the day in stale mall air and Nicholas and I couldn't wait to leave, so Kyle had been tasked with keeping us calm while Francine perused the store to kill time.

In front of the photos loomed Francine's typewriter.

I sat down at the desk. Whistling softly to myself, I pulled a tack hammer from my pocket. Then I smashed the keys down into the box one by one. The force of the bending stems and heads colliding with the box cracked it through, leaving the entire thing a mess of tangled metal.

Satisfied, I left the office and went back downstairs just in time to see Nicholas's new present: a remote control car with a spinning front axle that allowed it to tumble around the room. He rammed it straight between my weak legs and then away, circling me. Francine came in from the kitchen.

She cleared her throat and held a gift out to me. I accepted without response and let Francine watch as I unwrapped it. It was a copy of Updike's *Rabbit Run*.

Her words were tentative. "I think you'll like that. It's one of my favorite novels."

"Neat," I said, turning the book in my hands. I opened it to a random page. Then I brought up every bit of gunk I could from my chest and dripped a huge loogie into the pages. I pressed the book closed and handed it back to her. "You read it then." I turned a tight one-eighty and hobbled away to my bedroom.

Francine never mentioned this—nor the destruction of her typewriter, though I found it in the outside garbage the next day.

July 8, 2019

At school I worked on the newspaper. I talked to Mare Bear more often. We even ate lunch together, with Sheila and Rhiannon and some of their even older friends.

Mare Bear and Sheila and Rhiannon became my sounding board for stories. Ones that would run in the paper. Mr. Short was a shrewd negotiator when it came to word count, but it was agreed that twice a year I could go "balls deep." Those weren't Mr. Short's words. They were Sheila's to Mare Bear as they played a game called "fireworks," in which Sheila tried to make Mare Bear so uncomfortable she'd explode. Mr. Short said "all in."

Rhiannon and Sheila had gone to a Renaissance fair over the weekend and were talking about how fun and weird it was. Sheila told Mare Bear the people were just "*so* in character."

"Rhiannon and I kind of stopped on a whim," she told Mare Bear. "And it was wild. We didn't have costumes or anything and it felt like we were total psychos. There was a really funny blacksmith, though. He called Rhiannon 'Future Ma'am,' and me, 'Madame Time Traveler,' the whole time."

I'm letting the memories of the conversations get pretty loose now. Probably not what the slang would be in the 2000s but language is a tricky mistress.

Mare Bear laughed. "I've always wanted to go to a ren fair."

"Really? They're in town again this weekend! We should totally check it out. I'll be buying a costume, though. You can be Madame Time Traveler, if you want."

"That sounds really fun. I have to check with my mom and dad, though."

"Oh, please. Papa Turnton *adores* me."

"Ew," Mare Bear said. "Your crush on my dad is so not cute."

"Agreed," said Rhiannon.

Sheila shrugged. "K.J., you should come too."

I panicked. "I've gotta go."

I pushed myself away from the cafeteria table and took moderate steps to the differently-abled accessible bathroom around the corner. The one real perk of the legs in high school was this bathroom.

Per my after-lunch routine, having the bathroom all to myself, all the time, I rubbed one out to Sheila, who today was wearing a heather grey *AC/DC* t-shirt that made those three little folds across her chest when she needed a break from her cell phone and stretched backwards. Halfway through, her image shifted of that to a pretty typical busty medieval barmaid.

I thought about taking her up on the offer to join them at the ren fair. It could actually be a lot of fun. And it would be a nice chance to spend a little more time with Mare Bear, without the pressures of high school society and the eyes and gossip that lurked in every inch of the blue-locker-lined halls.

I came out of the bathroom feeling relaxed and focused. Glen waited outside, leaning on the wall next to the door.

"You take the longest poops," he said.

Mare Bear, also running late to class, walked by and said, "Don't be gross, Glen."

Glen rolled his eyes. Mare Bear smirked. We all headed to our Spanish class.

I zoned out pretty hard in class, worrying the idea of going to the ren fair. I made the decision not to go. I started to write.

When I was cleaning out some old shit after Kyle did his suey (yes, that's how I'm fucking saying it), I found a bunch of old school newspapers he'd saved. This was my first "balls-deep" story, edited to how I think the original probably read. I'm stapling it in here because I want to and it's my fucking journal. Eat it, Diamond.

Future Man

Tony stopped at a Renaissance fair on a whim. He left his electrical job early that day. His routine dictated a trip to the bar. He drove a winding, mountain road in a rusty blue pickup truck. Most days, he was unaware of the road's shoulders. The environment in totality. Today, his point-A-to-point-bar journey suffered a distraction in the form of a hand-painted wooden sign on the side of the road. Tony slowed and made a tight right-hand turn onto a narrow dirt road.

The oaks made the road dark and claustrophobic despite the early afternoon sun. The width of the road made turning around feel like more of a chore than it was worth. Tony followed the road for about three miles, until his tunnel opened onto sun-soaked gravel.

There were no cars on that gravel circle, rather a plethora of horse-drawn wagons. Tony parked away from them, towards the back right of the circle. He lumbered out of his truck and stretched in the sun. His flannel, appropriate for the chill fall morning but too hot for this afternoon, was already partially sweat-soaked. His jeans felt loose, his work boots a half-size too small.

Tony walked with a meandering gait through the wagons and carriages, up to a post fence with a central opening, at which sat a man in a coarse tunic and rough-looking trousers. A small table rested beside the man, a small wooden box with a slit at the top the only garnish.

The man greeted Tony, saying, "Good day, stranger. What brings you to these parts? And in such strange garb."

Tony smiled. "I'm just here to check out the fair."

"Why, yes! Of course you are. Admission to the festivities costs 200 shillings."

"..."

The man whispered, "Ten bucks."

"Cool."

Almost under his breath, the ticket taker said, "If I were you, I'd buy a costume and keep your phone out of sight."

"Sure, okay," Tony said.

Tony rustled a crumpled wad of cash from his back pocket and peeled a ten from somewhere in the middle. He handed it to the man, who deposited the money, turned sideways, and opened his arms to admit Tony to the fair.

Two small children ran up to him. To Tony's eye they were somewhere around eight years old. They bore dirty faces and what Tony assumed was peasants' clothing. *Urchins* was the word he searched for and eventually found.

"A pittance for two downtrodden orphans?" the little girl asked.

"Go ask your parents for cash," Tony said.

Both children frowned. The little boy said, "We got no parents. Don't you know what an orphan be?"

Tony rolled his eyes and walked around the children, who shook their fists at him as he passed. Tony walked a short grass path towards two rows of booths bordering a wide expanse of cobbled ground. The smells of the fair struck him. Tony had heard on some barely remembered podcast that people used to wear woolen underwear. He passed an outhouse with flies buzzing around the door.

He watched the people in front of the booths as he approached. Everyone wore costumes. People laughed and spoke in accents and ate greasy cuts of meat with their bare hands. It looked like a good time.

To get more into the swing of things, Tony reached the cobbles. His boots made dull thuds. Several people turned to look at him. Their eyes grew wide. They turned and whispered to one another. Tony tried to eavesdrop as he passed but couldn't grab any of the words. He stayed to the right side of the booths and skipped the first couple, one selling indulgences, another hawking wooden prosthetic limbs. He listened in passing to attendants' vocabularies, trying to form a character in his head. People used a lot of "thee"s and "thoust"s. He thought general thoughts about what "commitment" meant and came up feeling shallow and a little empty.

Four booths down was a woman in a tight-laced bodice. Tony stopped there. She sold costumes in the style of the fair. She greeted Tony in a hushed tone.

"Such odd garments you wear," she told him. "Might I interest you in something a touch more...usual?"

Tony snorted. "Yeah, okay, I'm the weird one."

His banter fell flat.

"Sir," the woman said. "I highly recommend you adjust your appearance."

Tony examined a price tag. "Uh, I think I'm good."

"Sir," the woman said. "I can assure you, you are not—as you say—'good.'"

Tony bade her good day and continued on. As he strolled, the pressure of human eyes began to weigh on him. He took his phone from his pocket to check the time, found he had no service. He sighed and jammed the device back into place.

He heard a whisper, "Future Man," but when he turned to see the source, there was no one in his immediate vicinity. He shrugged.

Hunger gurgled Tony's stomach. There was a large replica inn with a torch burning next to the doorway. An ornate white sign jutting from a post named the place, "The Good Days Inn."

"A bar after all," Tony said to no one. He looked over his shoulder. There were two groups of people standing back in the distance. When his head turned towards them, they looked away. Again to no one, Tony said, "This place is so weird."

He pushed the free-swinging doors in and stalked to the bar. Again, the smell. Vomit and sweat.

He said hello to the woman tending the long, dark bar at the front, making sure to speak in a cheesy accent.

The woman smiled at him with yellowed, crooked teeth. "What interesting clothes you wear, stranger! Be you in need of a room for the evening? We offer strong libations and the most wonderful company a man could want."

The bartender lifted her chin towards the side wall. Tony followed the motion, which was directed towards a tall brunette woman in a burgundy gown. Beside her leaned a small blond man in tight black pants and a loose white shirt.

"Nice touch," he told the bartender, feeling the pressure of eyes on his back again. "What beers do you have on tap?"

His instincts drove his eyes up to the wall behind, where he looked for a chalkboard or something with a drink menu, despite having already asked the question. There wasn't one.

"Only the finest ale," the bartender said. "Dark and hearty." She leaned her elbow on the bar and whispered, "Which be how I like my men." She winked at Tony and chuckled. He smiled and said ale would be fine.

The bartender poured from a tap into a pewter tankard and slammed it down in front of Tony.

"That's one hundred shillings," she told him.

Tony did some quick math. "That's five dollars?"

"Dollars?"

He sighed and handed the woman a five from his wad.

She said, "Thank you much, good sir," and shoved the bill down her shirt.

Tony took his drink and found an unoccupied table with a long bench near the inn's company for hire. He sat with his back to the wall against which they leaned. The ale was warm. Tony gulped it down and didn't grimace.

A man with a bald pate and narrow eyes sat down next to Tony. Tony side-eyed him and sipped at the empty tankard.

"Good day," the man said to Tony. "I am called Reginald. Who might thoust be?"

"Name's Tony," said Tony.

Reginald turned pensive. "An odd name."

Tony snorted.

"Such strange garb," Reginald said.

"Flannel and jeans?"

Reginald peered under the table. "And thoust's shoes."

"They're boots." Tony pushed his palms down on the table and stood up. He checked his phone for the time.

Reginal gasped. "What be this you have?"

"A cell phone?"

Reginald pieced out "cell phone," slowly with his lips. He whispered, "Future Man."

Tony said, "Holy shit. I need another drink."

Reginald hissed. "The forbidden word of S."

Tony rolled his eyes and went back to the bar. The pressure of strangers' eyes doubled. Before he could order, Reginald arrived on his left side. Another man appeared on his right. Tony could feel two more bodies close behind.

"Future Man," Reginald said. "The bards sing of thee."

Tony slapped another five down on the bar and the bartender, eyes edged with worry, filled his tankard and stored the bill in her blouse. Tony drank down half his ale.

"Good songs, I hope."

Reginald grew very serious. "Terrible, terrible songs, I fear."

"Alright, man," Tony said. "I get the whole 'stay in character' thing you're doing, but I really just want to have a drink or three in peace. Okay?"

"When the Future Man arrives, there shall be no peace."

Tony turned on Reginald. He had about five inches and maybe thirty pounds on him. "Listen, I'm sorry I don't have a costume and don't want to play along with the whole medieval-whores-at-an-inn thing. If you wanna start shit—" again Reginald hissed "—I'm sure we can find a way to make it happen."

He felt the other three men inch closer.

"Alright, alright," Tony said. "I'll go. Jesus."

Reginald's voice rose in pitch. "The Lord's name! In vain!"

Tony grunted and shouldered past the men standing behind him. They offered weak, startled resistance. Tony stalked through the doors and back into the sun, happy for the break from the more intense smells of the inn. Outside was a crowd of people, with the two dirty children in front.

They both pointed at him. The little boy yelled, "Future Man's a miser, he is!"

Tony pulled out his phone to check for service. A chorus of quiet *Future Mans* arose. He stormed through the center of the crowd that was blocking his way to the parking lot. He heard the inn doors swing and doubled his shoving pace until he emerged on the far side of the crowd. There was no one standing at any of the booths, no one milling around the walkways. They were all behind him now.

Except for the ticket taker. He made an urgent wave at Tony, mimicking a third base coach signaling a runner to put their head down and run.

A cry arose from the crowd, which had begun following a short distance behind, matching Tony's pace. In one frenzied voice, they shouted, "Future Man!"

"Bro," the ticket taker called. "Move your ass!"

Tony broke into a sprint. He heard the pounding feet of the crowd behind him. Reginald screamed, "The Future Man must not escape!"

Tony stumbled as he jammed his left hand in his pocket to get his keys out. The pounding feet behind gained ground. Tony passed the ticket taker, who yelled for Tony to get to his car, promised to stall the mob. Tony heard the ticket taker scream. Tony glanced back over his shoulder and saw the man disappear beneath the feet of the crowd, trampled. The crowd gained. Tony put his head down and raced back to his truck. His heavy boots had trouble on the loose gravel. He hammered the unlock button on his key fob. The truck beeped twice in acknowledgement. The crowd only yards behind him,

Tony threw his driver's side door open and grabbed the .38 he kept under the seat. Tony left the door open, shoved his back against his truck, and pointed the gun.

The mob stopped, several people towards the back colliding with those in front of them.

Tony, breathing hard, said, "Alright. Everyone calm now?"

Reginald shoved through to the front of the mob. He said, "Future Man. What shall you do? What is this apparatus? It resembles...what? A small cannon?"

"Enough! Enough with the character shit. What is wrong with all of you? You're so in character you chased me down for not buying a costume? Or for checking my phone. I mean, god. This is absurd."

The mob hissed at the forbidden "S" and Tony's use of the word "god."

Reginald held his hands up in placation. "Future Man, Future Man. Such anger. Please, please, let us speak."

"You see my gun? Say, 'gun.'"

Reginald sighed. "Though I am unfamiliar with this word, I will do as you say. 'Gun.' Are you pleased?"

A cry came from behind Tony. He looked up. Standing on top of his truck was the dirty little girl. Before Tony could back away, her arms came down, her hands gripping a heavy club which collided with Tony's forehead.

Mare Bear finished reading the story at our lunch table. She blinked and said, "I also liked 'The Lottery.'"

"Too on the nose?" I asked.

She shrugged. "Maybe a little? I don't know. It's funny. Not, like, jokey funny. But irony funny. I think. Also the ending. It's not cathartic. Mr. Short says endings should offer catharsis."

I thought, "You want catharsis? Fuck you."

I didn't say it.

I distinctly remember that after Mare Bear read the story, she said, "What I don't think is that Mr. Short will let you write *shit* in the school paper."

"I refuse to change it to *crap*."

Mare Bear shrugged again and took a heaping bite of her turkey hoagie. She ate the same meal every day for lunch: turkey hoagie, bag of sour-cream-and-onion chips, chocolate milk. Mouth half full, she turned to Sheila. "Have you been writing anything?"

Annoyed at the loss of attention, I turned my gaze down to the printed story I'd shown Mare Bear and pretended to be absorbed in the words.

Sheila said, "Kind of sort of. I've been reading a lot about the 'Pink Tax.'"

Mare Bear asked what that was.

Sheila said, "It's how they mark up products marketed towards women. How pink razors 'made specially for women's legs' are marked up anywhere from twenty-five to as much as sixty percent. And don't get me started on tampon prices."

"Don't forget makeup," Mare Bear said. "Have you been to Sephora lately?"

Sheila waved her hand in front of her face. "Nope. I refuse. Half the reason I never wear makeup."

Mare Bear frowned and then laughed. "You have lipstick on right now."

Sheila shrugged. "Well, that's different."

"But…it's not."

"Meh. I feel pretty. Fuck off."

They both laughed.

I caught Mare Bear's attention. "Do you think the story's underwritten?" I asked.

She rolled her eyes. “Maybe a little. It’s good, K.J. Mr. Short will probably be able to give you better feedback.”

Glen Sanders walked up. He said, “Hi, Mary.”

She blushed, answered him with a quiet hello.

“Glenny Poop,” Sheila said. “What up?”

Rhiannon waved.

Glen said, “The fair was fun this weekend.”

My friends agreed. Mare Bear blushed a little deeper. Then the bell signaled the end of our lunch period and everyone stood up to leave for our next class.

“K.J., come on,” said Glen.

I told them I’d catch up and buried my head in my story.

After school that day, sitting in Mr. Short’s classroom—him on the front edge of his desk, me in my chair before him—Mr. Short said, “You can’t say *shit* in the school paper, K.J.”

“Why the fuck not?”

He rolled his eyes. “Don’t smirk. And that’s the last time you get to use that language with me. Understood?”

I nodded.

Mr. Short bit his lip. “Well, you certainly took the minimalism we went over to heart. Did you read the Aaron Gwyn story I gave you?”

I nodded.

“You like it?”

I nodded.

His eyes drifted back to the story. He said, “Change the forbidden word of ‘S’ bit and I think it’s good to go.”

“But that’s a good bit.”

He shrugged. “Use it somewhere else. This is a very Christian town, K.J. Parents would throw a fit if we started printing things with swear words in them. And capitalize the g in god."

I looked hard at him. "No."

"You realize we're going to anyway when the paper comes out?"

"What about freedom of the press?"

"You're a high school student. You'll get over it."

"But I really like that joke."

Mr. Short sighed. "Kill your darlings."

The story was printed with *God*, and *crap*, and *the forbidden word of 'C.'* Ugh.

July 9, 2019

It's Nicholas's birthday today. He's twenty-two. We're going to go to some steakhouse he likes in Philadelphia, my treat. He promised not to drink too much. We'll see.

July 9, 2019 (cont.)

He got absolutely shit-housed and I made him give me his keys so I could drive us home. He snored and gurgled a little on the ride. The way his head rested back against the headrest worried me. I thought he was going to choke to death on his own puke or something. When we got back he stumbled out of the car and went straight to bed. I don't know what to do with him. I'll ask Diamond, I think. Meh, no point, she'll say something about "radical acceptance" that will piss me right off. I need some sleep.

July 11, 2019

Skip ahead to winter break of 2009. This was right before school started up for the back half of my sophomore year. I'm still so stuck in this time of my life. I don't want to move on. I'm comfortable in my resentment. I know it's not doing me any good…thought loop, thought loop…

I'd ditched the crutches by now.

Between the new house and my parents' habits, along with Kyle putting his income straight into the local bars, like Bowie on a coke binge, money started to thin out. By winter 2009, I thought it had to be almost gone. But Francine never worried; she'd just take another hefty disbursement from her trust fund without telling us.

January 10, a week or so before my birthday, I was in the living room of Francine's house, reading on the floor in front of the lit fireplace, when Kyle asked if I wanted a party.

"No."

"Well, maybe we can make a small dog house for Paws, then? We could turn the unoccupied part of the cabin into a shop to stay warm."

The request was timid, uncertain. We hadn't even discussed, let alone started, a project since the accident.

"No."

He cleared his throat. I went back to my book.

Such a pivotal moment in our relationship—the olive branch hanging in the air, dropping in slow motion from Kyle's trembling fingers—and I still can't remember what that book was. I've tried and tried. Repression works in funny ways.

"Well, all right," Kyle said, choking the words out. "If you change your mind, or want to play a hand of Gin—"

Francine walked into the room. Kyle, as was now his habit upon seeing her, washed an Oxy down with bourbon from his flask. They nodded to one another. Kyle left. I didn't know the last time they'd spoken. Maybe the day he'd slapped me.

The next day, unlike the book, was a memorable one, though I can't quite place why. Some things maybe just stick in our heads for whatever reasons they do. The images are so vivid at times and so vague at others.

Diamond Says: It's okay to not remember things perfectly. Imperfection is like variety, the cumin and paprika of life.

A Saturday. Francine sat inside with her new typewriter. This one was even more antique, with longer keys and a manual slide. She'd gotten it about a week after I declared war on the old one, which by now was a little over a year ago. Francine clicked away slowly at the keys. She believed using the typewriter made her consider each and every letter—unlike a computer, which had "no accountability."

I'd recently been entertaining the possibility that this was all *total* bullshit, but later that day I heard her talking to someone on the phone about her writing. She knew some literary agent in New York. She'd left the phone on the kitchen counter, on speaker, so she could busy herself with other things during their conversation.

I remember this agent—a woman who sounded ancient—telling Francine how well the manuscript was coming along. How much she'd grown as a writer. How "insanely talented" she was.

I remember that it made me want to puke.

My actual birthday, my sixteenth birthday—sans party—was the following Sunday. I'd taken to sitting outside in a lawn chair no matter the weather, wearing a wool cap, ear muffs, down-stuffed jacket, and two pairs of sweatpants. Though the cold didn't penetrate as deeply into the legs as it once had, I didn't want to get sick. So that's what I was doing on my birthday. I was sitting outside, and I was drawing. I liked drawing when I needed a reprieve from words, even though I had no real knack for visual expression. Paws huddled inside my jacket—which I zipped up over her—occasionally popping her head out to flick her tongue across my face.

While light snow and the scent of burning logs drifted around me, I made distorted versions of Francine's house, depicting it how I thought Kyle, strung out and incoherent, must see it. With agony. With abstract coloring or shapes or words scrawled over the front. I drew it hanging from the jaws of a giant Reptar; with Francine dangling from the front door, screaming. Sometimes I drew it with the whole family smiling as we stood outside it. In those drawings, I stood on straight, stable legs.

So, I was on the lawn, making gothic monsters out of Francine's roof shingles, brushing snowflakes off the page and blowing on the water marks to dry them, when Francine threw her front door open and came running down the ramp. She didn't say happy birthday or anything, though I hadn't expected her to. No: her manuscript, after dozens of rejection letters, all followed by drinking binges, had been accepted. Her "memoirs"—if you could call her shameless self-aggrandizing that—had finally been sold by the wheezing agent she was always talking to. This agent had told her that, if she was open to several minor revisions, she could get an inordinate sum of money for the story, based on the agent's track record with bestsellers and the market's climate at that time. She told Francine about potential film deals. The compelling nature of her traumas. Blah blah blah. And so, this date, January 19th, my birthday, one of the only things I had left, became the anniversary of Francine's first big break and was celebrated as such from then on.

The only thing I enjoyed—now shamefully—that day was Francine running over the frost-tipped grass to the cabin and banging on the door. Kyle opened it, bleary-eyed with a fifth of Maker's Mark in his hand. The bottle was three-quarters empty. I hadn't looked at him closely in a while. Probably because it hurt so much. He was nothing like the man with whom I had begun to build a house. Now emaciated and jaundiced, Kyle was perpetually dirty, beard long, clothes unwashed. His T-shirt hung from the points of his shoulders. He swayed in his open doorframe. Francine exclaimed to Kyle that someone wanted to buy her manuscript. She told him all their problems were over. She asked him how great it all was.

Kyle brought the bottle to his lips and knocked a huge swig back. The house inside him was shedding timber and there was no one there to pick it back up.

"Bully for you," he said.

He closed the door in Francine's face.

July 12, 2019

The spring of 2009 was quiet and I had developed a comfortable routine at school. I woke up at five fifty in the morning, showered, and shaved—always moving the razor against the grain of thick hairs sprouting on my chin and neck, how Kyle had taught me. Then I dressed in one of a variety of vintage band T-shirts, always too big, handed down from Kyle; some sort of zip-up sweatshirt; and jeans. I took to wearing a knitted cap at all times. To be, you know, cool and artsy or whatever. The bus picked me up at the bottom of the drive at six twenty. I limped up the steps, greeted the goblinesque driver with a singular wave, popped in some earbuds with whatever pop-punk or sad-toned female singer/songwriter I was into at that moment, and doodled in my sketchbook or read over story ideas in the dim morning light, ignoring the eyestrain and reveling in the headache it brought on.

The bus made two more stops for kids with whom I'd never attempted to make eye contact. The bus arrived at the school building at seven, plus or minus five minutes. I had Mr. Short for homeroom and English again sophomore year. He'd moved up a grade at the same time I did, which was nice. I rolled into his class, still always the first in, and he would gauge my energy level. If I seemed tired, he left me alone. If I gave him any sort of greeting, he told me about some stories he'd enjoyed and handed me printouts. Sometimes I'd bounce story ideas of my own off him. He ruined a lot of them by telling me about other stories or shows or movies of which the ideas reminded him. If a concept got through without those comments, I underlined it in my notes. Then other students would begin filtering in and our conversation would die. Mr. Short always tended to each student in whatever ways they received attention most comfortably.

Mare Bear Turnton would always arrive surrounded by friends. Before sitting down she'd detour over to my corner to say hello, and we'd chat about inconsequential subjects until Glen arrived, dropped off by his older brother. Glen's hair was always styled in those days, his clothes clean and free of wrinkles, and he smelled subtly of a sporty deodorant. When he showed up, Mare Bear shifted her attention to him and would sometimes try to force him into our conversation. As the days went by, our morning interactions became more and more about Glen. She'd tell me "this funny thing that Glen said," or "Oh, my god, wait, Glen yesterday," or "Glen is running late today, but he texted me he'll be here." And with each one of these diversions, we drifted a little farther apart.

At lunch, I sat with Rhiannon and Sheila, who were now seniors, and a few of their friends. Mare Bear no longer joined us, opting to spend as much of her time with Glen as humanly possible. Sheila and Rhiannon, however, became staunch friends. We had a group text on our Blackberries—holy throwback, Batman—where they took pictures of funny things they found on the internet and sent them over. This was before Facebook. In my day, this is how memes got done, y'all. Sheils and Rhi drove me home from school every day and we talked. I got to know them both well. Rhiannon's mom had died when Rhi was eight. Once, I made a joke about how lucky she was. Neither she nor Sheils laughed; they made faces of quiet concern. I noted it and kept future comments about my parents on the inside. Sheils had two older sisters. Rhi joked about what smoke shows they were, to make Sheils mad. Sometimes Rhi and Sheils fought, but never in the way Kyle and Francine did. The aggression was playful, naïve in its adolescence, and never lingered...at least, not in ways that I could see.

I really miss them both sometimes. It's so strange. There was never any falling out or anything, just...life. Sigh. Why don't the good things last. The nature of our very existence is finite. Everything is finite.

The way I'm feeling right now—like screaming and shredding this journal and burning Francine's piece-of-shit house to the ground—is finite.

I'm going to go back to writing about high school until I can figure out what it is that I need to process next.

Thursdays at school were my favorite. That's when the school paper met. It was when Mare Bear focused on the task at hand and we could talk, at least for five minutes at a time, about what we were thinking creatively. Mare Bear got really into feminist poetry that year, authors like Audre Lorde and Marilyn Hacker. I didn't have much interest or attention to spare for poetry, but it was nice to see Mare Bear excited about something other than Glen, so I did my best to listen.

To be honest, it kinda sucked. Mostly, what I enjoyed on Thursdays was talking shit with Sheils.

She understood my dark humor, wasn't put off when I went a bridge too far, and had a simple way of not making me feel judged.

She never invalidated me. It seemed like insane behavior. She saw me as human.

My emotions are valuable and my needs matter. Lol.

In the spring of 2009, Sheils talked a lot about what hot fucking garbage—her exact words—gendered wage inequality is. How she was going to work so hard in college and still end up getting 30% less. She was passionate about it. Rhi was apparently oversaturated with these conversations, because she would always end up zoning out. And fine, Sheila's takes may not have been original. But they were poignant and well-articulated.

She was overall a breathtaking human being. Sometimes it was the diffused gold of the sun backlighting her hair, sneaking through strands. Sometimes it was the breeze wafting the scent of that same hair. Rhiannon made fun of her for using tear-free watermelon-scented kids' shampoo, but I thought it was magnificent.

Sometimes it was the movement of the glint in her eye, the placement of which shifted with her moods. A mischievous sparkle was lower left. Concerned, upper right. Passionate, just below top middle. Etc. But always, *always*, it was the way she listened and spoke back. Our conversations had no ulterior motives or objectives. We...spoke. And though I was definitely in love with Sheila, I never wanted anything romantic with her. It terrified me that our relationship might change in any way.

One Thursday in mid-spring, Sheils and I were trying to figure out what my big, "balls-deep" story for the end of sophomore year should be when Sheils got a text from her mom that Brown University had accepted her off the wait list.

She and Rhiannon celebrated in Mr. Short's room, joining hands and jumping in a circle. Rhi was going to Northeastern and the two weren't far apart, I guess. I feigned happiness and sang made-up songs with them. It hadn't occurred to me in full until that moment that they were going to be gone soon.

My brain tried to reach out to something higher for answers. Some—any—part of the universe that might give insight. Any clue or hint as to why no one stayed, or if they ever would. I found nothing.

As they drove me home after school that day, I asked Sheila and Rhiannon something we'd somehow never discussed. "Do you two believe in god?"

Rhi's brow furrowed. She opened her mouth to produce what were clearly going to be overthought, pseudo-prepared words. Sheils cut her off.

She said, "Religion, 'god,' all of that—it's nothing but shit."

Holy Shite

It started with a capital *H* in the toilet. In Times New Roman font.

There are defining moments in a person's existence. Things that happen that change you forever. Stuff that can't be explained or denied.

My moment came in the bathroom on a Friday morning. I shouted for my wife, Analyn, to come share in the glory.

She called back, "No. I'm done looking at your poops. They're so gross. Seriously."

That's sometimes the thing about revelations, though.

I took a picture of the *H* for my records.

The next day, I let out a lowercase *e*.

This, while interesting, wasn't nearly as distinguished.

Then a lowercase *l* next to an uppercase *L*.

Monday came with an *O* encircling the entire bowl.

I told my wife that it felt like it couldn't be mere coincidence.

Analyn stared into the bowl. "It's definitely weird. Also, we need to address your diet. This is disgusting."

Odd that she was confusing disgusting with impressive. Again.

Pinching her nose, Analyn asked me if I was willing to acknowledge that my butthole probably wasn't trying to tell me anything.

"An uppercase *H*," I said. "Just think of the physics, the accuracy! I didn't do that. I couldn't have. Not in a million years."

I shoved my phone under her nose.

Analyn swiped back and forth through my pictures. She chewed on her bottom lip. She said that maybe she could kind of see it from certain angles, possibly.

I took the phone back from her, got my laptop, and opened up each picture, cropped, rotated and enhanced.

"Analyn," I said. "Come on."

The pictures next to each other, they read: *HelLO.*

It was so clear.

Analyn said that I should really see a doctor.

"How can you not see it?" I asked her, closing the laptop.

The next week passed without a sign. Without a letter. Without so much as a distinct punctuation mark. The photographed poops shed no additional light. They were just clumps, piles, twisted masses of digested foods. Analyn was probably right.

What man could possibly be blessed with a sentient butthole?

Then, on Thursday, the sign was painfully large.

IT.

Followed that night by a stringy *'s.*

On Friday morning, two weeks after the *H*, came an *M* of equal majesty. At work that same day, there was an emergency that formed an *E*.

In bed, staring at the blue light of my phone, I read the bowel movements over and over.

HelLO. IT's ME.

I think it was the loud humming of Todd Rundgren that woke Analyn.

"Sweetie," Analyn said. "What are you doing?"

I shut the screen off and told Analyn not to worry about it. To go back to bed.

"Weirdo." Analyn rolled over and nestled her chin into the crook of her elbow.

If I thought she'd believe me. If I thought she'd understand. If she weren't a biologist, focused on empirical reasons for every little thing, maybe I'd try to explain it. But some things defy all reason.

There are moments when you quite literally have to choose between the comfort of your warm bed, next to the woman you love, and shite. These decisions have the ability to define. Equally to destroy. Whether that destruction is physical or something else, it's impossible to see that far ahead. Sometimes instinct takes over.

I rolled out of bed and tiptoed to our attached bathroom. I eased the door all the way shut before flicking the light switch on, opened the toilet bowl, and stared into it for a full five minutes. I pulled my Cookie Monster pajama pants down to my ankles and sat on the porcelain. With closed eyes and folded hands, I tilted my chin down.

I asked my butthole what it wanted of me.

Nothing happened. I knew I had to go. I tilted my chin up and asked maybe if it was God trying to use me as His vessel.

There was a painful contraction, a grunt, and a loud plop in the water.

I looked down between my legs.

It was a human ear, perfect in shape, unmistakable.

I flushed and took a deep breath. God wanted me to listen.

Unfortunately, the message tunnel was out of fuel. I crept out into the hallway and down to our refrigerator. I piled up corned beef, turkey, Swiss cheese, and mayo on two pieces of rye bread and hustled back upstairs. Analyn slept peacefully.

She thought there was "never an appropriate time to eat a sandwich on the toilet, for the love of God."

I dropped myself down and ate with large, mouth-stretching bites. When the sandwich was down I asked God again if I should listen.

It was harder work this time—getting the message out—what with the need for deep breathing exercises and a slight rocking back and forth. But with experience comes foresight, so I pinched before fully expelling.

Floating in the water, ***y***.

Flush.

This time, I asked if it was really God.

I let more out.

y.

Flush.

"Why have you chosen me?"

Nothing.

There was a bright flash behind my eyes as I started to push harder, followed by a moment of panic. I flexed my abs. I held my breath and focused all my energy on forcing something out until I saw spots. I pushed until I felt a blood vessel pop in my left eye.

There was nothing left.

But I needed the answer.

And then there was no decision left to make.

I had to go.

I wiped, pulled up my pants, threw the door open with no regard for Analyn's sleep, whipped a bathrobe around my shoulders, and took off down the stairs.

She shouted about what the hell was I doing. I was already gone.

When I threw open the door to my Jeep, I realized I was barefoot but decided there wasn't time to go back in the house. The garage door rolled open and I rammed the car out, clipping the bottom of the door in my rush.

The 24-hour pharmacy was generally a 20-minute drive. I made it in 14.

I parked illegally on the sidewalk. The kid behind the register greeted me without looking up. I slammed my palms down on the counter.

I needed Metamucil and I let him know it.

He jerked his head up, did a double take. "Dude, what—"

"Metamucil! Where is it?"

His voice shaking, he said it was in aisle 12.

I found the sign and sprinted towards the back of the store. I grabbed a plastic can in one hand, got a water and a sandwich from the wall refrigerator, and ran back to the front.

"You have a bathroom?"

The kid had his cell phone pressed to his ear.

He was saying that there was a crazy guy in the store with one red eye shouting about fiber powder.

I slapped the phone out of his hand. His eyes went wide.

"The bathroom," I said. "Where is it?"

His mouth opened but no words came out. I set the Metamucil down and grabbed him by the lapels of his blue vest. I told him to pay attention. I said I was clearly a man in need. I asked him if he didn't understand how important this was? That I was shite-ing the word of God. He realized, finally, that if I didn't get to the bathroom I was going to beat him until I could use *his* shite to find out what the Lord wanted to tell me.

He raised a shaking finger and pointed to the back corner of the store. He squeaked that the bathroom was next to the pharmacy and the door code was 1, 2, 3, 4.

I grabbed the Metamucil and ran. The bathroom door clicked open. The toilet loomed large and dirty before me. I heard automatic doors open and close at the front of the store.

The seat of my throne was cold.

I unwrapped my Italian hoagie and ripped into it, shredding bread and cured meats and cheese with my teeth. Onions and tomatoes and lettuce sprayed the room.

Sirens wailed in the distance.

The top of the Metamucil can ripped away, taking a lot of the wrapper with it. I alternated dumping water and powder into my mouth until the can was empty. I sat tall to keep my digestive tract straight, to offer the path of least resistance.

The faith coursing through my digestive tract guided me.

There was a banging knock on the bathroom door. A man announced that he was one of two police officers responding to a reported disturbance. He asked me to come out and try to explain myself. He said that it had been a long night and he really didn't feel like spending the rest of it having to talk a guy off the toilet. He asked me what exactly it was I was doing in there.

I asked God for a sign. To pass along the message that my humble lips could not.

His answer came in the form of a massive shift in my bowels. The cops told me this was my last chance to come out on my own. I screamed in pain.

The code clicked, 1, 2, 3, 4. The bathroom door opened. One cop, a lanky guy—his badge said *James* on it—covered his nose and mouth and exclaimed, "My god."

"You don't know the half of it," I said.

The other cop, thicker around the middle, his badge said *Tiger* on it. He said, "Alright, guy. Come with us."

I stood without pulling up my pants and stepped forwards, holding my wrists out for the cuffs. Tiger stepped around me to the toilet, muttering something about courtesy flushing. He stopped dead in front of the bowl, eyes glued to the water.

"James," Tiger said. "Get a look at this."

"Come on. Haven't I seen enough of your shite at the station? I wanna go home."

"Damn it all to hell, will you just look at this?"

James told me not to move a muscle and shifted around me to look into the holy water. He began to stammer. I turned to watch Tiger cross himself. I smiled down upon them.

I asked them, "What do you see, my children?"

James and Tiger looked up at me. They proclaimed that the shape in the water was, in fact, the exact image of the

Virgin Mother. James took a crucifix from within his uniform and kissed it. He asked his partner if he thought this could possibly be true.

Tiger shook his head in disbelief. "Call it a gut feeling. Call it a hunch. But by God—and that might just be what this is—I think it's the real deal."

"Would you like proof, my children?" I asked.

I handed them my phone. They looked through the pictures. Through the letters. Through the word of God.

They determined that each picture was the same toilet. They inspected the photos for signs of Photoshop. They checked the date and time stamps and saw that they had not been altered. That there were no markings on the poop to show physical tampering. This was a clear message. The face of the Virgin Mother proved it was from on high.

They looked at me in reverence. "Please, sir," they asked. "What more would your divine colon have us know?"

I rubbed my stomach. I wasn't sure. I told them to ask me a question.

"Should we tell anyone about this?" they asked.

"That is not for me to decide, children."

So I turned the question to a higher power. Unfortunately, there was nothing happening down below.

"For Christ's sake, James," Tiger shouted, slapping his partner in the chest. "Get this man a box of Fiber One bars!"

James went and returned, slightly short of breath, an open box of granola bars in his hand. He unwrapped one for me and presented it, hand trembling.

I asked to whom God would like his message spread and ate the offering. There was an immediate and horrible gurgling. I didn't have time to make it back to the throne. I doubled over in pain. The world went black around me and

His message burst forth.

On the wall behind me, in brown and yellow speckled writing, was one word.

EVERYONE.

Tiger and James called the local news. Said they needed to get down to the pharmacy now.

By the time CNN showed up on the heels of the local affiliates of Fox and ABC, I stood on the sidewalk in my clean white bathrobe, barefoot and gazing into the distance. Tiger and James stood on either side of me.

CNN wanted to know if this could have been a one-off incident; if I thought science was responsible for this event.

Fox wanted to know if I'd been devout all my life or if I thought my being chosen was coincidence.

ABC asked about my diet. Would I possibly be willing to do a divine cooking segment?

Most of the reporters poked fun at me. They all wanted to know how I could be sure that I was receiving the word of God.

The cops promised they'd witnessed the miracle themselves. That they were present when God used me as a vessel. That, no, there could be no question that the Virgin Mother had revealed herself unto me.

Reporters went into the pharmacy, where more police stood by to protect and serve.

Each newsperson went in with a cameraman and came out shaking their heads in disbelief.

MSNBC said I was some sort of moron and that there was nothing more to it than poop.

The Washington Post wanted to know who would possibly care about this.

The New York Times said they guessed if there was room past page 17, maybe they could mention it.

Of course, skepticism appeared. But it would fail in the face of my divine truth.

The reporters demanded to see the photographic evidence of the rest of my message. They had me text all of my pictures to their analysis labs. They murmured to themselves. Were they truly in the presence of the sacrosanct? This guy has to be out of his mind, right? Would this be a good time to reflect on their lives, just in case? They mulled over ratings and called their producers to gauge interest.

Action News came to cover the story in full.

A platform and podium were constructed on the sidewalk for me. Microphones were attached to it. Cameras focused on my face. By now, the road had been taped off to thwart the gathering masses who had come to see if this was, after all, an act of God.

I refused to speak any more until Analyn arrived.

She was let through the barricades, led through the clamoring newscasters. Analyn reached the platform and looked up at me from the street.

She asked me if I was kidding.

She demanded I tell her just what in the name of decency I thought I was doing.

She pleaded with me to please, just please, stop showing everyone my shite.

"I mean, Christ," Analyn said. "What is happening to you?"

"Nothing is happening to me. Something wonderful is happening to us all. Something important. And maybe—maybe—something perfect."

"Is this because you don't get enough attention at home? Because, look, this is not the right way to go about getting it."

I hissed that she never understood what I was doing.

That she couldn't.

That her waste was only that. Waste.

Mine was nothing of the sort. I was now Pooping.

Analyn turned bright red. She started to speak, then realized there were cameras everywhere. "We will talk about this when you get home."

Tiger leaned over and announced that I was ready to make my public statement.

My voice amplified a thousand times by surrounding speakers, I told the crowd what they heard was true. That yes, God chose me as His vessel. That my butthole was blessedly immaculate.

The journalists began shouting their questions. A jumble of "What did you eat that led to this," and "How can you be sure," and "Why you?"

I told them God works in mysterious ways.

I informed them that out of the north comes golden splendor; around God is awesome majesty.

I said unto them that we have such a high priest, who has taken his seat at the right hand of the throne of the Majesty in the heavens.

When I returned home, escorted by Tiger and James, Analyn was waiting in our living room. She sat in an armchair in the corner, bottom lip turned out.

She told me it was time we talked about this seriously.

"What part of this do you think I haven't taken seriously?" I asked.

"Goddamnit! You barely even believe in God."

A laugh forced its way through my lips. I told Analyn I was no longer the same man. That I was special. That obviously God had presented himself to me because He knew I could deliver his message objectively.

"This is actual shite," Analyn snapped.

Tiger and James began to bristle at my sides. I placed hands on each of their shoulders.

I asked them to please wait outside.

They deliberated for a moment and then acquiesced to my request.

Analyn and I proceeded to yell in one another's faces. Her about how I couldn't just arbitrarily decide to worship shite. Me about, why does everything have to be so cut and dry?

"I can't talk to you when you get like this," Analyn said.

I told her it wasn't that she couldn't talk to me, it was that she wouldn't.

"Well, they're basically the same thing, here."

After the impasse, after another hour of arguing, after Analyn brought out a whiteboard and drew me a chart of the human digestive system, I was exhausted.

I needed some fresh air. I needed to know what was to come. I drove to Taco Bell.

I spent thirty dollars at the drive thru and returned home. Analyn was in our bed, reading a book about the ethics of evolutionary biology. I raised an eyebrow at her and closed the bathroom door behind me. She called that she'd be downstairs on the couch if I needed her, that she wasn't going to listen to my shite all night, that this was not a fair punishment for her perfectly reasonable doubt.

Fire sauce coated my food. The red packets soon littered the floor along with discarded paper wrappers and bits of cheese. It was not long before I felt God welling up inside of me. I asked what I should do next.

The letter B.

I ate another taco.

Pat.

I asked who Pat was and ate.

IeNt.

B PatIeNt.

Who was I to question divinity?

The next morning I awoke to Analyn screaming up the stairs.

We had guests. I stretched and put on my bathrobe. A disheveled man came to the bedroom doorway, but Analyn blocked him from entering. She looked at me, her face red and ripe.

"This," she said, "is one of your followers."

The man knelt down and bowed his head.

I asked, "What may I do for you, my child?"

He looked up at me. "I wish to know the Lord's plan. I have brought you this offering." He produced a Styrofoam container of what smelled like Halal-cart food. "It is lamb over rice," he said. "With extra white and hot sauces."

I nodded and told him to follow me.

We entered my bathroom and I took my seat on the throne. I ate with the weak plastic fork provided. I sprayed rice in my fury. I sat back as my new disciple offered to wash my feet. He said his mother was sick and her doctor couldn't determine why. He wanted to know what was wrong with her.

God engorged my stomach and flew from within me.

I stood and let my follower look upon God's message. I asked him what he saw. He said that it was a kidney.

"Does my mother need a new kidney?"

I told him there was only one way to find out, to take her to the doctor and see. He thanked me, pumped my hand, promised he'd let me know the results. I nodded to him and told him Godspeed.

The doorbell rang. I went to the stairs to see who was there. Analyn was shouting *No, no get away from our house, you're all idiots.*

"Analyn," I said. "Who is at the door?"

She looked over her shoulder at me. "For the love of... you'd better come deal with this shite."

Analyn stormed past me on the steps and slammed our bedroom door.

There was a line leading from our front door across the property and down the driveway. At the sight of me, my new disciples began shouting for attention and rushed forward. I closed the door in their faces and locked it. I called the police station. Tiger and James showed up minutes later amidst sirens and flashing lights.

From behind the curtains, I watched Tiger and James shove people out of their path until they reached the front door, where the most aggressive of my followers had gathered. They squeezed through. I let the officers in.

They said, "Yes, of course we'll manage crowd control."

Order returned to my home. Tiger and James let one person in at a time, tasted their offering to make sure it was not poisoned, then nodded them through to come see me upon my throne. The downstairs bathroom became a place of holy answers. I was brought fuel of fast food hamburgers, homemade tamales, prunes and beans, chicken tikka masala, coffee—anything that would expedite God's plan.

Analyn sat in the living room and made scathing remarks

at those coming to seek truth. Things like, "You've got to be kidding me," and "Talk about a real dumb-dumb," and "What a ridiculous excuse for a human you are."

As more people filed in, her ire grew. She invited other scientists over. They cut through my line of disciples with large whiteboards on rolling stands. They set them up in the living room. They filled the house with constant lectures on physics and nutrition, arguing that, no, of course my butthole was not speaking to anyone.

I agreed, my butthole was not speaking. My Butthole was Writing.

The next day, the man with the sick mother returned. He shouted in Analyn's face. He told her that the doctors wouldn't have checked his mother's kidneys in time, and that his mother's life might now be saved thanks to my willingness to serve as God's vessel. He thanked me with a roast pork sandwich.

A week went by like this. More of the devout showed up. More detractors as well. Analyn put a line of tape through our house. A friend of hers from work, some doctor or other, put up posters all over their side, declaring them "the Rationalists."

Those who sought the real truth stoically ignored the Rationalists' insults.

Another week went by and the news, who had previously only mocked, showed up to cover the growing conflict. They set up trucks and cameras outside the house. They interviewed the people waiting in line to come see me. They interviewed the Rationalists, who couldn't wait to spew their discontent.

The Rationalists grew louder with frustration. They quoted Charles Darwin and Albert Einstein and Marie Curie. They shouted all day and whispered theorems all night. Not one amongst them could shake my followers' faith in the divine Butthole.

Heavy bags began to darken Analyn's eyes.

It was the Sabbath when she came to see me on my throne. Tiger and James allowed her entrance. She told me she couldn't keep living like this and asked would I please, for the love of her sanity, give up this idea that my shite was special.

I told her I could not ignore what was right in front of me.

She told me I'd been ignoring what was right in front of me for years, pleaded that I knock this shite off, asked how it was possible that me, someone who'd never taken an interest in God, science, or meaning at all, how was it possible that I would be the one chosen to be the messenger for a higher power?

"Analyn. It is very simple. The Lord needed an objective canvas for His divine message. I am sorry you cannot see His wisdom. That is your shortcoming, not mine, nor His."

"Fine," she said. "See if you need God or your Butthole or Whomever to answer this question. Am I leaving you?"

She walked out. I sighed. All men must make sacrifices.

The very next day, Tiger and James brought me three holy men. A priest, an imam, and a rabbi.

They walked into the bathroom.

Together, they exclaimed, "Holy shit!"

At the school paper meeting, Sheils said she absolutely fucking loved it. Rhi was noncommittal.

Mr. Short, biting his lip, said, "You can't say *shit* in the school paper, K.J."

"It mostly says *shite*."

He rubbed his forehead with his palm. "It's the same thing."

He went on a bit of a tangent about the optics of producing a story with this sort of content. Then he said, "It also needs some narrative and detail work. This is more of a framework than an actual story. I see what you're going for here with the really drawn out joke, but it feels incomplete. Maybe add more of an ending?"

I thought, "You want catharsis? Fuck you."

I didn't say that, though. Instead, I shrugged. I told him the only other option was to kill the main character with the most gruesome case of IBS ever recorded. I found I didn't care about the criticism like I once had. The more I wrote, the more confident—or arrogant, more likely—I became. The page was where my self-esteem lay. It was the place where I trusted that I was smart. That I was creative. That a modicum of control existed. I became more and more resistant to the opinions of others—especially regarding what made an ending "satisfying"—and learned that no one, in reality, knew what they were talking about. We all just faked it until we made it. Fade it until we made it? Maybe I'm not as good as I thought. But I knew I *was good.*

Mare Bear said, "K.J., you can't equate god with shit. You know that, right? You know god is up there watching over us. Why would you even write something like this? It's so offensive."

I said, "I don't *know* that, Mary. And neither do you. And it's fucking stupid to say so."

Sheila came to my defense and said the story wasn't really anti-religion. It was a farce. It was literally a seventeen-page shaggy dog story and it was hilarious. Mare Bear stuffed her things into her backpack and stormed out of the classroom.

I'd find her and apologize a few days later. Say I wasn't trying to offend anyone or take a shot at her or anything like that. But I thought the story was funny and I didn't think the way either of us thought about god should hurt our friendship.

She mostly agreed, but her face retained a flicker of contempt.

She said, "I'll never understand why you can't get close to the line without cruising way past it."

"I don't think I've crossed any lines, Mare Bear."

She frowned. "Don't call me that. And you did cross a line, K.J. The fact that you can't see that makes me sad."

"Well, I'm sorry you're sad, then."

"Yeah, me too."

We small-talked after that and shared a couple jokes back and forth.

July 15, 2019

Going back to the moment where I thought I lost Mare Bear has been difficult. It's gotten me to reassess a lot of my current friendships. I do have a lot of friends, which is cool. I wonder how much they actually know me, a lot of days. Diamond calls what I do "masking." Saying I'm having a good day when I'm not. Keeping things superficial. Smiling and taking care of others at my own expense, etc., etc.

My friend Ronnie is a big-time disc golfer. I go with him sometimes when he texts me enough and I get tired of saying no to him. That's unfair. Not when I get tired of saying *no*. When I want to spend time with my friend. He's persistent in a way that's not pressuring and never communicates disappointment at the response. He's a good friend. We talk every couple weeks. He always gives me a hug when he sees me. Most people, no. Don't touch me. Ronnie is a genuinely good person. He's also in therapy. We talk about the work we're doing on ourselves. Nothing feels judged or misunderstood on my end. I like to think it doesn't on his, either.

What I appreciate the most about talking to Ronnie is there's never a push towards competitive suffering. I can tell him my problems. He can tell me his. There's a lot of active listening.

This is already getting into the weeds from where I wanted to take it.

So, I'm out disc golfing with Ronnie. He's *really* good. He's hard on himself, though. He celebrates it when I throw a shot anywhere near the target and pumps me up on the positive aspects of the throw. I'm terrible at the sport, but we don't keep score, and it's nice to get out into nature.

Ronnie will throw some ridiculous shot and use terminology I don't understand: words like *hyzer* or *flip* or *lift*. He'll throw one within twenty feet of his target and look pissed off. I've learned not to compliment him on those throws. His standard for himself is different. He wants perfection.

We're out in the woods playing yesterday. We catch up to another pair on a wide open hole where Ronnie can "finally let the arm out away from those fucking trees." The two in front of us tell us to play through. Ronnie tells me to go first. I throw this terrible floaty shot that goes straight up in the air, moves about a hundred feet forward, then dies and falls way left. Ronnie respects my request to not worry about coaching me and to simply let me throw the thing.

The twosome tells me that was pretty good. I thank them without much sincerity. Ronnie steps onto the tee, a wooden box filled with pavers. This fairway is maybe eighty feet wide, with a thick expanse of trees all the way down the left side and high grass lining the right. There's a treeline in front of us. Ronnie says it's about 325 feet to the trees, and then a hundred more to a wooden pyramid, atop which sits the basket. Ronnie gets onto the back of the tee and eyes up his target and takes a practice swing. He takes three steps, right foot, left foot crossing behind his right to turn his hips back, right foot planting parallel to the target, and then he reaches back straight and rotates fast from his core. The disc rips out of his right hand, drifts through the air, gets to a gap in the tree line, veers back to the left, and flare-skips off the ground all the way to the bottom of the pyramid, approximately 425 feet away.

The two guys we caught up to, a father and son, it turns out, look at Ronnie with slack jaws. Ronnie stands on the edge of the tee and turns around, his mouth turned down.

"That was amazing," the father says.

Ronnie asks if they mind if he throws a second.

The father and son urge him to please, go ahead.

He repeats the process with a different disc and this time hits the pyramid in the air.

"Okay," Ronnie says. "*That* was a good one."

The son asks him how he did that, and suddenly Ronnie is teaching them throwing mechanics while we all walk down the fairway. I kind of zone out because I'm not particularly interested in getting better at disc golf, although the son looks enthralled by the conversation.

The father chats idly with me while we walk. He asks me my name and I tell him it's K.J. He asks me what that stands for. I don't know why I lie to him. I tell him my name is Kaleb Junior. Then I say, "Its Hebrew meaning is *dog*. Isn't that interesting?" He nods and smiles. I think his name was Joe. I forget.

Ronnie volunteers us to play a few more holes with the father and son, to my chagrin, which I keep to myself. After three holes of Ronnie teaching these two about throwing form, he picks up on my minor annoyance and tells the father and son we're getting tight on time and have to move ahead. The father and son thank us so much for taking the time to throw with them.

The father—maybe-Joe—asks me, "Kaleb, are you a believer?"

I don't bother playing dumb with a blank look. I tell him I was raised Jewish but no longer practice. I don't know what I believe, but if someone's intentions are moral and they approach the world with a level of kindness, I doubt they'll be punished if there is, in fact, any sort of afterlife.

He nods and smiles. He says, "When you said the Hebrew meaning of your name, I thought you might be a man of faith."

I shrug.

He tells me Jesus loves me and that he believes I'm a good person. He says the same to Ronnie. The smile I give him is a sincere one. Ronnie shakes both their hands.

Why is this on my mind when what I really want to write about is Mare Bear? Well, A: it was yesterday. B: this father's approach to his faith, I found it to be more than palatable. He seemed like a person full of love and enjoyment.

The "Holy Shite" story essentially alienating me from Mare Bear was such a different take on faith from both of us.

The story is a scapegoat, obviously.

What was it that actually drove us apart?

There were a lot of things. One of the big ones was my refusal to participate in larger social events. Mare Bear *always* invited me. Unlike with Ronnie, I never said yes. Mare Bear never stopped inviting me, though. It absolutely took a toll on our relationship. Her extending herself time and time again and me rejecting her time and time again couldn't have felt good. I was so wrapped up in the ways in which I didn't feel good that I didn't give her emotions due consideration. When my friendship was supportive. When it wasn't. I always blamed Glen for the times that it wasn't. It wasn't about him either. Ugh.

But if I want this story to feel complete for myself, neither Mare Bear Turnton nor Glen Sanders can remain so fucking flat.

They were important people in my life. I can admit that. I can admit that, right? I'm admitting it. For fuck's sake.

Let's start with Glen, because, honestly, his role in my life dwindled over time. His importance to my emotions was entirely attached to how he affected Mare Bear Turnton.

Glen was the youngest of three. He had two older sisters. His parents were, by all accounts, sweet people who loved having Glen's friends over. His mom made big dinners every Friday night so when her daughters' or Glen's friends came over, there was enough to feed an additional ten. I was invited to a couple of those dinners—by Mare Bear, never Glen—and went once. I don't remember what Glen's home looked like, or what the smells were, or even the general vibe. I do remember the look of surprise on Glen's face when I arrived. He looked caught off guard, but not displeased. He held the door open for me and welcomed me into his home. This would have been, oh god…2009, still, I think. I walked in and faced a storm of anxiety that nearly got me to turn on a heel and walk back out. Then Glen's mom gave me a hug. A big, warm hug. She introduced herself and told me to please grab a plate of whatever unremarkable food was there. I probably thanked her and apologized for showing up empty-handed. I am sure that Mare Bear jumped up and gave me a big hug and said how happy she was that I made it. I remember Glen clapping me on the shoulder and echoing the sentiment, to my chagrin.

I wound up spending most of that night with Glen's father, Joe, whom Glen, his sisters, and all their friends affectionately called Joey Bags. Joey Bags was an avid reader. I remember him sitting in a brown-upholstered La-Z-Boy in the corner of the living room under a floor lamp. He was reading *Citadel on the Mountain* by Richard Wertime. I hadn't read it and asked him about it. It was the memoir of an English professor reminiscing on and grieving the loss of his father.

Woah. Hadn't made that connection.

It was a good book. I should revisit it, sometime.

Joey Bags had lots of nice things to say about the book. He mentioned that Glen and Mare Bear had told him at some point that I was a writer. He asked me what I wrote about and we chatted for a while. I remember him making a couple of very sharp quips that tickled me.

I guess this is all to say that Glen was in no way a bad person. As we grew up, I realized where most of his arrogant façade came from. Glen was insecure, like every high-school boy with any amount of self-awareness. Though Glen had a girlfriend and played a sport, he still didn't know who he was, just like the rest of us. He knew he wasn't going to play in the major leagues but had still committed himself to baseball and didn't know what he wanted for when he would inevitably be talented out of the game. He was intelligent. He struggled with purpose and the future's uncertainty. He covered that up with preppy aesthetics and a poker face.

My distaste for him was mostly jealousy. Glen was funny in a childish way. He liked to make fart jokes and high-five his friends with a juvenile chuckle. He liked to say things like *snap* after a particularly bad joke. He understood how to make people smile.

He was the one Mare Bear chose. He was the one who received the majority of her attention. He was a higher priority for her than I was. That's all it came down to. I'd say I forgive him, but the reality of the situation is that I owe him an apology. Glen, I'm sorry. There.

Mare Bear Turnton…

I can't right now. I have an appointment with Diamond in a couple days. Maybe I'll ask her for advice.

July 17, 2019

Dear Mare Bear Turnton,

I haven't done you justice. It's a problem. I'm so obsessed with myself because I can't figure out who I am or who I was or who I'll ever be.

When I talk about how I had no friends in high school, I experience a lot of what my therapist calls "fictionalized nostalgia." I'm choosing to remember things in certain ways. I focus on how sad I was back then. Then it's easy—comforting, maybe—to blame external factors for my misery and exaggerate them. I'm not sure how it got so easy for me to number *you* among those factors.

Okay. Things I understand—understood—about you. Robby was your only sibling. Still is, I think? I don't know how often your parents get freaky or if they've been responsible over the years. Hey, Mare Bear, picture your parents *doing it*. Lol.

I don't think I've ever given you enough credit. In any regard. I know how much pressure you were under in those days. A good example is when, freshman year, I found you crying under the strairwell before lunch period. I heard someone in distress and crutched my nosy ass over to see what was happening. You were sitting like an egg, your knees pulled up under your chin, arms wrapped tight around your shins.

I said something like, "You know, if you don't drink water or shower, you can dehydrate yourself enough to stop this kind of thing from happening."

You looked up at me, embarrassed, eyes wide, mascara smeared, and said something like, "Oh, hi, sorry. I was trying to be quiet."

I asked you what you were sorry about, said there was no need to apologize.

You said you wanted to be alone.

I left you there.

Later on that same day you found me and said you were sorry I saw you like that.

I reminded you there was nothing about which to be sorry.

You told me not to say that, to let you apologize if you wanted to.

I remember that was the first time someone gently demanded I let them be themselves. It was formative.

Dear Mare Bear Turnton, this isn't supposed to be about me. I can't seem to be anything but obsessed with myself. Thought loop…thought loop…

Dear Mare Bear Turnton, you were always willing to gently demand people respect who you were. Who you are? How do those verb tenses match up? Does it matter? Do you still have answers for most everything?

You found me and apologized and told me you could be sorry about whatever you wanted. I asked you why you'd been crying. You were reticent. I told you that you obviously didn't have to tell me if you didn't want to. You said you knew that. That you didn't need permission to communicate how you wanted. I remember you being angry when you said it. I remember you taking a deep breath and saying sorry again. I remember how intentional I had to be to stop myself from deflecting this apology.

You took a deep breath. You told me how you were just overwhelmed or whatever. How it was so actually stupid that you'd even been crying. You told me you had a bit of a "menty b." You rambled a little more and finally said how you'd been crying about an essay we'd gotten back from Mr. Short.

You'd gotten a B+ and it was just *so* unacceptable.

"I've probably got too much on my plate," you said.

At the time you were juggling the school paper, FBLA, volleyball, and working part-time at your dad's store.

I think I shrugged or something and said, "Yeah, maybe. But it's a B+. It's not like you failed the assignment or anything."

Your face turned red and you teared up a little. "You'd be pissed with a B+."

"Yeah, but I don't have as much going on."

"That's what I'm saying, K.J.! Why is everything so contrarian with you?"

"It is not."

I remember how you crossed your arms and raised an eyebrow at me.

I remember saying, "Touché, Mademoiselle."

"Don't you take Spanish?"

"Yeah, but that's only because I get A's in English."

You punched me in the arm and smiled. I remember how you smiled because I was the one that made you do it. I was able to turn your tears and embarrassment into a smile. It was a huge victory for me. Self-obsessed, I fucking know.

But yeah, you smiled and it solidified something between us. That tension we'd both felt up to that point, of "can I share what's going on with you or not?" sort of just…melted away.

Dear Mare Bear Turnton, you were the first friend who ever made me feel comfortable enough to speak freely.

To a point, of course.

I'm sorry I worked so hard to keep you at a distance.

I'm sorry I never told you what happened with the legs.

I'm sorry I couldn't be the friend to you that either of us wanted.

I remember you asking me about the legs, in that first week of school, freshman year. I know I totally stiffed you. I can imagine that was quite the turn-off, person-to-person, not even romantically speaking. Earlier, when I talked about my fantasy of you sticking up for me publicly and accepting me for god and the other kids to witness, I wasn't fair to you. You asked me what happened and there was genuine concern painted on your face. Your eyebrows were up, cheeks tight, chin a little slack. You said something like, "K.J., what happened? Are you okay?"

I said something like, "I'm great, Mary, thanks for asking. I have to get to class." I didn't even ask you how the rest of your summer had gone after that awkward double date with our dads at the diner.

I said that to you in front of all your friends. If there's such a thing as social cache, I certainly took some from you that day. Getting iced by the crutches kid in front of a group of judgmental teenage girls, hoo-boy. That must have stung. Or I'm aggrandizing again, thinking that my actions have such a sharp ripple through the world.

Even though I was cold to you, you saw something in me. I never had the confidence to ask what that was, although I always wanted to know. I've come to accept we'll never have that conversation.

What did I see in you?

I saw a person with a deep intentionality in their core. Your filial relationships were purposeful in a way that other teenagers' weren't. You mentioned several times that your mother's labor on the day you were born was an intense struggle. A thirteen-hour ordeal that led to your emergence. You said to me once that you thought that labor was what gave your mother such high expectations of you. Your father as well. It was hard work bringing you into the world. It created some unusual sense of obligation between you and your parents. Your mother worked hard to get you here safely, which meant you had to work hard at everything you did to repay the debt. That's what made you cry so hard about a B+. It was the fear that you'd not met your purpose to be the very best at all times.

I wonder if you hated me for doing better at school than you while I made such an effort to appear like I didn't give a shit about any of it. I wonder if I somehow resented you for being comfortable making it known that you did care.

Meanwhile, you had Robby at home. No one cared if Robby fucked up. He was charming and laughed and had an easy manner. Your mother didn't snap at him to clean up or make sure his homework was done. He didn't have to work at the store if he didn't want to. Did you want to work there? Did you like the incredibly high standards to which you were held? Were you rewarded according to your efforts? Questions I can't remember if they were answered. Questions that don't necessarily need answers. Questions I'll never have answers to.

There are so many questions for which I know I'll never have answers...thought loop...thought loop...

Once, I think maybe junior year, after the legs had gotten "better" and left me with only my permanent limp, I was having a terrible day at school. This was a period when I was hardly sleeping. I'm sure other people took notice, but you were the only one who said something to me.

It was after school paper, I remember that much.

Dear Mare Bear Turnton, I recently read about the correlation between sleep and how humans code memories. I wonder if I can trust any of what I'm writing. Any of what I think is true. Any of what I "know." Did we even participate in the same reality?

So, after school paper, leaving Mr. Short's room, you called after me in the hallway and I stopped. I was dragging and bleary and half-alive. You asked me if I was okay. I remember how you said it. You asked, "K.J., you don't look great, for a couple weeks now. Are you okay?"

I grunted and nodded.

Your voice resonated with notes of authenticity. "K.J., you can always talk to me if you need to."

It's interesting that you said *need* and not *want*. You understood my needs better than I did. You understood people. That's weird. It's probably a gift. Definitely sometimes a curse. Despite your immense workload and your mother's refusal to accept anything but greatness from you, you remained empathetic. You remained caring. You remained committed to being there for people. I cared about you, too. I hope you know that. I just didn't have the tools in my belt to make sure you knew. My toolbelt is missing so much.

Okay, I just now hit what I'm trying to get to in terms of what I meant to tell you.

I want you to forgive me.

I don't even know if you think about me anymore.

I won't ever know, probably. That's okay.

Also there are some things for which I'd like to thank you.

When you told me there was nothing I couldn't talk to you about, you meant it. The statement wasn't marred by ulterior motives or dishonesty. It led me straight into a panic attack. In the hallway outside Mr. Short's room, I jammed my back into a locker and slunk to the ground. My breath became tight and I started seeing spots. It wasn't my first panic attack, but it was a bad one. Your voice came from far away while you repeated my name and asked me what was going on. Tears welled and I tucked my chin tight against my chest, threw my hands up hard against my eyes. You asked me if you should go get someone. I viciously shook my head. You sat down next to me and wrapped your arm around my shoulder. I forced air deep into my lungs. I wiped away the water on my face. I looked over at you. I assured you I was okay. I said, "I'm okay," over and over. You laid your head on my shoulder. We sat there. A couple people walked by and stopped, concerned. You waved them away and said you had things under control. And you did. You really did.

Once I was human again, you showed me your phone. The screen displayed the symptoms of a panic attack and what to do when a loved one was experiencing extreme stress around you.

"Does this help?" you asked.

I nodded and we sat there.

This was embarrassing for me, by the way, to display what I perceived as weakness in front of another person, in a public setting no less. You made me feel safe.

Sigh.

Dear Mare Bear Turnton, there was another time, before the public panic attack. It was summer between sophomore and junior years. It was a lazy, foggy night and I was at home reading or writing or drawing or something. My phone buzzed. It was a text from you asking if I was busy. It was a rare occasion where I said I had nothing going on. You asked if I wanted to do something and I said sure. I went over to the cabin to ask Kyle if I could take his truck. I found him passed out inside and swiped his keys from the hook on the wall where they lived. I had a learners' permit at the time but didn't much care if anything happened. What were my parents going to do? Ground me? Lol to that, Madame.

I met you at the basketball courts adjacent to the public pool. You were waiting, sitting on the hood of your dad's truck, the floodlights that lit the parking lot glowing yellow and casting a multi-faceted shadow of you. You had a Budweiser that you'd swiped from your parents' fridge. You got off the truck and gave me a hug. A tight, comforting hug with our lower bodies bowed back to avoid that kind of contact. We walked over to the playground a few hundred feet from the blacktop, went across the woodchips, and sat on the swing set.

I asked how you were doing. You shrugged and said, "Not great, I guess."

I asked what was going on.

You'd been fighting with Glen and were taking a break.

My heart fluttered. I wanted to be there for you and you let me.

I wanted to tell you I was in love with you and that you deserved someone who wouldn't make you feel that level of stress. I didn't say that, obviously. I'd romanticized you to the point where I actually thought that's how a relationship could work. That things would just start themselves without me needing to do any self-advocacy. That there would and could be no room for conflict. I think I was more comfortable with that illusion than real human intimacy.

We sat on the swingset and you told me how Glen had been acting with Frieda Perry. How you'd seen them flirting and called Glen out on it. How he'd dismissed you as jealous and told you to back off. That he was allowed to have female friends.

Glen and a bunch of friends had gone bowling while you were working the front of your dad's store. Frieda was there. She was, naturally, the touchy type. Apparently Glen had ribbed her about being a terrible bowler and she had pantsed him for vengeance, which everyone, Glen included, thought was hilarious.

"He doesn't understand why that would upset me," you said. "I mean, it's literally another girl taking his pants off. How crazy is that? Why wouldn't that piss me off?"

"That's wild," I said.

"Right?" You took a sip of beer and pushed yourself back on the swing. "Love is hard," you said.

I said, "No kidding."

We twisted on our respective swings for a bit.

You asked me if I liked anyone. In my head I said, "Yeah, you, dumbass." Out loud I said, "No, not really."

"What does that mean?"

I shrugged.

"You know," you said, "Courtney Galleri is totally into you. I think her exact words were, 'I'd smash.' Not very subtle."

"She's cute," I said.

Your voice became tentative. "You should ask her out."

I made a noncommittal sound and said, "I don't know why, but I'm not interested in dating the way everyone else seems to be."

You sighed. "I just want you to be happy, K.J. It's nice to have someone, you know? Even though Glen and I are taking a break, I love him. He makes me feel…I don't know, complete? Not that I need another person to feel whole, but we balance each other out. I know he can be a little intense, but…anyway. I wish you two got along better."

"We get along fine," I said.

You scoffed.

I said, "I'm just not super interested in the drama."

You looked down. "You'll find someone cool who makes you feel good about yourself. I'm confident in that."

I wanted to tell you that person was you, but I didn't.

Jesus Christ. High school. Sometimes I dream that I'm still there, only doing things differently than I actually did.

You took a big swig of beer, asked me if I wanted some.

"Hard pass," I said.

You smiled. You told me some funny stories from home. You told me about a ridiculous customer that came into the store the other day. You told me about yourself in those ways. Communicated what you valued in people, what irked you.

The aptitude you had for assessing others and yourself—insight, I guess—has always stuck in my mind.

And of course you were lucky in that puberty was very kind to you, aesthetically speaking. You mentioned how ugly you felt at times but knew you technically weren't.

"People tell me how pretty I am, but it grosses me out. Men are creepy. Like, you know Mr. Richardson?"

"The science teacher who looks like Jay Leno?"

"Yes! He's the grossest," you told me. "I was wearing a red blouse one day last year and I bent down to grab a book or something off the ground and when I looked up he was *staring* at me." You made a disgusted sound. "I hate being objectified. But I'm also weirdly competitive about it. I hate being looked at, but sometimes I don't."

"Well," I said, "maybe you should be less hot."

"Ew, K.J."

"You're like Marissa Tomei in *My Cousin Vinny* but the hick version."

You punched me and I grinned. You said, "You're so fucking annoying."

"No," I said. "I'm K.J." I stuck my hand out for a shake. "Nice to meet you."

You groaned. We spent hours that night talking. You drank two Budweisers. We left in separate trucks.

When I got home I had a text from you. It said, "Thanks for tonight. I feel a lot better. I hope we start hanging out more, but I get it, with the anxiety and everything, if you don't want to. I won't judge you."

I texted you, "Thanks. That means a lot to me."

And it did.

Dear Mare Bear Turnton, I have friends now with whom I have respectful, reciprocal relationships. Mature mutual friendships.

I still miss you.

July 21, 2019

Faith.

Icky icky gross and sticky. Faith.

I am not a man of faith. I never have been. There was a time pre-2007 when Kyle and Francine made attempts to force religion upon me. Probably Nicholas, too. I wasn't attentive to that and don't have a good feel for what his experience was. He didn't have a Bar Mitzvah when he turned thirteen, so that's telling, in a way.

Fuck. Why is it so hard to get this going.

Faith.

A long time ago, in a land called Randolph, New Jersey, there was a couple with a toxic marriage. Their names were Francine and Kyle. They had no spiritual beliefs. They'd both tried religion and found it too convoluted or hypocritical or tragic. God was at best a nebulous idea to them, but they still looked in his general direction when they wanted comfort. What they knew for sure was that they had a hollowness inside that couldn't be filled. They didn't want that to be their children's experience. Francine and Kyle decided the missing component was god, despite there being no way for them to lead by example.

When their firstborn son was seven or so years old, they sent him to Hebrew school on Sundays, despite his protests about trouble sleeping and having too much homework. When their firstborn asked why he had to spend his Sundays at school when other kids got to have a weekend, Francine and Kyle told their firstborn, "Because."

Ugh, this isn't working for me either.

Okay, so yeah, I got sent to Hebrew school. I acted out a lot because I was pissed. I was punished regularly for how I spoke to the moms who volunteered to teach the classes. Then, when I told Francine and Kyle I didn't believe in god and that the whole thing was stupid and no one could prove god existed, they added in more Hebrew school on Tuesdays. So after my full school day on Tuesdays, from the time I was seven until I was twelve, Francine picked me up and drove me immediately across town. It was about a twenty minute drive. Then I'd have to sit with the same volunteer moms for three more hours until Francine came and got me.

One time, in Tuesday school, probably 2002 or 2003, one of these volunteer moms—I can't remember her name, but she looked like a paunchy frog with bright red hair—told the class that if we didn't want to be there we could leave. This idea, somehow, had never occurred to me. I stood up and walked out of the room, then out of the building, then through the open gate at the edge of a wide parking lot, and sat myself down on the curb to wait for Francine. Paunchy Frog Lady came storming out of the building a few minutes later, screaming bloody murder.

She demanded I return to class. I remember feeling very calm as I told her she wasn't my mom and couldn't make me. I think she really wanted to smack the shit out of me. The school's windows looked out onto the street, and there was a strong chance people were watching, which is maybe what made her think better of it. She commanded me to get up and return to class. My response was a crowning achievement of my life. I leaned to one side on the curb and let out an absolute ripper of a fart. See, I've always been funny.

Anyway, PFL stormed inside and called Francine, who arrived at the school in record time, screeching her brakes in front of where I sat. She got out of her car with an anger-reddened face.

She opened her mouth to yell but screwed her eyes shut to stop it. She hissed that I had no idea how my behavior was making her look. This was pretty formative: the realization that my actions weren't, to Francine, about my needs. That was so incredibly secondary to how my behaviors reflected on her. The optics, if you will.

Francine told me to get my ass back inside and apologize to PFL and the rest of my class. She escorted me in. I walked beside her, head hanging low. I mumbled, "I'm sorry." Francine made me say it again with more sincerity (guess it's always good to teach children to lie effectively). Then we left. Francine screamed at me the whole way home. When we got there, Kyle laid me across his lap and spanked my ass red with an open palm.

Faith.

Why am I trying so hard to avoid the subject that *I* decided to write about today? The past doesn't matter. It's happened. There's no changing it. I guess I wonder a lot about, if god were real, then why? Just why? I don't have any profound questions or points of view that haven't been worked, reworked, considered, and written since there have been concepts of gods or brains.

I had a weird phase in my freshman year of college where I developed a passing fancy for superstring theory. The dumbed-down version I was able to conceptualize was basically that our universe consists of at least thirteen dimensions, maybe as many as twenty-six depending on where you do your research or if you fully understand it, which I admittedly do not.

Alright, whatever. Basically, the first dimension is our X-axis. Second is the Y-axis. Third is the dimension in which we understand the world. Height, width, and depth. Boom.

The fourth dimension is already beyond any true human reasoning, in the way it would function, that is. The fourth dimension is time. We experience that linearly, even though it's its own whole dimension somehow. Bear with me here, because it's hard to think through something that a human language itself can't really encode thanks to the limitations of our perception.

Deep breath.

First dimension: X. Second dimension: Y. Third dimension: Z. Fourth dimension: time. To me, it would stand to reason that if the third dimension can support self-aware, organic life, the fourth certainly would, based on how the first three dimensions build upon one another. So if there are fourth-dimensional life forms, living on a plane of existence close to our own but outside it, our lives would appear to them how the second dimension appears to us.

We're essentially movies to fourth-dimensional beings who exist independent of the confines of time. They would appear to us as "gods," if we could develop any real awareness of them. I have no idea if that's possible or not. My gut says we just can't comprehend anything like that. Also, Zeus hasn't come down to try and violate a bull on camera or whatever gross shit that dude was always getting into, at least not in quite a while, so empirical evidence is scarce.

Okay, for conceptualization's sake, let's say something like Greek gods are a stand-in for fourth-dimensional life, with the immortality and all that. They don't quite work how timeless entities would, because Greek gods were made up by people, and people, under no circumstances…

I'm getting off track here.

First: X. Second: Y. Third: Z. Fourth: time. Fifth: a plane of existence that contains every parallel—earth? universe? I don't feel like looking up what the right term is and am not going to—with the same set of starting variables.

This is the dimension where time has the same starting and end point. Or is the same-shaped circle, more accurately. So here, every possible earth exists with the same parameters of physics and life. This is where every version of me exists. The one with good legs. The one with no legs. The one that died at birth. The one that cures cancer because his family had entirely different lives. The one whose parents had children because it was the right decision for them and they were prepared for the responsibility of developing an emotionally stable and healthy child. All of it. All the time.

Six: every possible earth but with *different* starting variables. Here is where dolphins evolved faster than humans and now they ritualistically feed us to volcanoes to keep the water warm. Here's the world where neither humans nor dolphins ever existed. The one where the sun exploded and our entire planet became nothing but an arid rock floating in the infinity of space.

Seven: okay, this is where I get foggy and start to lose interest, to be honest. It's the amalgamation of the fifth and sixth dimensions, so all possible versions of earth, but also with any and all potential laws of physics. I use the word potential because it's impossible to wrap our heads around. I think of it simply as, "Okay, so in this dimension, gravity pulls up instead of down. Then add infinite everything else that would break our understanding of the physical world."

Now I'm going to fast forward to the part that interests me. One: X. Two: Y. Three: Z. Four: time. Five: Earths with same starting variables. Six: Earths with different starting variables. Seven: Earths with all starting variables plus any and all variants of physics. Then life forms from eight through twenty-six would stack in perspective and ability accordingly. Every prior dimension would appear, to the higher dimension, as two dimensions appear to us, or even more limited.

So, accelerate my rambling to the twenty-sixth dimension. Here would be a being I see as the best candidate for a Judeo-Christian-Muslim "God." A being so overwhelmingly advanced as to be ubiquitous. Omnipotent, without a doubt. I've spent a lot of time chewing on the idea of how could such a god be so obsessed with variance. Why he'd have some people suffer when they seem, for all intents and purposes, "good." At the same time great things are happening for, let's say, Mark Zuckerberg, who got rich by starting a marry, fuck, kill website in college and then screwing over everyone close to him on his way to literal billions of dollars and an empire of misinformation. He got there on the back of capitalism and hardcore exploitative economics. To me, that's bad. And yet.

Why do "good" people suffer and "bad" people thrive?

This has nothing to do with theology. It has everything to do with motivation and control. The twenty-sixth-dimensional being(s) would have every concept of it and simultaneously none at all. Talk about a mindfuck. A twenty-sixth-dimensional being would experience every last bit of pain anyone could ever imagine, and also none at all.

Why would that kind of thing concern itself with us at all?

It wouldn't.

And it wouldn't be able to stop.

Faith isn't theology. People want to equate the two but they are fundamentally different. Faith is about surrendering control. It's about allowing yourself to fully trust and believe in someone or something. Surrender control.

So then, how does someone have faith in themselves?

Is that what I'm missing? Is that the hollow thing inside me I can't seem to touch?

When I write, my brain feels like it's firing. Never totally, not how it used to at least, but there are sparks.

Do I write to build faith in myself, or to make myself god?

Faith does not equal god, but our society ties the two so closely together. In what do I have faith? How much further can I deconstruct this? Can I Derrida it?

Okay, I've got an actual thought, and then I'm checking this box as explored. Here's a thing I have faith in as "true."

In *Living to Tell the Tale*, Gabriel Garcia Marquez wrote about a village doctor who examined a frustrated young writer and thought his madness "was splendid proof of an overwhelming vocation: the only force capable of competing with the power of love. And more than any other the artistic vocation, the most mysterious of all, to which one devotes one's entire life without expecting anything in return. It is something that one carries inside from the moment one is born, and opposing it is the worst thing for one's health."

I believe in that.

July 22, 2019

I was mean in the fall of 2009, as my junior year started. But apparently in a funny way. People liked my quips and phrase-turning, at least when whatever shit-talking I had to do wasn't directed at them. I was also the school's most successful student, grades-wise, and had gained further admiration from my peers thanks to my (outward) I-don't-give-a-fuck attitude. If I'm being honest, even Glen and I spent some time on rather good terms that fall.

He'd realized by this time that he wasn't the natural stud of a baseball player he'd always fantasized himself to be, but he did have a quick wit when he was engaged in conversation, and he thought he could use that to help his team. There was a day when Mare Bear and I were chatting before a class we shared with Glen, who generally showed up a few minutes late. This particular day, he was a couple minutes early and sat down with us. He and Mare Bear were back together. He sat next to her and leaned over to kiss her on the cheek.

Timid, he said, "K.J., can I ask you for a favor?"

"Um, sure?"

"Would you teach me how to talk crap?"

I laughed despite myself. "You'd like to learn the noble art of shit talk, young sir?"

He blushed and kind of side-eyed Mare Bear. He nodded. "We played an exhibition the other day and they had this guy who couldn't catch an infield fly. But he wouldn't shut up, and it was getting in our guys' heads. It threw everyone off a little bit. I wanna be able to do that, too."

"Glen," I said, "it would genuinely be my pleasure."

The bell rang. Mare Bear and Glen went to sit at the front of the room.

At lunch that same day, Glen waved me over to sit with him and some of his friends. I didn't have opinions about any of the other kids at the table; I wasn't interested in gaining their friendship nor in making enemies out of them.

I focused on Glen and asked if he was ready.

He said, "Oh, yeah. So, I thought—"

I held my finger up to stop him. "Don't think," I said. "Insult one of your friends."

He looked across the table at—I think his name was Tobias, and he went by Toby? We'll call him Toby. Glen looked at Toby, then back at me. He said, "What?"

I said, "Make fun of Toby."

Glen said he didn't want to. Toby looked totally confused but had his mouth full and didn't say anything.

I asked Glen what he thought of Toby's ears.

Glen looked blank. I grunted. "Here," I said, "I'll show you. Toby don't take this personally, okay?"

He swallowed his food and asked what was going on.

"Toby," I said, "I didn't know your mom was into bestiality. Wild that she fucked Dumbo to have you."

Toby turned bright red and the rest of the guys at the table laughed. Toby said, "Fuck you, Fiveskin."

I didn't miss a beat. "See, I don't think you'd be interested, since I'm human."

Toby flushed brighter. I looked at Glen, "See? We call that a *bit*. Pick something to insult someone and double down on it no matter what they say." I looked a couple people down and pointed at the chubbiest kid at the table, who had also laughed the hardest at the crack about Toby's ears. We'll call him Gary. Gary had on a t-shirt with black and white horizontal stripes. "Glen, what do you think about Gary's outfit?"

Glen looked hard at Gary. "Gary," he said, tone soft. "Did, um. Did you just get out of jail?" Then Glen snorted, pleased with himself.

"Good one," Gary said.

"No," I said. "Like this, Glen. Hey Gary, what did they arrest you for, robbing a Taco Bell, you fat fuck?"

"What would they arrest you for, Fiveskin? Using your dick as an excuse to get handicapped parking?"

I clapped my hands. "Nice one, Gary! A good comeback won't help you as much as picking up your phone and dialing 1-800-JENNY20, but that was pretty funny."

The table roared with laughter. Gary picked up his lunch tray and left.

"See, Glen? It's all about tone."

Glen had taken out a notebook and was scribbling in it at a haphazard pace. Once he was done, I told him to shit-talk me, pull no punches.

He cleared his throat. Before he gave it a go, I told him to say it like he meant it. He nodded and took a second to think. "Hey Fiveskin, nice limp."

I waggled my hand. "So-so. Sharper tone, try again."

Glen put a little poison in his voice, repeated himself.

"Better! Now let's get a little more in-depth. What's your bit?"

"Hey Fiveskin, nice limp. Is that why you couldn't beat me to dating Mary?"

My eyes went wide. The lunch table absolutely howled. I swallowed.

"Good, Glen," I said, "that's some A+ shit talk right there. Have fun using your new skill staying a nobody townie with a ceiling the same height as my basement."

"That's the basement I'll be in with Mary all night."

I think I held my poker face? I hope I did. I put on my happiest, most impressed face. "Great job, Glen. You picked it up quick."

"Was that too much?" he asked. "I'm sorry, K.J., I didn't mean to—"

"Glen, Glen, Glen. No apologies in shit talk. Say what you say and own it. Apologies or 'no hard feelings' speeches let your opponent back in. Throw your knockout punch and make sure it's done."

He nodded and took more notes.

The bell rang. I pushed back from the table. "And Glen, don't forget you're a fucking idiot who lucked into peaking young. The future is all downhill from here, buddy."

I clapped him on the shoulder and walked out of the cafeteria.

I knew he'd won, and boy fucking howdy did it make me angry. But I also know my closing comment stung him deep. Mare Bear and I had talked about Glen a bunch, solely because he was important to her and she was important to me. She'd opened up to me about Glen's fears of being average, forgettable, et cetera, et cetera.

I knew deep down he'd wanted to hurt me. To win. I'd wanted to win, too.

Word about what Glen and I had said to each other inevitably reached Mare Bear. She knew I'd breached her trust. She also knew exactly what Glen had called me out on, what had made me react that way. In hindsight, I'm pretty sure Mare Bear knew I was in love with her the whole time.

I'm not convinced she didn't feel, in certain aspects, the same way. That didn't matter. She loved Glen, truly, no matter how she may or may not have felt about me. If it ever came down to me or him, I knew who she'd choose.

July 22, 2019 (cont.)

There was a time Mare Bear had faith in me when I couldn't, maybe.

This is still the fall of junior year, after my shit-talk lesson with Glen Sanders. We had this new English teacher for AP Lit, Mr. Giacomelli. He looked sort of like if a turtle fucked a jackal and had an ugly-ass humanish child. Then that child grew up with intense frown lines and a transparently unfulfilling life.

I sat in back of the classroom, per my habit, away from the door. I sometimes paid attention but mostly did my own thing. My notebook was full of ink-pen doodles. I drew based on my meandering preoccupations, on this particular day settling on representations of Mare Bear Turnton, as I did whenever my mind drifted to how intensely lonely I was.

Mare Bear sat front and center but raised her hand a lot less than the other AP kids. I was drawing her as an anthropomorphic bear, which was one of my staples, crafting her with over-large eyes that went with an anime style I liked. In this picture she wielded a sword with a pencil for a blade and a notebook shield. It was only when I finished that I realized how quiet the room was.

Mr. Giacomelli, first name Kelly, by the way, scanned the room with a slight frown. He had a habit of letting silences permeate for at least two minutes before cold calling, creating an uncomfortable, shameful atmosphere. I raised my hand.

Mr. Giacomelli's voice rasped. "Mr. Green, please, rescue us."

"What was the question?"

He sighed. "What is the origin of Rumpelstiltskin? And not the terrible rendering presented by network television, as thought by Ms. Turnton." A pointed look at Mare Bear. The back of her neck blazed red.

I said something like, "The Grimm Brothers popularized the character, though they put together the plot of their story from other European folktales. The Grimm Rumpelstiltskin spun straw into gold for a princess until—because the girl was locked away by her father—she was desperate enough to trade her firstborn. Then she tried to talk him out of it once the kid was born, but he wouldn't. Then he probably ate the kid or skinned it for a nice jacket or something, I don't know."

Mr. Giacomelli said something like, "Very good. Aside from that last little bit. Always the imaginative one, Mr. Green. Ms. Turnton, I noticed you weren't writing, did you get all of that?"

The back of Mare Bear's neck scorched even brighter and she shifted in her seat while writing at a brisk pace. Mr. Giacomelli resumed his lecture for ten minutes until the bell rang. I didn't leave right away, since I was busy drawing Mr. Giacomelli's hybrid parents watching as he battled Mare Bear and her pencil sword.

I moved to the door, still doodling as I limped, head down in my notebook.

Mare Bear walked by me with Glen.

On his way out, shoulder-to-shoulder with Mare Bear, he said, "Real nice job today, Rumpelfiveskin."

Tone hostile, I asked, "What was that?"

He stopped before the door. "You heard me."

I arched an eyebrow. "Glen, don't try to act tough."

"I'm not."

"What are you gonna do, dude? Break my legs? Go for it, you fucking idiot."

He turned bright red.

Mare Bear said, "I don't have time for this. I'm going to class." She left the room.

A stern-faced Mr. Giacomelli walked up to us. "Can I help you, gentlemen?"

We shook our heads. Mr. Giacomelli told us to move along.

Later that same day, I walked by the table where Glen and I had practiced talking shit. Mare Bear was there too, though I don't know why. Glen said something about what a prick I was. I slowed down to eavesdrop, since Glen's back was facing me and none of his friends had the tact to shush him. I heard him call me Rumpelfiveskin again. Then Mare Bear Turnton said, "Don't forget the legs. It's more like Crumpelfiveskin."

I decided not to make a scene.

I decided friends were for suckers.

I decided I hated Mare Bear Turnton and Glen Sanders and promised myself I would never speak to them again.

July 25, 2019

Francine wasn't home very much once fame struck her in early 2010. Honestly, I preferred things this way. It left space for me. I didn't have to look at or hear her. It let me move away from intrusive thoughts, rather than obsessing.

Francine's publisher had turned her memoirs around in a lightning-fast six months. She toured the country, doing readings, interviews, and what-have-you for the next year. This was when I was sixteen, Nicholas was twelve, and Kyle was thirty-six but looked sixty-three. Kyle, Nicholas, and I ate our dinners in the cabin. Ramen noodles or peanut butter and jelly, most nights. Then Nicholas and I would go to sleep in Francine's ghost-quiet house while Kyle stayed behind. I was excelling in school. I knew it was thanks to Francine's initial lessons, and in some sort of parallel universe, maybe I could have thanked her.

It's so easy to focus on the negatives with Francine. To demonize her. And she should be demonized, for certain things. But not all of them. I believe that deep down, at her core, she loved me. That she showed it in ways that didn't meet my needs because she couldn't even meet her own. I've been clawing for positive memories of her at the insistence of Diamond. Nothing's coming to mind yet, but that doesn't mean they don't exist. After all, her life was never easy. And she did her best as a parent. She did. Even if she sucked at it.

Francine was an abuser from being abused. All about control because she never had any. I hate her for never trying to accept that. She didn't know it was possible to accept the things we cannot change. And she wanted to change everything about herself and everyone else to fit the person she always wanted to be and wasn't.

I don't blame Francine for my legs as much anymore. I don't blame anyone. It is what it is. My therapist keeps telling me to give myself credit for how hard it's been to get to this point. After Kyle's suicide and all. My childhood. The things I've done that make me feel shitty about myself. AKA everything. And I am trying.

After Francine abandoned her duties as a mother in a more physical way, Nicholas seemed to have a cloud of impending doom following him around. He and Kyle had never been close. I was Kyle's and Nicholas was Francine's. That's how it always was. But then she wandered, spending three weeks of each month on the road, whether she had some sort of engagement or not. Sometimes, when she did come home, it was with strange men. Kyle resented that, but I don't think for the obvious reasons. That his wife was having sex with other dudes wasn't the worst part for him. It was the specific type of guy. Men with ponytails. With berets. With thick eyeglasses and blazers. They presented as somehow refined in ways Kyle wasn't and had never tried to be. If Francine were bringing back guys that looked like farm boys and left the "g"s off of their gerunds, Kyle wouldn't have cared half as much, so long as Francine's money kept the Oxys and bourbon flowing.

It was this "sophisticated" type of man—Kyle referred to them as "la dee da"—the kind of man who read Francine's work and understood the allusions—that set Kyle off. He would get out of bed at night, leave the cabin, and scream at the house, empty bottle in hand. He yelled things like, "She's got herpes, you know!" or, "Her pussy has teeth and the juice is toxic!" or, "That bitch will steal your soul like she did mine!"

What he meant was, "Francine, I love you so much, I'm too fucking stupid to say it, but it's true. Please come down!" But when Francine's bedroom light flicked on, he scurried back to his cabin and locked the door.

Kyle's substance-driven screaming, it was maybe the least disturbing part of the conflict. On a hardness scale, if Kyle's feelings were freshly hatched ducklings, Nicholas's were diamonds. He followed every new man Francine brought home closely. Literally, physically followed them. Nicholas stepped on their heels, trying to ruin their shoes. Or he'd wait around corners to try and trip them. Or he'd tell them to their faces that they were worthless and if they tried to spend the night in his house, he'd kill them. Sometimes Francine sent him to his room. Sometimes she dragged him there by his ear. Sometimes she forced him to go stay with Kyle in the cabin. That was the worst punishment of all. Kyle was so out of it all the time that he either didn't notice Nicholas drinking or didn't care. I told myself it was the former.

Most of the men Francine brought home were one-offs, stopping in with her on the way to their next destination. Generally, I wouldn't waste my time on them. There was, however, one repeat patron of Francine's bed. Brayden Huntsman.

Hunt's fifth visit to our home was his last. It was also the first real interaction he had with Nicholas or me. He and Francine arrived around noon on a Sunday in March of 2011. Keeping the timeline in order ceases to interest me at this point. Time is weird anyway.

This Sunday, when the days were warm but the evenings chilly, Francine walked in wearing a white button-down and a blue pencil skirt, Hunt a step behind in white polo and dark slacks. Hunt had a jaw that could cut glass and light-brown hair in perfect order. He was tall, lean, and built like a Grecian god.

By this point, Francine and I only spoke when I needed something for school, as she'd grown immune to my mischief and I'd gotten bored with it. There was something about Hunt—the set of his shoulders, maybe—that aggravated me. I didn't like him tramping into the house like he belonged in it. My upper body strength was substantial from compensating for the legs. From tossing Paws into the air and catching her when the bleak atmosphere of home brought her low. From lifting weights to offset bloating and assist my metabolism.

Francine walked past where I sat on the living room sofa, curling forty-pound dumbbells, to kneel down next to Nicholas. He lay on his back, picking absently on an acoustic guitar which he was getting really good at playing. Francine laid her hand on his cheek. He sat up, took notice of Hunt, hit a dissonant minor chord, and turned away from Francine. She sighed and invited Hunt in from where he waited by the door.

"Oh, take off your shoes first," she said.

He pried his boat shoes from sockless feet and padded barefoot into the house. I put my dumbbells down, stretched tall, and stood to block his path. I stuck my hand out.

"Kyle Junior," I said. "And you are?"

He looked past me, then down, and moved to shake my hand. I cut his handshake short, catching his fingertips on which there were no calluses, and squeezed.

He winced. "You can call me Hunt. Quite the grip you have there, young man. We've met before, if I'm not mistaken."

I did a pompous affectation of his voice. "Yes, yes, of course, old chap. You see, there are just so many dicks in and out of my mother's...house, that it gets hard to keep track. You understand."

He frowned and sniffed. I gave his fingers one more squeeze before breaking my grip. He moved on, trailing the scent of his oversweet, French-hooker cologne.

Hunt detoured to my brother. "And you must be Nicholas." He extended his hand.

Nicholas hit another dissonant chord and said, "Move on, fuck face."

"Nicholas!" Francine shouted.

He lowered his voice to Hunt. "Watch your ass."

Hunt followed Francine into the kitchen. Their conversation carried, picking up where they must have left off about Italian renaissance painters. Hunt talked in an overconfident voice about Dante Gabriel Rossetti only painting women to "throw off the scent of homosexuality that bathed him," totally omitting any mention of his infatuation with his sister, Christine. His way of speaking, stating his opinions as sheer fact, irked me, but he wasn't worthy of my direct opposition.

Paws crawled out from her customary spot beneath Francine's sofa and leapt into my lap, made a tiny muppet sound of satisfaction, and curled up. I picked her up, cradled her to my chest, and walked into the kitchen. Francine was sitting on her granite countertop beneath the cabinet, her feet resting on Hunt's hips. He leaned subtly towards her as they talked.

"Did Francine tell you how I got my limp?" I asked.

He looked sideways at me.

"She shoved my head into a shoe rack. Because I had a dog." Paws whined. "Not this dog, mind you. She had the other one sent off. Who knows what happened to him. His owner supposedly got him back, but he's probably in some dogfighting ring or something."

Francine stared. To my knowledge, this was the first time she'd heard me state the events out loud.

"That's not what happened," she whispered.

A harsh laugh burst from my lips. "Whatever." I turned to Hunt. "She may fancy herself sophisticated enough to give you lobsters instead of crabs, but either way, you're going to leave here with something pinching your nuts."

Francine's voice regained strength. "Don't listen to him. The accident he was in gave him brain damage. He doesn't know what he's saying."

In the name of pure honesty, there was a moment there where I wondered if she was right. How fucked is that? Just because it was my mother who said something gave my brain the natural inclination to listen.

Inside I screamed *fuck you* at her but my lips remained shut. I wondered when she'd become a pathological liar. If she'd always been one. If it was the only way left for her to live her life. Regardless, I bottled my rage and found another direction for it.

Francine's feet fell from Hunt's hips and she hopped off the counter. I turned and left the room. Nicholas was standing out of sight on the other side of the threshold. He made an almost imposing figure, what with how big he was for his age. It gave me an idea.

Nicholas's plucking on the guitar grew louder and angrier.

"I know how you can make that guy leave," I murmured to him.

I waited out on the lawn with my sketchbook, Paws having scampered off into the property to run circles and dig. I doodled Hunt's BMW, him on hands and knees behind it, sucking on the tailpipe, while Francine sat on his back holding a riding crop. It was only fifteen minutes until Nicholas came out of the house with blood on his shirt, crying. Feeling somewhat responsible for his exile, since I'd given him the idea to stab Hunt with a salad fork, I went with him to Kyle's. I made a lazy pace over the grass behind Nicholas as he trudged to the cabin beneath spitting clouds. Nicholas threw the door open as hard as he could and stomped in.

Kyle grunted to us from the sofa by way of greeting. "Make yourselves at home." Then he laughed, which turned into a deep wheeze. The cabin stank of cigarettes and stale beer and what I could only imagine was fermenting vomit. The furniture was the same as always but tinged with grime and overrun with dust bunnies.

The day wasn't cold but it wasn't warm, that strange in-between time when spring hadn't quite sprung but was considering it. The place needed fresh air like Garfunkel needed Simon. I went around and opened all the windows. The breeze washed in and took some of the cabin's reeking air with it. Once all the windows were open, a pleasant cross-draft started. It was when I turned back to the room that I saw Nicholas pouring scotch into a can of ginger ale. Kyle was looking at nothing in particular. Nicholas sat right down next to him and belched. Kyle held up a half-empty glass. Nicholas clinked his can against it and they drank together, staring at the television. The screen was black.

The two of them were just so fucking pathetic. I thought about a fight between two Dalmatians back in the days of the dog business. It took everything Kyle, Nicholas, and I had to pry them apart, both animals coming away with puncture wounds, one on its chest, the other its hindquarters. Francine had broken down into tears and fled into the cabin at the onset. Both dogs wound up partially lame. The first with rasping breath and a woozy stride, the second with a permanent hitch in its gait. They were both forever scared, their tails tucked down between their legs.

I asked if Kyle and Nicholas wanted to play a couple hands of Gin Rummy. They agreed.

Kyle walked to the very same plank table where he'd told us about smashing a chair on his stepfather's back. Now crowded with empty beer cans and open liquor bottles, the table didn't have any space for us to play. Kyle unceremoniously planted a forearm and swiped everything off. The cans and bottles clattered against the floor, spilling residue. The suction of my sneakers to the floor suddenly made a lot of sense.

"There you go," Kyle mumbled.

He dumped himself into a chair, Nicholas following suit.

I went to the kitchenette and retrieved a bottle of surface cleaner, an unused roll of paper towels, and an unopened deck of casino cards. I stuck the cards in my pocket and sprayed the table liberally with cleaner. It took more force and elbow grease than I expected to scrub it smooth, but it got done.

The cellophane on the cards was old and stuck to the box as it peeled. I pocketed the plastic, pulled the Jokers from the deck, gave the cards a dozen bridge shuffles, stripped them, shuffled again, and put the deck down for Kyle to cut. I dealt out hands. Neither Kyle nor Nicholas gave me much of a challenge. They weren't tracking cards, rather taking and throwing them at random, which drove me crazy. We had to stop after every hand or two for Kyle to freshen his drink. Nicholas looked at the booze with a kind of wistful contempt and made no efforts to sneak any more.

"Deal me out for a couple," I said.

Kyle shrugged and dealt to Nicholas. The kitchenette waited. Garbage bags filled the cabinet under the sink, side by side with the other unused cleaning solutions. I rolled through the cabin, filling bags with cans and bottles, empty or partially full. I would have chucked the full bottles too—if I'd found any. The fermenting vomit was in the corner of Kyle's bedroom. I decided to leave it, not wanting or knowing how to deal with the orange-pink goo.

When I rolled out of the bedroom with three full trash bags, both Kyle and Nicholas were crying. I put a pair of screwdrivers, a hammer, and some fishing wire in my pocket and left without saying goodbye. Hunt's Beamer was gone. I wanted someone to talk to about my shitty family. To lean on while I cried. To tell that my legs hurt every single day. But it was just me and Paws. I thought about texting Mare Bear Turnton or Sheils—Sheils had left for college by this time and was hardly ever in contact anymore. I heard Mare Bear's voice echo *Crumplefiveskin* in my head. I pictured her and Glen making out on some basement sofa somewhere. I fastened my eyes shut against the oncoming tears.

Before returning to Francine's house, I sat outside and drew Kyle's cabin, positioned at the bottom of a deep ditch. At the upper rim of the hole stood Francine, the same size as the cabin, looking down with a shovel in hand. Then I erased the shovel and made it so she was holding her hand out, an offering. In the direction toward which her fingers reached, I drew myself, holding the shovel out to her but looking the opposite way.

Why didn't Kyle and Francine get a divorce? The answer was simple and the very same as their approach to parenting. They were lazy.

Or laziness is a myth and they were too deeply wounded and didn't have any spoons left to give.

No matter how hard I tried to dampen my emotions, they still existed. I needed to let some aggression out.

Francine had left with Hunt, I think. That's not important. The important thing is that she wasn't home. I strode into her kitchen. After the first few times I'd destroyed her booze collection, she'd moved everything into a locked cabinet. Until now, I hadn't felt a repeat performance was worth my time.

I planted a palm on the counter and hoisted myself up. I wedged the flathead of a screwdriver between the base of the lock and the wood of the cabinet door. I hit the base of the screwdriver hard with my hammer and smashed the lock out, splintering the wood. The door swung open. Bottles packed the top two shelves. I got down and jammed a step stool beneath the cabinet. I climbed back up. Then, with my Phillips head screwdriver, I unpinned the liquor cabinet from its next-door neighbors and, whistling "Popeye the Sailorman," started removing wood screws.

Ten screws in total held the cabinet to the wall. When the higher eight were gone, the cabinet wobbled on the stool balancing it. I dropped from the counter and tied one end of the fishing wire to a stool leg, strolled into the living room, and pulled the line taut. Paws scuttled out from under the sofa and looked at me with tilted head.

"You're not going to love this sound, my tiny princess."

I yanked on the fishing line with all my might. The stool came free. The crashing of the cabinets and shattering bottles filled the house. Paws barked in panic and dove for cover.

July 26, 2019

Today is an important anniversary to me.

The rest of junior year was uneventful both socially and academically, and I have few vivid memories from that time. I'd been trying so hard not to feel anything that I became my own autopilot. Wake up, brush teeth, shower, dissociate through the school day, let my brain pick up the pieces to get good grades, do homework to kill time. I didn't hate school as much as some of my peers. If not a sphere of safety, it was at least somewhere to be other than home.

I did make a friend about whom I reminisce fondly from time to time. A freshman who joined the paper. His name was Nate. His last name was Bennet, but whenever someone asked, he would say, "Just Nate." So he became Nate Just Nate, or N.J.N. We got along so well because this kid could not be even moderately bothered to give a fuck. He was very intelligent but a pain in everyone's ass, which he told me was why he and I got along so well. He could see that I held constant pain within myself. He would try so hard to get me off balance with whatever nonsense or offensive statements he could muster. I didn't care so long as he was himself around me. His family life wasn't good either. He smoked a lot of weed despite his age.

He had shoulder-length auburn hair and a pointed jaw. He liked to describe himself as "svelte and sylph-like." His poker face was decent. As you got to know him, you learned to read his thoughts by the glint in his eyes. It reminded me of Sheila.

At school paper, Mr. Short either loved or hated him, depending on the day. When N.J.N. turned on the charm, he was as likeable as could be. But it's worth mentioning a second time: he didn't usually care.

His favorite game when we were together was telling me his "brilliant ideas," in which he went to places in his mind that I couldn't seem to access in my own. The corners with the darkest jokes and most deplorable ideas.

After high school, he joined the army and flew attack choppers overseas to piss off his parents and stepmom. He died, shot down over some desolate expanse of sand somewhere, fighting a fight he didn't believe in or fully understand. That was five years ago today.

Nate Just Nate isn't integral to this story, but I did love him and I miss him terribly.

July 30, 2019

Something happened to Kyle after I emptied out the alcohol from the cabin and Francine's house. Bottles didn't immediately reappear. There were two weeks in which Kyle sweated uncontrollably and shook violently. Nicholas and I were convinced he was going to die. We spoke about it through looks, but never words. It was the only way we communicated anymore. There was a tacit hatred between us. That's what I thought at the time. I think now it was more like looking at each other made us both sad. It made us hurt. It made us see ourselves and that was, a lot of the time, too much pressure. We had an impenetrable bond that only siblings trapped between rocks and hard places can understand.

After those weeks of withdrawal, Kyle became more active than I'd seen since the summer of 2007. The cabin, a cluttered yet somehow also barren monument to failure, shifted along with him. The textures of the floors changed. No more suctioning residue lingered. The soiled rugs disappeared, replaced with lush blue carpeting in the living room and hardwood in the kitchenette. In the "dining room" area, the cracked, round tabletop was given pride of place, with a conspicuous three placemats set at all times. Kyle filled in the chips and splits with epoxy and finished the surface with a dark stain and wax. The wood grain shone bright against the contrasts. A steampunk sort of candelabra with a cybernetic skull for a base adorned the center. I asked about it in passing. Kyle told me every cabin should be at least a little spooky. The cabin's dirty, blue-grey walls were repainted a bright Swiss Coffee white. The couch—sagging, with fractured supports—was made whole by Kyle's hand, stripped of the ratty green fabric and reupholstered with pale leather. A new recliner appeared to match it. The bunk beds were disposed of, replaced by a single queen bed on low posts that Nicholas and I were "welcome to, anytime either of you maybe wants to spend the night at the old man's place," in Kyle's words. Our father's gaunt frame began to fill back in.

The changes happened quickly. Or I didn't pay enough attention as they happened gradually.

The three of us sat down in the revivified cabin to eat dinner on a cold Chanukah night during the winter break of…2011, I'm pretty sure. Kyle had, at some point, figured out how to cook at least a few things. The table was loaded with chicken thighs, potato latkes, and a kale salad with tomatoes and feta cheese in a large mixing bowl. The food wasn't what you'd call "good"—thanks to Kyle's insane seasoning experiments—but it was edible, and there was an air of consideration and hard work around it. It was our best family meal in years.

Nicholas, headphones in and loud enough to make sure Kyle and I knew he wasn't available for conversation, drummed his fingers loudly on the table to whatever screeching guitar and vocals deafened him. Kyle asked me if I wanted to light candles.

I asked, "Why would we bother with that?"

He shrugged. "That's always been my general feeling."

He saw my empty plate and offered me seconds.

There was a Band-Aid wrapped tight around his middle finger. I asked him what happened.

"Hm? Oh, I got myself on the grater when I was making the potatoes."

"So you're feeding us your blood?"

He shrugged. "It's running through you anyway."

"Don't remind me," I muttered.

He laughed. I felt my face turn hot. I had an unexpected, long-missed reaction to that laugh. My father's old laugh. The one in which I used to revel. My eyes welled up suddenly. I wiped at them.

Kyle grew concerned. "You okay?"

"Hm? Oh, yeah, my contacts are a little dry is all."

"I didn't know you wore contacts."

"He doesn't," Nicholas said.

Neither Kyle nor I had noticed when the headphones went away.

I said to Nicholas, "Fuck off."

My brother let out an angry exhale.

Kyle placed a palm on the table. "We're not doing this tonight."

The authority of the words was unassailable.

Nicholas and I apologized without thought, first to Kyle and then to one another. Nicholas and I exchanged a wide-eyed look.

Nicholas, to Kyle, said, "What was that? Are you a witch?"

Kyle laughed. Nicholas wiped at his eyes.

I said, "His contacts are dry."

"Eat," said Kyle.

Nicholas eyed the food tentatively.

Kyle sighed, grabbed Nicholas's empty plate, and filled it up. He added a side dish and plopped apple sauce and sour cream down for the latkes. Nicholas took his first bite, made a puzzled face at the flavor, and then wolfed down the food. Kyle, without question, refilled the plate. We sat in silence while Nicholas stuffed himself.

An air of contentment filled the room. I stretched backwards in my chair and let out a small, high-pitched yawn. Paws leapt from the couch where she had nested on a soft blanket and ran up to sit beside me. I took a leftover latke from the table. I ran Paws through her commands of "sit," "paw," "touch," "eyes," and finally, "gentle." She sat with her mouth slightly agape and let me place the food on her tongue.

I said, "Okay."

She closed her jaws on the latke and bounded off to the edge of the kitchenette where her bowls rested on a purple rubber mat. She lay down with the latke and chomped it away.

Now that Nicholas was paying attention, Kyle asked if we should light candles for Chanukah.

Nicholas nodded. Kyle cleared the dirty dishes in one go, bringing them to the kitchenette sink. He rubbed Paws's belly while she lay on the cool wood floor, the latke devoured. Then he stretched up to the cabinets overhanging the counter, reached far back into the rightmost, and came out with a dusty Chanukiah.

It had a baseball diamond for a base, little baseball bats for candle holders, and a baseball with the Phillies logo top center where the Shamash candle went. Kyle set the Chanukiah in place of his spooky candelabra and fetched a box of blue and white candles. He set one in the center and one to the far right.

Why do I remember this so well? Like I'm back there. Like I'm desperate to relive any sense of ease and peace. I'm remembering that those feelings are possible and it's terrifying. Where does it come from? Where does it go? Where does it come from, Cotton-Eyed...thought loop, thought loop…

"Nicky," Kyle said, "do you want to lead us in the prayer?"

Nicholas nodded. Kyle handed me the matches and the three of us sang, getting the Hebrew mostly correct, while I lit the Shamash and then the first night's candle.

After the ceremony, Kyle told us there were gifts.

Nicholas and I waited at the table while our father vanished into his bedroom. He returned with two small rectangles wrapped in cut-up paper bags. Nicholas's name was scrawled on one, mine on the other.

Kyle handed us each our gift. The two were identical in dimensions.

I said to Nicholas, "Same time?"

He nodded.

We counted to three and ripped the paper off.

Both were packs of playing cards. Images of Greek mythology decorated Nicholas's cards. The suits were drawn to resemble letters of the Greek alphabet, and the face cards had Hermes for the Jack, Athena for the Queen, Hades for the King, and Zeus on the Aces. The backs of the cards hosted the artist's rendering of the Acropolis.

Nicholas fanned through the cards, his face bright. He looked up at Kyle. Kyle said, "I know you like all the philosophy stuff, and Greece was the place for that—back in the day. I hope I got it right." Then a long pause, followed by an uncertain, "Did I?"

Nicholas nodded. "It's awesome, Dad, thanks." He stood up and hugged Kyle, who squeezed his younger son tight against him with one arm.

The whole thing was so fucked and weird that I was sure it was a dream. I pinched myself hard. Nothing. I looked down at my own cards. The suits were shaped from quills and ink pots, and the backs of the cards had the quote "The process of revision should be constant and endless," attributed to Salman Rushdie. The face cards had Mark Twain as the Jack, the Bronte sisters as the Queen, Hemingway as the King, and Shakespeare as the Ace.

I hated Hemingway.

I looked up at Kyle, into his expectant, loving gaze. A cold fury washed through me.

I said, "I hate Hemingway."

"Oh," Kyle said. "I can always take the cards back and exchange—"

Ahhhh, now I remember. Here it is. Here's the good old guilt and shame spiral. The fury is back. It's at myself. I'm so angry at myself all the time. I remember exactly what I told my father.

I said to Kyle, "No. Fuck you. Fuck you and fuck this. What? You're suddenly a dad again? You give a shit about us now? About our interests? You've been nothing for…forever. What was next? We all sit here and play Gin Rummy with our pretty new cards? Try this game." I sprayed the cards at my father. "Fifty-two pickup. That's a fun one."

I exited the cabin. Blustering wind assaulted my face, shocked my chest and arms—I'd left my winter coat inside—and Paws's feet scrabbled over the cabin floor as she raced to catch me. She hopped around me on the lawn. I paused so she could jump into my arms and we went to the lightless void that was Francine's house.

That night, I slept in Francine's house with only Paws for company, sporadically moving between bed and desk, looking out my bedroom window at the Phillies Chanukiah shining in the cabin's front window.

I'm feeling steamed out but I have to keep going. I have to get this out. I have to look at it without turning away. I've numbed myself for…I don't know. I've just been numb for so long.

So the morning after I cursed Kyle out, after a fitful sleep that proved not at all restful, I woke to the smell of coffee. I rubbed my eyes, shifted my body to the night table where my phone charged, scanned some heinous text from NJN about a cult that provided "corn in EVERY orifice," and checked the time. It was seven in the morning, which was late for me but early for Kyle or Nicholas. I reached into the clothing pile on the floor that I'd been using instead of my closet, pulled on black sweatpants and a white t-shirt.

I can see myself there in the mirror. I remember staring into my own bloodshot eyes. I remember cursing myself out so intensely that I knew, in my heart, I was the meanest person in the world. I actually recently had a friend tell me she wished I could see me how other people do. I didn't think to ask her how that was in the moment. Diamond told me I could just ask this friend directly what she did, in fact, see when she looked at me, if I wanted to know.

My friend said she saw someone who cares deeply about people, with a wicked sense of humor and a deep sense of sadness. She said she wishes I'd take my mask off sometimes. That it's always on and it makes her feel like I don't want her around or she's not a good friend. I cried in front of her.

I hate myself. I told her that. She told me she loved me. I cried even harder. She wants me to learn to love myself. I don't know how. Talking about it helped, at least. I told my therapist about that too. She said I should give myself credit. That it was a huge emotional growth moment. Then she hedged the word "should."

I'm doing the avoidance thing again.

Thought loop, thought loop…

Back to the morning after I tore into Kyle and stormed from the cabin. I was staring at myself in the mirror, saying things like, "You dumb fucking crippled piece of human filth. You're nothing. You'll never be anything. You're useless and everyone knows it. You're too pathetic for anyone to tell you the truth. Loser." I stayed lost in the mirror until Paws poked her head up from under my covers at the foot of the bed. She let out an excited squeal of a yawn, tail thumping against the mattress.

"I know," I told her. "It's later than usual, I'm sorry."

She popped off the bed and sat in front of my closed bedroom door. I stepped over and opened the door for her. Paws went straight from my room to the front door. I let her outside and closed the door against the morning air, setting the timer in my head for about four minutes. That was generally how long it took her to do her morning business and come back. When I turned around, my father was standing across the living room on the threshold to the kitchen, a steaming mug in his hand.

He said, "Do you drink coffee?"

I shook my head.

"Okay. I probably made too much, then."

Nicholas squeezed by Kyle with his own mug.

I commented on how Nicholas was almost definitely too young to start drinking coffee.

Nicholas said, "It's hot chocolate, dick."

Kyle frowned.

Nicholas dumped himself on Francine's sofa and flicked the TV on. He put on his favorite show, *Adventure Time*, and sang along with the opening credits. Kyle, amused, observed. I stared daggers at my father. I turned around to let Paws in; she arrived right on time.

Paws ran up to Kyle and circled his feet twice.

"I can feed her, if you want," Kyle said.

"I've got it."

He stepped aside to let me into the kitchen, where Paws had an identical eating station to the one she used in the cabin. On the floor of the pantry slumped a five-pound bag of kibble for small-breed dogs. I scooped out half a cup and dumped it in Paws's bowl, where she sat, tail swishing the surface of the tiled floor.

Kyle leaned against the kitchen counter with his coffee. He said, "You've really got things under control around here, huh?"

Every fiber of my brain screamed to tell him what I thought about the concept of control and if I had any. I took a deep breath. "Sure do."

"Last night was nice," he said. "You know, right until all the *fuck yous*."

I said, "Fuck you."

Kyle nodded, sipped his coffee. "Get it out, kid. Say what you need to say to me."

I tilted my head at him. My thoughts fired through all the most hurtful things I could come up with. In the end all I said was, "There's nothing to say."

It turns out I picked the right one. Kyle swiped at his eye. "Contacts must be dry." He swallowed hard. "Can I say something?"

I looked at him. All I wanted to do was break my father's heart.

I can't right now. I can't keep going there. Why do I have to be this way?

July 30, 2019 (cont.)

"Oh, my god," I screamed at Kyle. "Could you be any more useless? You wanna talk? Talk!" Paws stopped eating and fled. "You want to try being a father? Have at it. Let me spoil the ending. You fail. You fail at being a parent like you've failed at everything else. What do you want from me? Approval? Sympathy?"

Kyle nodded. "Okay." He sipped his coffee. "It always makes me crazy, too. When someone asks for permission to speak instead of just saying something."

A wordless scream burst from my lips as I left the room. Nicholas looked away when our eyes met. An urge to smack him in the head tightened in my chest. Instead I went past and found

Paws curled in a ball on my bed. I slammed the door behind me, pulled myself onto the mattress, and wrapped myself in blankets with the dog.

I'm done. I'm fucking done.

August 1, 2019

It's been three weeks since my last entry in here. I think I've cooled off enough. I just reread the last two entries. They aren't making me want to burn Francine's house down with myself inside it anymore, so I'm going to go back to the same day. Might as well. I can't stop dreaming about it.

So it's that day in the winter of 2011 when I said everything I could think of to break Kyle's heart and watched him take it. Paws got hungry around five in the evening, which is when she was accustomed to eating. She army-crawled from under the blankets and stretched. I told her *no* in a gentle voice. She paced up the side of the bed, sat beside my head, and bent down to lick my face. I rolled onto my stomach. She let out a compressed whine. I told her *no* in a gentle voice. She made a little muppet sound from deep in her throat. I sighed and threw the blankets off.

Paws squeezed through the bedroom door as soon as the opening was wide enough. There was no one in the living room. She excitement-hopped over to her place mat and bowls. I filled her dish and told her, "Okay." She gobbled the kibble and let out a belch.

"You gross," I said. Then I listened to the silence of the house, thinking maybe Nicholas was upstairs in his room. I strained my ears, listening for his guitar. There was only the tiny abandoned creaking sound of the house settling. I let the dog out into the winter twilight. Across the land was Kyle's cabin, windows bright. Paws made a beeline for the glow. I grimaced, turned back into the house, and put on a heavy hoodie to follow.

She reached the door well before me and let out one sharp bark. Nicholas answered the door and squatted down to greet Paws. She bounded past him. Nicholas turned without looking into the lawn and shut the door.

I stopped where I was and thought about turning around to go back to Francine's. All my anger towards Kyle welled up again and I decided, Fuck him. He can come to me if he wants to try and talk.

I guess he did technically try already.

Nope, if Nicholas wants a relationship with our father, then he can be Kyle's new favorite and effectively only son.

I looked back at Francine's. The little light from my bedroom lamp glowed weakly through a single crack in the curtained first-floor window. A soft yellow glowed from the semi-circle of glass above the front door where I'd left the living room light on. Brown-leaved vines clung to garden lattices on the side of the house, untended. The whole structure seemed to sag under its own weight.

Francine's topiaries were only bushes now, bloated remembrances of what she'd wanted this land to be. It had never served her purposes. Never received the attention it was due.

I looked up at the sky's thin grey strings of shattered velvet floating softly towards the tree line on the horizon. Behind them daylight was vanishing at a faster and faster clip, while the moon took its place and let things freeze down for the night.

I turned back towards Kyle's.

I started slowly. A cold gust of wind blew straight into my face. I whipped my hood up and quickened my pace. Before I even reached the door, it opened, and Kyle stood against a backdrop of bright but soft white light, his frame nearly filling the door, his features unreadable. Warmth emanated from the wood stove burning behind him. Not breaking gait, I limped past. His body shifted in a smooth motion to clear the entrance. He closed the door behind me.

I miss Kyle. I really do.

Nicholas lay prone on the sofa with Paws wedged in a ball between his armpit and the back cushion. In his left hand he held a book under the beam of a large table lamp, which had a carved wooden base. The lamp gave off a subtle smell of cut pine, fresh stain, and butcher's wax. Kyle had stained it a deep cherry rosewood, starting at the square bottom that looked to be double routed with a roman tip around all the edges. Atop it was an elaborately detailed sea turtle, the shell etched with swirling filigree patterns, the nose pointing up to a circular, cream-colored lampshade. It was beautiful. I hated it.

I said Paws's name and she leapt out from snuggling Nicholas and stepped over his back to come to me.

"What did you do that for?" Nicholas asked. "She was comfortable."

I ignored him, asking Kyle, "Where's the lamp from?"

He told me he'd found a couple little DIY kits and spent the last few months whittling it into shape. "That one's Nicholas's," he said. "Second night of Chanukah and all. Yours is right there." He motioned to the kitchen table. A lamp with an identical square base, but the face and head of an elephant for the body, stood there. It was stained a much darker walnut color, polished with wax to bring out the grain of the wood, and had the same kind of filigree running up the elephant's trunk and around its brow and ears. It was beautiful. I hated it.

That's a lie. I loved it. I still do. I'm writing this under my elephant lamp's light. Kyle put so much effort into this lamp. So much care. So much love. I wanted—still want—to resent this elephant, so badly. I don't, though. I can't.

Sometimes I think about Francine's shoe rack. How it somehow embodied her. This lamp is mine. Made by Kyle to embody me. A lot of days, I want to find wherever Francine is nowadays and bash her skull in with it. Turn about is fair play, right? Thought loop…thought loop…

My hand is pressing this pen into the pages with way too much force. The paper feels like it's going to rip. Back to the second night of Chanukah in 2011.

Kyle told me he'd made the lamps while we were at school so they'd be a surprise. He said Nicholas told him sea turtles were his favorite animal, so that one was an easy choice.

"Why did I get an elephant?"

Kyle said, "Because, apparently, they never forget."

No words came to me.

His voice became quiet. "And they're the only other species besides human that digs graves."

Paws quivered once in my arms.

Kyle asked if I was hungry. "Nicky and I were thinking pizza tonight."

My stomach gurgled. I looked over at my new lamp.

My mouth moved without conscious thought. "Where the fuck did all this EQ come from? What is going on? Who *are* you?"

Kyle folded his hands behind his back and took a rasping, Darth Vader breath. "I am your father."

"Not funny!" I screamed. Paws leapt away from me to take shelter beneath the sofa. "How are you making jokes right now? What part of anything in this family seems comedic to you?"

"None of it," he said. He went to the table and pulled out a chair. "There's something I need to tell you. Why don't you join me at the table?"

"I'm good right here."

He nodded. "I've been seeing a therapist. And I've been going to AA meetings, I don't know if you've noticed. I tried NA, too… didn't like it as much." He rubbed his forehead with the heel of his hand and stopped talking.

Bent over the table, his forehead in his hand, his breath tight, tears on his cheeks, I realized something about my father. I had made him a paragon. He was the best or the worst. There was the Zeus of a man I knew in the summer, before the legs, and there was the pestilent shade that showed me everything a person should aspire not to be. Now, there was just some guy. Just a regular fucking human man with a broken family, trying to piece some semblance of a life together with a wife who had left him and two sons who far outpaced him in intellect, the younger of whom had started drinking before his teenage years and the older who—on most days—refused to so much as make eye contact with him. I felt my gaze was made of daggers and a flame burned in my solar plexus. The blades dulled. The fire shrank.

Without looking up, Kyle said, "I know I've been the worst father there has ever been." He swallowed. "But I promise to try and be better."

My brain fastened to the idea that this man did not deserve the comfort for which he begged. My heart, aching to have my father back, shoved my head aside. I went to Kyle and put my hand on his shoulder. His hand floated up from the table to rest atop mine. I squeezed him.

“There have probably been worse dads,” I said. “I’m pretty sure Ted Bundy had a daughter.”

“He did,” Nicholas chimed from the sofa.

I said, “I can’t imagine her being super happy about that.”

Kyle snorted. “It’s all relative, I guess.”

“Moral relativity is a lie,” Nicholas said. “Things need to have an absolute delineation to be considered good or evil.” Then, “I guess cultural relativism exists, though.” He groaned. “Dad? Does life ever get less complicated?”

My father laughed and it seemed like he was alive again. It was beautiful. It was the way I want to remember him. Is this grieving? Have I now grieved thanks to this memory, so vivid in my mind’s eye that I feel physically warm?

Diamond says grief isn’t a linear thing. That the whole DABDA—denial, anger, bargaining, depression, acceptance—stuff cycles and ebbs and flows. Right now, I feel good. The next step is feeling good about feeling good. Not seeking out the negativity. Not spiraling into resentment. Does life ever get less complicated? Hell no.

August 2, 2019

Francine did a radio appearance in 2012 that I listened to, I think because I missed her. I remember her talking passionately, intently, about her writing. About the labor of love and the tireless hours spent practicing her craft. I remember feeling a type of way that grudgingly included respect. Once again, Francine, on paper, made sense. She'd found her way to a new life. Her creative pursuits—I'd wanted to say she wasn't good at them. I wanted to call her lazy and feckless and a myriad of other shitty things. But she never quit on herself. And I'm sure that was hard. Or not, because, you know, narcissism. Maybe she also prioritized herself at our expense but…what else could she do when she was in so much pain?

In her interview Francine talked a lot about finding one's personal connection to creativity, however that looks for a given individual. It's the only way to write in an authentic voice. This played a duet with her voice in my mind saying, "Write what you know." I didn't and still don't *know* anything.

Creativity, though. I value it with a feral joy.

Diamond reminds me that there's no wrong way to do a grief journal. She told me that celebration and mourning are two sides of the same coin. They fill our universal human need for joy and remembrance and something else that isn't coming to me at this exact moment.

Joy.

This is a story I found yesterday in my old senior-year English binder. It was the last balls-out story I got to write.

It's been a long time. Finding this story, rereading it, it brings me a modicum of joy. I want to hold that in my hands.

Even though I've found some respect and empathy for Francine over the years, probably because absence makes the heart grow fonder, I've kept wanting to prove to her—to myself—that creativity is not tethered to the sum of one's experience.

I don't know where this story came from. The muse works in egregious ways. I plugged into a different side of myself. A kind of authenticity that only comes from letting go of preconceived notions. I had no idea at the time, but this story was a way of practicing self-compassion. It was me letting me be me, for the first time? I was a creator again, not an amalgamation of physical and emotional trauma. I only realize that now, but it happened when I put this on the page.

When I formulated the idea for this story, Mr. Short said to me, "Go all out. Do whatever you want. I'm leaving at the end of the year."

Imaginary Friends

Ronnie, he's my dragon. He's not a dragon like Smaug from *The Hobbit*. He's a dragon like Mushu from *Mulan*. Except he's purple with golden eyes. He likes to sit draped around my shoulders. He spits hot fire.

But only if you give him sixteen bars.

Ronnie's been my best friend since I was maybe five years old. He likes to breathe his rhymes into my ears. I don't think he realizes that he just rips off popular tunes and changes the words. Or he does know and doesn't care. He spends a lot of time talking about artistic license.

He's at his best when he's doing "Copacabana."

Ronnie is the one getting me through high school. I'm going through this phase where I don't sleep a lot and it's hard to stay focused.

I go to public school, but a suburban one. People probably say it's pretty nice, especially by public-school standards. The problem with nice schools—for kids who don't sleep and aren't super interested in remedial math—is that sometimes the teachers actually care.

The teacher, she goes by Ms. Rachel. She's not a teacher like the love interest from *Billy Madison*, Veronica Vaughn. She's a teacher like that guy in *Ferris Bueller's Day Off*, the one played by Ben Stein, in that she's boring as sin. I think her last name's Bass or something, like the fish or the former pop star, not the instrument. Or maybe she just has a fish face.

Anyway, she's one of those people that insists you call her by her first name, even though she clings to the "Ms." I guess as a way to symbolically hold onto her authority or something.

She starts in on me about do I need anything from her. And how are things going at home. And have I considered talking to the guidance counselor. She can't make me but strongly recommends it. She's a pain in the ass.

Every time she really gets going with this, Ronnie picks up the Barry Manilow.

—Her name was Fish Face. She was a teacher. And she could never butt out, because her face looked like a trout—

I whistle along while Ronnie sings, until Ms. Rachel gives up and goes back to writing on the board about who-cares-what.

Here's the other thing about public schools. They need public funding. To get it, they have to have kids graduate. And yeah, my school's in good shape, but there were teacher strikes last year. Something about not enough money in the budget. I can't really remember.

So I graduate on the merit of this creative project I do. I put on this black-box, one-man show in the theater for Ms. Rachel, the assistant principal, and the volunteer theater director from the local Church. Ronnie is my sounding board throughout the whole thing. The show is about the characters being created by this guy with extreme insomnia. Each made-up character has a key personality trait through which the main guy tries to cope with all the underlying horrors that keep him awake. The character makes a big deal about not going into the issues he's repressing. He says how far down he's shoved everything. He goes on and on about keeping his real issues safe and removed from anyone, even someone as far away as an audience member he'll never meet.

Because of this, he won't go into details about the father that he watched kill his mother. His brother who, at the age of 14, smoked himself into paranoid schizophrenia. He won't tell you about his crippling inferiority complex. Or his inability to connect with actual human beings. There won't be anything more about his fear of letting anyone in because they'll leave.

He—the character—tells you all of this without really telling you any more about it. The story isn't about his past.

The whole thing's way too meta, but they wind up passing me, so that's pretty neat.

* * *

Bearenstain, he's my bear. He's not a bear like the bears from *Goldilocks and the Three Bears*. He's a bear like Yogi Bear. Except he doesn't wear a tie, he wears a leather jacket and smokes cigarettes. He goes by Bearenstain because he thinks the irony makes him sound cool. He doesn't have a great grip on the meaning of *irony*.

But wow, can he beatbox.

Bearenstain basically gets me through my associate's degree at community college. There are all these prerequisite classes that everyone has to take, no matter what. That's where I meet Bearenstain, sitting to my left, drumming on his desk and making popping noises between his cheeks and teeth. This wouldn't bother me otherwise, but it makes it so Ronnie never shuts up.

—His name was Bearenstain. But he was a bear. With a really stupid name, and he always dressed the same. With that dumb jacket, but never shoes on—

So we're sitting in this freshman comp class, and my head starts to nod and jolt the way it does when you're fighting to stay awake but can't. And of course, the only time my body is willing to sleep is during class. If only I were cool like that dude from *Fight Club*.

That's where Bearenstain sort of bails me out, I guess. In between talking about these contrived philosophers—guys like Paulo Freire and Michael Pollan—Bearenstain tells me jokes.

He leans over and whispers stuff like, what happens when you shove a pogo stick up a duck's ass?

He times it so that his question ends right when the professor says, "What."

He tells me you get a bouncing quack and tilts his chin towards our professor.

My head snaps up and I snort loud.

The professor and a couple other kids look at me. I avert my eyes. The professor looks a little less than happy.

He asks, "Is there something funny?"

Bearenstain leans over and whispers to me.

I say, "Knock, knock."

The professor stares at me. A girl in the front row of the class asks, who's there?

I say, "To."

The girls asks to who?

I snarl, "To whom."

The professor's lip sort of curls, like maybe he'll laugh. Then his face turns all hard.

He says, "Get the hell out of my class."

I shrug and sling my backpack over one shoulder, slouch out of the classroom. On the way out, Ronnie is singing.

—His name was Hard Ass. He had bad ED. And since he couldn't get it up, he could never get enough. Shouting at students, to o-ver-comp-en-sate—

The girl at the front of the class, she scoffs at the professor and does the universal sign for "suck it" before following Bearenstain, Ronnie, and me from the classroom. So I guess now I officially have my own posse or something.

The girl and I don't talk. She keeps looking at me while we walk outside and opening her mouth but not saying anything. Eventually, she shrugs, and that's that.

We all loiter under an ash tree until it's time for my Intro to Theater class. This class, I kind of like. We learn about some pretty neat people. Bearenstain likes Oscar Wilde and takes to quoting him.

He starts saying things like, the only difference between the saint and the sinner is that every saint has a past, and every sinner has a future.

He thinks it makes him sound real deep.

He says these quotes while drumming in weird time signatures, experimenting with 13/8.

The professor, she's a doctor. She's not a doctor like Henry Gray, the one who wrote *Gray's Anatomy*. That's *Gray's Anatomy* the essential medical text, not the overwrought TV show.

She's a doctor like Dr. Seuss. Her name is Frances Moyer. She smiles a lot.

She has us reading *The Importance of Being Earnest*. Bearenstain is beatboxing behind me at his desk. Ronnie tells me it's my turn to rap, but that I have to do it quiet so I don't disrupt class. The girl, she's not in this class, but she's here taking notes anyway.

I whisper. "Here with Ronnie and Bearenstain, my bear. I'd call him my dog but he's a bear, I swear—"

Dr. Moyer comes up to my desk.

She asks, "Do you mind coming with me to my office after class?"

I tell her, "Sure."

—Her name was Frances. She was a Ph.D. But it was in Theater Studies, so she might be a dummy. But what a rack on her, I'd love to see them things—

I flick Ronnie in his snout and follow Dr. Moyer to her office. While we're walking, Dr. Moyer tells me how interested she is in this one-man show I put on in high school. She read my personal essay about the play and wants to hear more.

Bearenstain tells me that there is only one thing in life worse than being talked about, and that is not being talked about.

We get to her office and I explain the character from my play. Explain to her Ronnie's character. How he loves Barry Manilow. That sometimes you love your best friends simply because you don't have to hide from them.

She blinks at me.

She says, "That sounds more intellectual than I would have expected from a high school senior with, quite frankly, terrible grades."

She chuckles and asks if I like plays by George Bernard Shaw.

I say, "I don't know who that is."

"Don't worry. We'll be studying some of his work in a week or two. He's a really great playwright."

Then she starts talking about Shaw's philosophy and approach to theater. I'm not listening. I'm more interested in the way her eyes sparkle while she talks. The little movements her lips form around vowels. The fingers flying through the air with her hand motions. How her French manicure reflects the light.

But I nod along as if I know exactly what she's talking about.

—There was some tension. And it was sex-u-al. With the hot doctor in her lair, and her perfect shiny hair—

Bearenstain waxes poetic: be yourself, everyone else is already taken.

When Dr. Moyer finally relaxes, her breath is a little short. I think, okay, yeah, maybe I can, like, talk to this lady, possibly.

So I say, "Would you want to get a drink sometime?"

The girl from comp is leaning in the doorway and her eyebrows go up.

Dr. Moyer asks, "How old are you, exactly?"

"Eighteen and three quarters."

She sort of looks at me sideways.

She says, "Then, legally, no drinks. Besides, you're my student."

Bearenstain tells me hear no evil, speak no evil—and you'll never be invited to a party.

I ask her, "What if I wasn't your student?"

I tell her, "There's more to life than sleeping through my classes."

I say, "Dropping out is always an option," and I wink at her.

I immediately wish I hadn't winked at her.

She says "You're too young." Then, softer: "Maybe when you graduate—if you're twenty-one—I'll buy you a drink to celebrate."

I try not to take it personally.

The girl steps into the room now. She points her finger at Dr. Moyer. She asks, what is wrong with her? The doctor, that is.

She calls Dr. Moyer a horrible person, asks if she's serious.

She talks about how much of a prick Dr. Moyer is being and can she really not see how hard that was for me? How lucky Dr. Moyer would be to go out with me? At the very least, to hedge her bets against me becoming the next Bernard Shaw, whoever the hell that is, she could throw me a hand job or something.

This whole time, I'm staring at the girl. I can feel all this burning heat in my ears. My eyes hurt from how wide they are.

Dr. Moyer is just looking at the girl with one eyebrow raised and her hands folded on her desk.

I stammer an apology and grab the girl by her elbow.

As we leave the room, the girl is still shouting at Dr. Moyer.

The girl, Gwenyth, she's my dream girl. She's not a dream girl like the girl in that crappy Dave Matthews Band song, "Dream Girl." She's a dream girl like if you wrapped up Juno from the movie *Juno* and Alison Brie and made them smell like daisies.

Gwenyth, she's getting me through this stay we're doing in a behavioral center for people with substance abuse issues.

She's there because she accidentally took too many Xanax. Then she decided to drive out and adopt a puppy. She crashed into a fire hydrant on the way.

I'm in for huffing glue and trying to hang myself with an extension cord.

The thing with Gwenyth is that her mom is Filipina and her dad is Jewish and she's beautiful. She has these thick cords of scar tissue on her inner forearm from middle school. They spell the name "Kurt." She loves Nirvana. Maybe she likes me because I smell like teen spirit.

Even I know that's a bad joke.

Gwenyth loves bad jokes.

I ask her, "What do you call an alligator in a vest?"

She pretends she hasn't heard it before and asks, what? She laughs hard when I tell her it's an investigator.

I can almost hear Ronnie and Bearenstain in her laugh.

Her laugh sounds like...

—Her name was Gwenyth. And she soon became. Our very good dear friend, and she will be till the end—

Her laugh is Bearenstain saying that man is least himself

when he talks in his own person. Give him a mask, and he will tell you the truth.

Gwenyth falls asleep on my shoulder during our daily classes. We have all these guest speakers come in. Guys with PTSD from Desert Storm and women who say they'll never truly beat their heroin addiction, but they know they won't be shooting up today, at least.

We watch episodes of ***Intervention*** after these guest speakers. Most of the other patients shout at the television. They yell stuff like, "Why are we watching this? It's triggering," or, "I can't watch her cut herself no more," or, "Tell him to stop talking to his brother, that dude is an enabler."

I don't understand why we watch them, either. No one here is getting scared straight. No one feels safer for the fact that other people have similar problems. No one evolves from watching these videos.

We watch a particularly graphic episode. One about an alcoholic, anorexic woman who was sexually assaulted as a child. She can't stop slugging down vodka and taking razors to her inner thighs. Afterwards, we get a little lecture to wrap up class.

The nurse who plays these tapes says, "The things we're most scared of are ourselves. The things we're most in danger from are ourselves. The only thing really holding you back is yourself."

What a load of horse crap that is.

Then we get dinner from a cafeteria. Then we come back and unwind in these surprisingly comfortable chairs. There are tables for doing jigsaw puzzles and a chess set and some other innocuous stuff. Gwenyth and I sit and color.

Gwenyth asks me, what do you get when you breed a horse with a rabbit?

I ask her, "What?"

She tells me it's a dead rabbit.

I snort but don't laugh.

She tells me to come on. That that's a funny one.

I say, "Too morbid for me."

She asks me why the girl dropped her cell phone.

"Why?"

She tells me the girl was an unfortunate victim of a drive-by shooting. She laughs from her belly and slaps her knee. She explains to me that these are a brand of comedy called "anti-jokes," in which the humor arises from the fact that they're not at all funny.

The explanation makes me laugh more than the jokes themselves, which I find to be in poor taste.

I get up to get us a bag of pretzels from a little snack alcove. I sit down across from Gwenyth and she says she wanted Raisinettes. I stick my tongue out at her and we split the pretzels.

There's a nightly AA meeting we have to go to. Everyone sort of goes through the motions. This guy Floyd with three piercings in his nose—one in each nostril and another in the septum—snores loudly from the back. The same people volunteer to do the readings every night, not because they're invested in the meeting, but because it gets us out quicker so we can all watch *Sanford & Son.*

After the meeting, after the two AA guys tell their horror stories about rock bottom, after the same three people from our group say the same three things they say every night, we walk up to shake the speakers' hands. Their palms are sweaty and their eyes are bulging out of their skulls from all the coffee they've been drinking.

Gwenyth says she's pretty sure she smells liquor on their breath. She says it's definitely whiskey. That the mix of bourbon and cigarettes makes her want to gag. A lot of the other patients complain about the same thing. They tell our unit's staff. The staff are pretty well used to these kinds of complaints and mostly ignore them.

Gwenyth and I sit by ourselves while everyone else gets their vitals taken.

Gwenyth tells me to drop some phat bars for her.

"Gwenyth and me, we're sitting at a table, she's so pretty that this might be a fable, but it isn't one, so it's more fun, and maybe some time we could go for a run—"

She giggles and tells me I really lost the thread there.

The nurse, she's a real eyesore, but I think her outside reflects her insides. She's not a nurse like Florence Nightingale. She's a nurse like Beverly Allitt. She's a nurse like Kristen Gilbert. She's a nurse like the nurses that worked for Dr. Mengele and smiled.

She says, "You need to stop singing and come get your blood pressure taken."

I say, "I wasn't singing."

I mutter, "You should mind your own business."

I tell her, "These new pills give me the night sweats."

She looks at me annoyed, shakes her head, and hands me a little paper cup with a white tablet and a green capsule. She makes me get up so she can take my vitals. She lets everyone out for a cigarette break. The smoke reminds me of Bearenstain, but of course, he isn't there.

One of the orderlies, the only one I can even moderately stand, plays music for us quietly, even though he isn't supposed to. He plays "Copacabana," per my request. I feel for Ronnie around my shoulders, but of course, he isn't there.

I turn for Gwenyth, so I can tell her about the joke I just thought of. An anti-joke about the president being a seventeen-foot-tall reptile in a human suit.

She isn't there.

My doctor tells me I'm set to go home right before Thanksgiving. I'm not listening to him.

I spend the next day idly saying yes to an IOP—intensive outpatient program—and chemical regimen, and pulling my pants up constantly because there are no strings or belts of any kind allowed inside the unit. Also taking dumps behind a curtain, because the unit's staff has to be able to check on me every fifteen minutes.

Then it's time for me to leave.

Usually, everyone does this weird, fake, lovey-dovey act of handing out their phone number when they get discharged. It's like a ritual. They tell every single person to call them. They promise they'll call the facility from the outside to keep things lively. They write the number down in green crayon on torn strips of paper.

It's all just for the appearance of having become a better person.

It's all a show.

It's all about as real as my friends.

Mr. Short did leave the year I graduated. I never spoke to him again. I distinctly remember his face: simultaneously pensive, concerned, and impressed. It was this weird expression: lips pursed and twisted to the right, eyelids at half-mast, brow neutral.

Out of that face, he said, "This is really good, K.J." A thoughtful pause. Then, "Where did this come from?"

I shrugged. "I don't know. I thought about, like…I don't know."

He asked, "Have you experienced things like this? It's very... specific."

I shook my head.

He sighed. "We've known each other a while now, yes?"

I nodded.

"May I ask you something?"

"No."

With no malice or disappointment, he said, "Okay."

I rolled my eyes. "May I ask you something?"

"Sure."

"Why," I asked, "do people ask permission to ask a question instead of asking what they want? Such a stressful set up. Who says 'no' to 'may I ask you a question,' honestly?"

He told me I had, about six seconds prior.

I said, "Noted."

He said, "Does this mean I can ask you the question?"

"You just did it again."

He nodded.

I probably said something like, "Fucking ask me, then," but I know I didn't say quite that.

What I do know was said next by Mr. Short—at least the gist of it—was, "Why are you so terrified of giving the reader a cathartic ending? Some resolution?"

"I'm not."

He arched an eyebrow. "Then why don't you ever try it?"

It was such a weird gut punch to take. I wish I'd said, "Because in real life, things just end. The way I see it, setting people's expectations that a story needs to end in a comfortable, familiar, or neat way sets them up for failure. Art mirrors life or whatever, and mirrors work in two directions. I won't give a story a 'cathartic' conclusion because catharsis has to come from within. You create your own meaning from stories. You build your own narratives.

All I do is Jacques Derrida this shit by putting lines and symbols on a page. Everything else is out of my hands. If a reader likes the wrap-up, chill. Great. Wonderful work for me, I guess. If they don't, sucks. That stinks for them. I guess I don't actually give a fuck. My artistic validation doesn't come from external gratification anymore. I write for *me.* You don't like a story? Put it down. Problem solved. Move on. Tight."

But I didn't say any of that. I didn't know it then. Instead, I asked, "Do you hate the ending?"

He shook his head. He said, "Do *you* like the ending?"

I bit my lip, nodded.

"Then this is how this particular story ends," he said.

August 3, 2019

It turned out the doctors had been right about the brain injury not ruining my cognitive abilities. Whether from self-induced friendlessness or the need to escape my parents—more likely, both—I graduated high school at the very top of my class. I slaughtered the SATs. Princeton University accepted me on early admission. With all the gossip that ran our small school, everyone was bound to find out the other students' plans for after graduation. I was our only Ivy League acceptance.

Glen still walked near enough to me in the hallways, but only because it looked good on his own college applications as community service.

I asked him where he was going to school next year. He rolled his eyes. "What do you care, Fiveskin?"

"Just making conversation, Fuckface."

His ears turned red. "You know," he said, "if you weren't such a dick all the time, we could actually have a conversation."

"And maybe if you were more intelligent than a sack of horse shit, we'd have something to talk about."

He made a disgusted sound and stalked in the direction from which we'd come.

I went to a quiet hallway and sat on the sill of its large windows, so I could eat my turkey sandwich alone with a book, like I did every day by this time—late spring of 2012. Mare Bear appeared before me and cleared her throat. She was unencumbered by her usual group of friends. The latter stages of puberty had been even kinder to Mare Bear than the earlier ones, and with her beauty become obvious, so grew her popularity. These days, we spoke little to not-at-all, based on our respective social ranks and lack of common interests. She was salutatorian.

"Hey," she said.

I looked up. "Yo."

"So, um, I heard you got accepted to Princeton. That's really cool. You always were too smart for it here."

I didn't answer her.

She shifted her weight from foot to foot.

"Do you need something?" I asked. "Or can I get back to my lunch?"

She rolled her eyes. "Look, you can be as mean as you want, but it doesn't change the past. I was wondering if you'd sign my yearbook. I can sign yours, too, if you want."

I hate myself for how I decided to treat her in this moment.

I told her that I didn't buy one but I'd sign hers, if she really wanted. She handed it to me. The back pages were already filled with signatures and long messages about how much people would miss her, imploring her to keep in touch. I took the pen she handed me and scribbled over the other signatures. In hard-pressed letters, I wrote, "You disappointed me." I signed it *Crumpelfiveskin*. I snapped the book shut and handed it to her.

She opened it, read my message, and left without a word.

I don't have any words for her now, either. Maybe *I'm sorry*.

Kyle drove me down to Princeton the following August, my wheelchair in the back. Nicholas, huge for his age and certainly the first kid in his class with armpit hair, sat between us. There was something poetic to the arrangement. We were sitting in the same order we did after my accident.

Shortly after I left for college, Kyle fell off the wagon. Apparently, he'd begun dating the therapist who'd gotten him on the right track, though their relationship was kept secret from me. When the therapist dumped Kyle, he spiraled really hard. In my head canon, she broke up with him because he finally, after years of telling her half-truths in a thoughtless man's effort to rebuild his self-esteem, came clean to her about what had happened to me. Francine. The shoe rack. Reptar. She couldn't stand to look at him anymore and left.

That whole story is unverified. I guess, now, with Kyle in the ground, I'll never know.

When I'd left for Princeton, Kyle and I had been on good terms. When I heard he was tearing himself back apart, I decided my hands were now washed. I'd like to write more about what his decline was like. I would detail how it went down, but I can't, because I intentionally wasn't there for it. I was mostly grateful for my absence. In part, too, I was so overwhelmed with guilt about that decision that I didn't know what to do other than shove the pain deep down and pretend it didn't exist.

Regardless, I shone throughout college. I didn't go home for summers or holidays, rather stayed with one of the few friends I made, none of whom made me say exactly why I couldn't go home. It's amazing the questions you don't get asked when you walk with a limp. This went on until junior year of college, when Francine swooped in to rent me an apartment. We didn't talk directly, only communicating through Nicholas. Distance had improved my relationship with my brother, and though we weren't friends, we answered each other's calls. Usually only to check in and make sure the other was alive. It was something.

Nicholas told me that Kyle was dead on April 3, 2019. At this point in time, that's five months ago today.

He said he'd found Kyle sitting in front of Francine's fireplace with an empty handle of Maker's, an empty bottle of Vicodin, a shotgun, and a flap of skin clinging to the shards of his skull. I thought of the body that once wrapped itself in pillows to tackle a raging dog. I thought of poetic justice. I thought that Kyle should have killed himself in the cabin where the rest of us died.

I think maybe it's okay to have those feelings. To have those thoughts. I don't think I can or will ever be able to fully control that kind of stuff. Sigh. My therapist says intrusive thoughts are exactly what they sound like. They're going to come. That doesn't mean you have to listen to them.

When Nicholas called me to tell me how Kyle "did a suey," as we now phrase the event, his voice was solemn. He sounded very, very tired. He didn't ask me if I would come home to tend to Kyle's funeral arrangements, but I said I would anyway. I took a train from Penn Station in New York down to 30th Street Station in Philadelphia. Nicholas drove almost two hours to the station to pick me up. He arrived in a GMC Yukon, dried mud caked on so thick that the paint beneath could have been dull green or dark silver.

Nicholas stepped out, fully grown now. He had Kyle's wide-set shoulders, broad back, thick forearms, and sandy hair, worn long. But he had Francine's bright-brown eyes and crooked mouth. He said, "Hi." He lifted me by way of a bone-wrenching hug.

"Can't breathe," I said.

He set me down and opened the passenger door for me. He popped the trunk, tossed my stuff into it, and circled around to the driver side. We settled into our seats.

"Where'd you get the car?" I asked.

"Twenty-first birthday present from Francine. Showed up in the driveway with a note on it. It's already seen better days by now."

"Why? It's only, what? Two years old? How's the mileage?"

He shrugged. "More than it probably should be."

"How is Francine?"

"Wouldn't know."

I gave him a questioning glance. Without meeting it, he told me about Francine's permanent departure from her house. Apparently, with all the fame and critical acclaim, her siblings were now willing to recognize her as family. It had taken the better part of a decade after her first manuscript acceptance. (There had been three novels since, all meeting general praise.)

A letter had come from her brother Michael down in Marco Island, telling her she had to come and visit. To meet her three nieces, one of whom was an aspiring writer herself. She'd asked Nicholas to go with her, but he hadn't wanted to leave Kyle. He wasn't sure his father would remember to feed himself on his own.

"How are you doing?" I asked.

Nicholas shrugged. "Got my license suspended, so there's that."

"And you're driving right now?"

"Someone had to come get you." He reached into the slot beneath the radio and took out Kyle's flask. "Cheers," he said, unscrewing the top with the heel of his hand and taking a swig.

I murmured, "Christ."

He held the flask out to me. "Want some?"

"I'm good."

"Your loss." He took another sip and replaced the flask.

He shifted the Yukon into gear and pulled carefully out of the pick-up area for arrivals. He made a left and then merged onto I-76

West, from which we'd pick up 476 North. I let Nicholas do the talking while he drove.

He told me Francine loved it down on Marco Island. She'd decided she should move there. The second time she went away, she didn't ask Nicholas to come along. She left him a note with the words *I'm sorry* and nothing else, then sent a crew in to move out her stuff. Despite how critics sucked her dick for the eloquence of her writing, that was all she had for her only real son. "I'm sorry."

"Funny," I said. "That she's still pretending to know what those words mean."

"Don't be so hard on her."

I stared at the side of Nicholas's head. "Are you fucking kidding me?"

He gave me Kyle's shrug for when a conversation wasn't going anywhere. "Still," he said. There was a long silence. Then he surprised me. He said, "The only difference between her and the rest of us is that she can handle her liquor."

It was everything I could do not to smash him in the side of the head.

Then he said, "Well, Dad and me, I guess. You've never been like the rest of us."

I stared through my window as highway ripped past. By the time we were fifteen minutes from home, evening was coming on. I watched as the trees we'd passed after the accident glided into view. They were as rich and green and dense as ever. Maybe even more so. Seeing those trees, so stoic and hardy as the earth was dying beneath them thanks to humankind, it was breathtaking. These were the trees that made lasting houses. They could weather anything. Even being cut down.

Nicholas drove through the open gate. We got out of the car. I stared at Kyle's deteriorated cabin, exterior chipped and streaked with dirt, the grass spreading white around it in a radius of decay. By contrast, Francine's house was magnificent. My legs faltered, as they still did from time to time. Nicholas hooked his arm under mine. I felt steady.

We started towards Francine's house. My eyes went wide.

"Stop," I said.

"What?"

"Fucking stop!"

Nicholas planted his feet, wanting to know if everything was okay. I barely heard. I stared at the space beside Francine's house. Another house. Two houses. Smaller houses. Doghouses.

"What are those?"

Nicholas cleared his throat. "Um, Dad and I made them."

"Really?"

"Yeah."

"Who're they for?"

Nicholas whistled through his teeth.

The flap at the front of the first house opened and out came Paws, her ears back, tail wagging in circles from the force of her excitement. Her snout was mostly grey and her hips were a little rigid. She bounded up to us and stood balanced on her hind legs. Then the strangest thing happened. She dropped onto her forepaws and jumped at Nicholas, who caught her and brought her to his chest.

"Sorry I was gone so long," he told her. "I'm back now, don't worry. You wanna see your dad?"

Paws's ears flattened all the way back and her tail slowed. Nicholas handed her to me. She whined, put her front feet on my shoulders and touched her nose to mine. Tears welling, I told her how sorry I was over and over before scratching her head. Her tail went wild and she nuzzled into the crook of my neck. I held her tight to my breast.

"Francine never got rid of her," Nicholas said. "She let her live in the house and even reminded me to go out for dog food when we ran low. Love isn't the right word for how she felt about Paws once you left, but it isn't the wrong one either, if that makes sense."

"I didn't think she'd still be here," I whispered.

"There was a lot you didn't think about before you left."

I cleared my throat. "What else?"

Nicholas whistled again, louder and shriller through his teeth. The other doghouse slowly opened at the front. From it emerged a fourteen-year-old brindle Staffordshire terrier, the fur a little long for the breed, the snout a little sharp. Paws's tail thumped gently against me. Reptar's eyes settled on me, went wide to show the whites all the way around the irises. His tail shook the entire back of his body. He trotted up on arthritic legs. Paws barked with excitement from my shoulder. I handed her to Nicholas and squatted down. Reptar picked up speed. He would have bowled me over if Nicholas hadn't braced my back with a wide hand. I sat down on the grass. Reptar bathed my face with his tongue, stood on hind legs, wrapped his forepaws around my shoulders, and rested his face against my cheek.

"He's a little deaf now," Nicholas told me. "Old dog."

I sat and cried against Reptar's face.

I choked out the words to ask Nicholas how the dog was back.

"I stole him out of the Millers' backyard."

"Whose?"

"The people that initially took him. I guess that ball player got traded to Milwaukee or something so he just left Reptar there."

"You shouldn't have taken him from his home, Nicholas."

"This is his home."

"The—did you say Miller?"

"Yeah."

"The Millers are probably heartbroken."

"Nah, they're real old. Pretty sure the wife has dementia and the old man is basically negligent. Reptar was filthy and too skinny when I got him. Now he gets his anti-inflammatories every morning and some calming treats every night. He's better off."

Nicholas put Paws down. Reptar let go of me. The dogs grumbled playfully at one another. Reptar rolled onto his side and mouthed at Paws while she hopped around him. Nicholas and I watched with gentle smiles. We made our way towards Francine's, the dogs in tow.

I asked Nicholas how things had been lately, hoping for a short answer, but Nicholas needed to talk.

This is his story. But it's *my* journal, and I haven't written anything new since I started this fucking thing, so I'm taking liberties with the details. This is what he said, but in, like, a fun(?) way.

After Francine left, after having read her note over and over, after realizing he was all alone in life, Nicholas decided he would be the one in the family who could handle himself.

On the Saturday in 2017 after Francine went to Marco Island for good, Nicholas woke up with Paws huddled beneath his covers. Nicholas stirred and stretched. Paws scuttled up to poke her nose from the top edge of the blankets, tail slapping the mattress. Nicholas rose, went through his morning routine, and searched in vain for signs of life, eventually sitting down at Francine's kitchen table and sharing a bagel with Paws.

He let her out onto the property, feeling the cool morning air of springtime, stepping onto the grass barefoot to let the dew well between his toes. He watched Paws do her business, scamper in circles, chase her tail, and fall down.

"Come on inside, girl."

Paws's ears flattened, tail dropped.

"Come on. In, in."

She whined and sprinted past Francine's house. With a long breath and a look towards the heavens, Nicholas trudged over to the cabin. Inside, he found Kyle, shirtless, skin clinging to his ribs, sprawled unconscious on the sofa. Nicholas picked up a bottle of vodka from the floor and took a long pull. He suffocated the ghost of a wince, checked Kyle's breathing, and shook him by the shoulder.

Kyle grumbled, cracked one eye, and swallowed down vomit.

"Hey," Nicholas said, sitting down beside his father.

Kyle grunted.

"Francine's gone."

"Where now?"

"Florida. Forever, I think."

Kyle stared at the ceiling. "She'll be back."

Nicholas put the bottle back to his mouth and then handed it to Kyle, who did the same. Nicholas said that the weather looked good today, according to his app. He asked, "You want to maybe do something outside with me?"

Kyle struggled to a seat. "What would we do?"

Nicholas shrugged. The two sat in silence, passed the bottle back and forth a couple times. Nicholas said, "We should get you into the shower. Then we can figure it out."

Nicholas waited outside, tossing sticks for Paws, who sometimes brought them back, sometimes not. Kyle emerged, smelling of soap but still rancid. Nicholas took in Kyle's T-shirt smeared with dirt and his jeans hanging off his ass.

"I have an idea," Nicholas said.

Kyle belched. "What's that?"

***

Nicholas drove down to the local lumberyard and came back with a loaded truck bed, the wood paid for with a debit card Francine had given him.

The rest of that day and the following Sunday, Nicholas and Kyle built a dog house for Paws. Really, Nicholas built it, Kyle sort of supervising but mostly scratching his head and measuring cuts three, sometimes four, times. Kyle never ran the saws. Nicholas stood at the chop saw, cutting fourteen-footers to length, doweling and gluing them into solid pieces.

"You're making them too big," Kyle said. "Gonna be too heavy. Easier to frame and then side the whole thing."

Nicholas wiped sweat from his brow. "How the fuck do I do that?"

"It's easy."

Kyle plopped down in the grass and talked Nicholas through ripping the boards until all the cuts were clean and square. "Can't rack the frame," he told Nicholas. "Or the house'll fall down in two days."

Nicholas grunted and sat beside Kyle. They shared a bottle of whiskey and fell asleep outside. Nicholas woke up around midnight, shivering, with Paws huddling in his armpit. He threw Kyle over his shoulder, scooped Paws up to his hip, and carried them inside.

It was the first time Kyle slept in Francine's new house. In her bed. But she still wasn't there.

Kyle milled around Nicholas as he drove the final nails into Paws's house. Kyle walked a circle around it, inspecting.

"Looks real good," he said. "Where'd you learn to do all this?"

Nicholas took a pull from the flask he and Kyle now shared, passed it to his father. "You pick things up, just watching people, you know?"

Kyle nodded, tested the swinging hinges on the top of the circular front door Nicholas had installed. He opened it all the way and checked on the burlap flooring, pushed at the dog bed inside. Nicholas closed it, held the doggie flap open, and told Paws, "Okay."

She approached tentatively, sniffing her way up to it. Nicholas, tired from labor and impatient, grumbled, took a treat from his pocket, and tossed it through. Paws chased. Nicholas held a treat on the other side until Paws's excitement forced her back through the doggie door. Two more times and she had it figured out.

"All yours," Nicholas told her.

Paws made a big show of going in and out on her own several more times, looking up at Nicholas to see if the treat stream had yet run dry. She settled inside her new house. Nicholas brought her bowls out into it.

The following Friday, Nicholas went down the mountain to a party at the Turntons' house, to which he'd been invited by Robby, with whom he was still close. Mare Bear was home from wherever she was living and working to watch the house while her parents were on a trip. Nicholas parked the pickup with the driver's-side tires up on the sidewalk, an hour and a half after the official start time, already buzzed. He walked across the fresh-mown lawn into the Turntons' Colonial without knocking.

He followed voices straight back into the kitchen. He poked his head in to find an older crowd of yuppie whoevers invited by Mare Bear, only a few of whom he knew. Nicholas stepped fully into the room and nodded to them. Mare Bear, standing at an island in the middle of the room, squealed and ran up to him.

Her lips were stained with fruit punch. "Nick! My gosh. You've gotten...you've gotten really big." She held a fist to her mouth and burped into it.

Nicholas took the cup from her hand and drained it. The drink was terrible. "Robby here?"

Mare Bear took her cup back. "Downstairs is reserved for all you little kids."

Nicholas rolled his eyes playfully.

She asked, "Heard from your brother at all?"

"Maybe. I'll see you later." Then he went through the basement door.

The basement, unfinished, held the more raucous crowd headed by Robby, who stood on top of a plastic folding table shouting out instructions for the coming beer pong tournament. He wore a flannel shirt tucked into jeans, a big belt buckle with "Tennessee" embossed on it, and cowboy boots. He looked towards the stairs, wobbled on his feet, and let himself down to the floor.

Robby announced Nicholas's presence by throwing his hands in the air and screaming "Woo! My pong partner's here! Let's get this shit going!"

The population of the room turned to see Robby clap both hands on Nicholas's shoulders. "You didn't get dressed up. It's cowboys and Indians, dude."

Nicholas shrugged, pulled at the chest of his T-shirt. "That's fucked up. And I don't think cowboys wore flat-brim hats, Robby."

Robby frowned. "I couldn't find a cowboy hat." He took off his baseball cap and smoothed his hair back from his eyes. Their other friends gathered around the folding table, set with pyramids of red cups at either end.

Nicholas eyed the light beer but didn't complain. He and Robby, as was custom, took their place at one end of the table. Nicholas, with his height, was a good beer pong player. He and Robby won three straight. But Robby was a smaller guy, only around five-six, and skinny to boot. He outdrank his weight and needed a break to lean against the wall.

"Someone jump on for us," Nicholas said. He stood before Robby and bent to get to eye level.

"How you feeling, bud?"

"Great." He swallowed and his eyelids fluttered. "I great feel. You're my friend...best friend. I want know you to that. Know?"

Nicholas smiled with the side of his mouth. "Why don't we get you to bed there, kid."

Robby insisted he was fine but didn't resist as Nicholas scooped him up and took him to his room. Nicholas came back down the stairs, still not drunk, only a little more buzzed than his standard. "More buzzed" wasn't what he'd come to the party for. He thought about going back down to the basement, but he'd be damned if he was going to get fucked up on light beer and Smirnoff. He walked into the kitchen where Mare Bear, five of her girlfriends, and their male counterparts drank and shouted at the table.

Nicholas approached the kitchen island with all the booze on it, checked labels. He scratched at the back of his neck.

"Mary," he called. Mare Bear's head rotated towards him and forced her off balance, though she caught herself on the kitchen table.

"Nick!" she shouted across the room. The guy next to her winced at the volume. "What's up?"

"Got anything better to drink in this joint?"

Mary scowled, wobbled over. "What's wrong with this stuff?" She steadied herself by grabbing Nicholas's shoulder.

He scratched his chin. "I'll show you. Hold tight."

Nicholas went into the attached living room and spotted the liquor cabinet in the corner of the room, a teak armoire with glass-paneled doors and edges routed with a quarter-inch round-over. The cabinet wasn't locked. Nicholas grabbed a bottle of Chivas Regal, racked his brains for something interesting to drink. There was no Drambuie in the cabinet—he couldn't make the Rusty Nail he craved—so he settled for sweet vermouth and bitters. He went back into the kitchen, ignoring all the lightweights, and rustled up an orange. Mare Bear told him he shouldn't drink her dad's liquor. That that was why they got their own stuff.

"Just tell him it was me," Nicholas said. "He won't get mad."

Mare Bear smiled. "That's probably true. You're his favorite." She lowered her voice. "Don't tell Robby."

Nicholas leaned in, extended his pinky. Mare Bear linked hers to his and they kissed the outsides of their hands to seal the swear.

"Now," Nicholas said. "You ever have a Rob Roy?"

Mare Bear shook her head. Nicholas grabbed two real glasses. He eyeballed two ounces of scotch into each glass, followed by one ounce of vermouth and a couple dashes of bitters. He cut two identical strips from the orange's peel with a paring knife, twisted one above each glass, and dropped them in for garnish, then stirred both drinks with a wooden spoon. He handed one to Mare Bear, who was gripping the edge of the counter with hooded eyes. She took the drink, clinked it against Nicholas's, and sipped.

Her eyes opened up.

"Holy fuck," she said. "That tastes amazing."

Nicholas sipped his own, bit his upper lip. "I've made better."

Mare Bear shook her head, fell back. Glen Sanders appeared behind her and wrapped his arm around her waist, steadying her.

"You good, babe?"

She nodded. "You have to try this drink Nick made." He took the glass and sipped it.

"Wow," he said. "That's really good."

Nicholas shrugged. "I'll be downstairs if anyone needs me."

"No," Mare Bear cried. "Stay and hang out with us. I never see you anymore."

So Nicholas stayed. He decided he didn't feel like making more drinks. He grabbed the Chivas bottle by the neck and took it straight.

He awoke on his stomach in Mare Bear Turnton's bed. She lay naked on her back, her white comforter askew across her lower half. Nicholas was in his boxers and socks. He looked at the floor, saw a discarded condom wrapper. His knuckles stung, the skin raw, dried blood in the creases. He rubbed his eyes and stood up. Mare Bear grumbled and turned over. Nicholas found his jeans and T-shirt, pulled them on, laced his sneakers, and padded out of the room. He pulled over on his drive home and puked on the mountain road. He leaned against the side of Kyle's pickup, wondered how it had stayed running all these years. He took a long inhale through his nose, felt the chilled, fresh air rejuvenate him some. He got back in the car.

When he got home, he found Kyle asleep on the couch, Paws was stretched out longways on his chest. Nicholas passed without waking them and went to bed.

"You had sex with Mary Turnton?" I asked.

Nicholas nodded. "And beat the hell out of Glen Sanders."

"Why?"

"He said something about you. Something not very nice, I imagine. Either that or he caught me making out with Mary and wanted to start some shit. I don't really remember."

"How did Robby feel about all that?"

Nicholas shrugged. "He forgave me after about a week."

I stared at the pile of ash in Francine's fireplace.

"You need to clean that out occasionally," I told Nicholas. "And close the flue, too. Did you close the flue?"

"No. Here." He handed me a slip of paper. "Kyle's little suey Post-it."

It read, "I spent my whole life killing myself for other people. It only seemed fair that I do something for myself."

Which, honestly, lol. I think he probably really did think it was true, though.

I read it over five times. "Kyle wrote *this*, and all Francine could muster up was, 'I'm sorry?'"

"Yeah."

"Christ." I rolled to my bedroom. The room looked untouched from when I'd left. There was a thick coat of dust over every surface, but it was unaltered. The same sheets, now musty, on the bed, old sketch- and notebooks scattered on my desk, an aromatherapy candle burnt down to the very last bit of wax.

The only difference was my nightstand, where two items that did not belong to me sat.

The first was Francine's memoir, *Exorcisms of Self*; the second, *Rabbit Run*. Tented atop the two was a sheet of paper that read, "Look inside the covers," with the numbers one and two on either side of the words, arrows pointing down to the books.

Exorcisms of Self was number one. I opened it. On the inside cover, it told me to skip to page 144. This was the seventh chapter of the story, titled "Words to My Firstborn."

If you have your first child by accident at nineteen with the wrong person, a person you love nonetheless, a person with beautiful eyes and a delicate soul to offset their rough exterior, and you try to make a life with this person despite realizing your mistake in the first six months of marriage—if this is a person who doesn't understand subtlety, or the fact that you ultimately stayed with them not out of love but from an untempered stubborn streak and fantastic ideals of an idyllic lifestyle—there is something here that may reach you. If you hate yourself and cannot find a disingenuous way to express this to others, as the façades you've created have wrapped you in so many layers of mask that you couldn't pick yourself out of a lineup—if it's a hatred for yourself that runs so deep, you project it onto the things that are most precious to you, because if there is one cliche that rings true, it's about misery and the company for which it longs—I hope you read this and feel, someday, like you are less alone in the world.

If you find yourself stuck with this person you married, and hate and treasure and resent them all at once, and don't know how to negotiate that space because they have locked you in a prison cell made from your greatest weaknesses and swallowed the key, this should all be making sense. If your own firstborn grows so competent so quickly that you feel they don't need you, and if the only thing you want to feel is needed, but they write you off and prefer the attentions of your partner, then I won't remain such an alien, such a hypocrite, in your eyes. If your partner uses your firstborn as a paragon in order to show you your own flaws, faults, and failures by comparison...if you destroy everything you touch, and the only way you can get through your days is by resorting to your family's hereditary vice (which is not an excuse for the others), so that you can wake up hoping the new person you've always prayed to be has magically inhabited your body...if you hope to redeem yourself with a second child and fail there too, then I'm sorry. I'm sorry you inherited these things from me. I'm sorry you became a casualty of my sorrow. I'm sorry I was never a successful parent, teacher, or provider, though I tried at all three.

In short, I am sorry for everything.

I read and reread, my eyes so wide they dried out. My head ached. Francine's handwriting at the bottom of the page told me to turn to the back cover. There it read, *Congratulations on the Magna Cum Laude. I'm proud of you. I know now that everything I've done and become is unforgivable. Please do not hold these things against Nicholas. He needs you.*

I set the book down and opened the bruised edition of *Rabbit Run*, its central pages crusted and stuck together. On the inside cover was Francine's handwriting again, the words faded from when she must have originally written them on the Chanukah gift I rejected so many years ago. *K.J., if you ever want to talk to me, though I understand if you don't, or if you want to murder me or have me disappear forever, look at the woman standing before you and say so. Love, your mother.*

I carefully rearranged both books and limped into the living room where Nicholas lay on the floor, staring at the ceiling.

"Hey," I said.

"What up."

"Would you mind coming with me to the cabin?"

On our way over to the cabin, I told him not to worry about arranging the funeral or anything, that I could handle it. He thanked me, then cleared his throat.

He asked, "And you'll do the eulogy, too, right? I'm not so good in front of people these days. I wouldn't know what to say at this point anyway, and—"

"Of course."

"Thanks."

He opened the door to the cabin. It was spotless inside. It looked just like it did on the day, eons ago, when we first moved in and Francine collapsed in tears. I stared at the shoe rack. I told Nicholas that I hated that fucking thing.

"I can tell," he said. "Your contacts must be dry."

He told me to wait outside. A loud scraping sound emanated from the cabin. Moments later, Nicholas emerged backwards, dragging the shoe rack. He pulled it across the dead grass and out to the center point between the two homes. Nicholas motioned me over. He opened the shoe rack door and took out a full bottle of Knob Creek.

"Clever," I said.

"Right?" He peeled the wax seal away and twisted the cap open with a crack.

"Do you have to?" I asked. "Right now? After Kyle just killed himself with the stuff?"

"*Dad*," he answered, "killed himself with a shotgun. Besides, this isn't for me."

He poured the liquor out onto the top of the shoe rack. He tossed me a pack of matches. I stepped up, lit the whole book, and threw the ball of fire onto the alcohol-coated wood. The oxygen in the air sucked past me as the shoe rack ignited and for a moment I couldn't breathe at all. Then the great *whoosh* and the whole thing exploded into flames. I shielded my face. Nicholas, standing next to me, left his hands in his pockets and watched the fire. Its glow painted his face orange and reflected in the unknowable depths of his eyes.

In a reverie, he muttered something to himself.

"What was that?"

He didn't look at me. "Nietzsche."

"What about him?"

"'He who fights with monsters should be careful lest he thereby become a monster. And if thou gaze long into an abyss, the abyss will also gaze into thee.'"

We watched the shoe rack burn until the sun set.

"It should be safe in there now," Nicholas told me, indicating the cabin. Then he smiled. It was his old smile. The smile from when we were kids. The smile that—on the rare occasions it revealed itself—could light a room on fire. It was somehow better now, the smile. Absence makes the heart grow fonder. (I have to find a better way to say that. Proximity takes the heart for granted? It almost works. Proximity makes you blind to beauty? Maybe I shouldn't try to go fully opposite just to mean the same thing. Distance shows us what we've missed the most?)

We went in to the old cracked and refinished table and sat across from one another. I put Kyle's suicide note at his customary place. Nicholas dealt out three hands of Gin Rummy.

It got me thinking about ghosts. It got me thinking about souls. It got me thinking about how the real victim of the family was always Nicholas. Things were amputated from Kyle and unwired inside of me, but Nicholas had been shattered and glued back together poorly. None of us was whole, but for the rest of us at least something was left.

No one drank while we played our final hand of cards.

My mind wandered to the ways in which things deteriorate. I wondered how long it had taken Nicholas to clean this place up. I wondered if Kyle would have been appreciative. I wondered, for the billionth time, about why he and Francine could never rediscover their love and work things out. Or move on in healthier ways.

I think it's the fact that she and Kyle spoke different languages. I think the miscommunication was actually quite simple. That he said *Stay* in German and she translated to *Drop it* in English. Everything else stemmed from that misunderstanding.

Everything. Including me.

Even with all the shit that went down in my fifteenth summer, at least back then we were all together.

I still can't remember it raining at any point that summer, though I know it must have.

Epilogue

Is that cathartic enough? If not, fuck you. Move on. Tight.

Acknowledgments

Donna, Rickathy, and Arthur Heaslip (in the first slot because I'm not putting up with Donna's SHIT FOR THE REST OF EVER).

Stephanie Feldman, Dick Wertime, and Chip Delany for all the invaluable lessons, literary and otherwise.

Christine Neulieb, for being so very much smarter than me, whatever, shut up.

Feliza Casano, for telling me where to be and when, and never being too mad when I need ten million reminders.

Amanda Thomas, for her kindness and generosity (plus remembering my name years after there was any reason to).

Christina Rosso and Alex Schneider, for putting up with being called Mom and Dad at incredibly inappropriate moments. Also, I guess, being incredible community builders and leaders and other way more important stuff, but I've chosen to focus on the part where they're patient with me.

Rianna Polin, Mia Jablonski, Dennis Jablonski, Tracy Venella, Kai Davis, Scott Gay, The Meg Ott, Meaghan Lynch, Cody Heaslip, A.J. Natale, Blake Vermandel, Adam Harris, Becky Harris, Kirsten Fuss, Mark Ducceschi, Alannah Dixon, Rickstopher Dennehy, Punky Holcombe, Tyler Beck, Courtney Straka, Nick Bravo, Matt Hickock, Devin Hughes, Mike Lash, Logan Mowl, Lauren Fischer, Daniella Santos, and Benji Halper, for being there when times are bad so we can celebrate when they're not.

About the Author

Andrew Katz is an avid reader and writer and thinks that the written word is a huge boon for people's mental health, whether they plan to do anything with their personal writing or not. He is a dog dad, carpenter, and disc golfer. He thinks there are other things about him that might be interesting but is trying to employ brevity here.